THE GIFT OF RIO

THE GIFT OF THE ELEMENTS SERIES

BY C.S. ELSTON

SHINE-A-LIGHT
PRESS

Visit Shine-A-Light Press on our website:
    www.ShineALightPress.com
    on Twitter: @SALPress
    And on Facebook: www.facebook.com/SALPress

Visit The Gift of Rio on our website:
    www.GiftOfTheElements.com
    on Twitter: @GiftOfElements
    And on Facebook: www.facebook.com/GiftOfTheElements

Visit C.S. Elston:
    cselston.com
    twitter.com/cselston
    facebook.com/cselston

Library of Congress Control Number: 2017909687

ISBN 9780997672237

Printed in the U.S.A.

For my beautiful bride, the kindest, sweetest and most naturally good person I know. Andrea, you are the greatest gift God has given me besides Himself.

Acknowledgments

As always, I would like to extend my deepest gratitude to my original proofreaders: My parents, Doug and Judy; my father-in-law, Craig; my sister, Jennifer; and my wife, Andrea. This time around, I added my good friend and fellow author, Greg, to the list. They have all been supportive in numerous ways, not the least of which is having read drafts of the book before publication and offering valuable feedback.

Table of Contents

THE GIFT OF RIO

THE GIFT OF THE ELEMENTS SERIES
BY C.S. ELSTON

When you pass through the waters,
I will be with you;
and when you pass through the rivers,
they will not sweep over you.

- Isaiah 43:2a

CHAPTER ONE
The Month Of Mei

The first few months of 1972 had been particularly difficult ones for sixteen-year-old Mei Akagawa. She was a good girl. A good daughter. A good person.

She was barely five feet tall and very thin, giving her an almost fragile appearance. Mei was quiet, shy, and even a bit timid. She always obeyed her parents, followed the rules and generally did what she was supposed to do. Unfortunately, this meant that she had never even begun to build a life of her own. She didn't have any close friends and she only showed interest in the things that she knew would make her mother and father happy. Until 1972, she had been content to make pleasing her parents her primary goal. But, what her father had asked of her this time had, so far, made 1972 the most challenging year of her young life.

Mei's father, Eito, worked at the Tanaka Corporation in the

Kita Ward of Osaka, Japan. Mei wasn't sure what the company did or even exactly what it was that her father did for them. Work was one of the many things that Eito kept to himself. But, Mei knew that the Tanaka Corporation was quickly becoming an important fixture in Umeda which was the major commercial and business district in Kita-ku, Osaka where the Tanaka Corporation headquarters was located. Now her father had asked her to marry the son of the company's founder. It would be good for her father's career. She understood that. And, he wasn't forcing her. Legally, he couldn't. But, the pressure she felt was immense.

So, as she usually did, Mei eventually obeyed her father's wishes and was soon engaged to someone she had met only twice. Sota Tanaka was a nineteen-year-old man who Mei found physically attractive enough. And, she could tell that he felt the same way about her. But, emotionally, he was as cold as she was shy and the combination made it very difficult for them to get to know one another. Their first two meets had involved very little conversation. In fact, the way Mei remembered them, she spent most of the time looking down at her hands and Sota was virtually expressionless, speaking in shorter sentences than anyone she had ever heard before. These meetings and the circumstance surrounding them were causing Mei a severe amount of anxiety. Had she not already been such a naturally discreet girl, her parents would probably have been able to tell that she was quickly slipping into a deep depression.

Awaiting their third encounter, Mei was sitting on a park bench near the Osaka North Port Marina, staring out at the Yodo River and feeling as though her world was crumbling around her. She was nervously anticipating Sota's arrival just moments before the unexpected event that would change her life forever. Instead of Sota arriving and taking a seat, an elderly woman nearly startled her into leaping off the bench as the woman seemed to appear out of nowhere and take a seat next to Mei.

"Lovely," the elderly woman spoke calmly to Mei in Japanese without taking her eyes off the river. "The water is just lovely, isn't it?"

"It is," Mei spoke back, also in Japanese, as she tried to slow her heart rate back down to a normal pace.

"It's no wonder God chose to cover most of the planet with the stuff," the elderly woman continued. "Just lovely."

Mei nodded her head as if she agreed but she was barely paying any attention to what the woman was saying. However, she did notice that the woman spoke with a warmth that seemed unique and inviting. But, what Mei was really doing, as she nodded her head, was trying to gain the courage to inform the woman that she was meeting someone at this bench and that her seat was being saved for him.

As if the woman knew exactly what Mei was thinking, she

suddenly reassured her. "Don't worry, Mei."

The woman's use of her name startled Mei as much as her sudden appearance had. But, what the elderly woman said next truly shook Mei to her core.

"I'll be gone just a few moments before Sota arrives."

"What?" Mei asked. She was so stunned she couldn't form full sentences. Only individual words. "How?"

"I know things about you, you don't even know yourself. At least not yet."

Mei stood up as if she was going to leave. Instead, she plucked out one of the many questions that were zipping around her brain and asked, "Who are you?"

"I'm no one of great consequence, Mei. Just a humble messenger."

"A messenger? Then who exactly was it that sent you?"

"The only one who can, my dear."

"I don't know what you mean by that."

"You will. Eventually. What's important now is the message. You need to hear this so that you can prepare appropriately."

"Prepare for what?"

"You will ultimately have two children. All children are special in the eyes of loving parents. But, your firstborn, your daughter, will be truly remarkable and you will come to realize that she's not just a gift to you, but to everyone."

Mei stared blankly at the elderly woman for what felt like minutes. Finally, she took her eyes off the woman and turned briefly to look back out at the river. What the woman was telling her sounded ludicrous. But, she had known her name and the name of her fiancé. Yet, as far as Mei knew, the woman was a total stranger.

She spun around again to ask the woman how she knew all of this but the woman was gone. She had vanished without a trace and the surrounding area left nowhere to hide. She hadn't disappeared into a crowd of people. She wasn't hiding behind a building or a tree. And, Mei had not taken her eyes off her for long enough that the woman getting up and walking out of sight would have been remotely possible. *Was she a spirit?* Mei wondered to herself. She could think of no other explanation.

Mei forced herself to sit back down and try to appear as if nothing had happened. She did not want to act or sound like a crazy person when Sota arrived. That could only complicate matters. But, to be fair, what this woman had told Mei would affect him, too. Surely, he would be the father of the children that this woman claimed Mei would have. Should she tell him about the encounter?

She decided she couldn't. At least not yet.

That was precisely the moment Sota stepped in front of Mei, startling her even more than the elderly woman had. She quickly stood and composed herself as they bowed in greeting to one another. She forced a smile for the man she didn't know but was engaged to marry and, with whom she would apparently, have a very special daughter.

CHAPTER TWO
Secrets & Lies

Although the religious lines had blurred in Japan since World War II, both the Tanaka and Akagawa families continued to identify themselves as practitioners of Shinto, the ethnic religion of the Japanese people since before Buddhism came over from the mainland in the sixth century. While the engagement between Sota and Mei was the result of an arranged introduction, a somewhat outdated method of finding a partner called "omiai," the couple still honored the common three-year courtship period.

Mei was not sure if she believed the elderly woman she had met briefly on the park bench. But, during her courtship with Sota, Mei decided that she could not risk having a child with him. Not if it was going to be this daughter that was a 'gift to everyone' as the woman had put it.

Sota was cold and calculated. His greatest concerns were for his own success in business. Sota wanted nothing more than to rise to the top of his father's company, ultimately making it more successful than it had ever been. He suffered from an unhealthy competitiveness with his father. It was something he kept hidden from his family but Mei had observed enough privately to recognize that a child could become a dangerous weapon in the hands of such a man. Particularly if that child was special in some way. So, she never told him about her encounter with the elderly woman. In fact, she never told anyone.

Mei felt trapped in the engagement. There was no way to escape without suffering consequences that seemed unbearable to her. But, there was a way that she could protect her unborn child. Unfortunately, the only way she could come up with was to never conceive the child at all. So, she illegally purchased birth control pills on the black market and began to take them about five months before the wedding ceremony. Every three months she would take the bus into Japan's largest slum, Kamagasaki, and purchase them from a man who called himself Yamashita.

Thirty-eight months, almost to the day, after meeting the elderly woman near the Osaka North Port Marina, Sota submitted the required family registration sheet with the city hall registrar to change their marriage status and legally give Mei the surname Tanaka. The ceremony was held in the main building of the Sumiyoshi Grand Shrine, approximately sixteen kilometers from the park bench where Mei had received the prophecy.

Family members, very close friends, and strategic business associates of the Tanaka Corporation were in attendance. Mei was elegant, painted white as a sign of purity before the gods and dressed in the same type of black kimono, patterned with colorful flowers, once worn at weddings of the nobility during the Edo period some two to three hundred years earlier. Sota, too, looked very handsome. He wore a black crested haori jacket and loose, skirt-like hakama with a vertical stripe. The kannushi performed a ritual purification for the couple and announced their marriage to the gods called the kami. The bride and groom took three sips each from three cups of sake in a ritual called "sansankudo."

The dinner reception and after-party was held in the banquet hall of Hotel Granvia Osaka, about 5 kilometers away from the Sumiyoshi Grand Shrine. Extended family members, more friends, and additional business associates attended, making speeches before offering gift money in a special envelope. It was everything Mei could have wanted. Everything except for the fact that she had a very deep secret she was hiding from everyone in her life. Not the least of whom, was the man she had just married. A man she knew she didn't love. Even worse, a man she couldn't trust to be the father of this special baby girl that she desperately wanted but was fighting not to have.

Newly married and surrounded by family and friends, it was the loneliest Mei had ever felt in her nineteen years of life. She continued to feel lonely long after her wedding day. Family and friends went home. Her husband remained emotionally cold, having little time for anything that wasn't work related.

Mei slowly became quieter and more internalized. She put on a happy face whenever her husband had to take her out in public for a dinner with people he needed to impress or spent an afternoon or evening with family. But, otherwise, she mostly stayed home by herself. The one exception was the quarterly bus trip to Kamagasaki to purchase more birth control pills from Yamashita.

As the months passed, Sota grew angry over the fact that Mei wasn't getting pregnant. When a full year had come and gone he told her she was embarrassing him by not giving him a son to carry on his name and his business the way he was doing for his father. He tried to force her to see a doctor but she refused. He didn't understand why she wouldn't go and she declined to explain it to him.

Sota's emotional cold front turned into a volatile storm of cruelty in the year that followed. He never physically abused Mei in the first two years of their marriage. But, one night, that changed. He came home drunk and began interrogating her over her inability to get pregnant and refusal to see a doctor about it. He made her sit in a chair at the kitchen table and would push her back into the chair if she tried to stand. He yelled at her until tears were streaming down her cheeks. Finally, he began to slap her across the face as he demanded answers that she would never give him. The interrogation lasted almost an hour. And, when it ended, it was only because Mei couldn't hold herself up in the chair anymore. He finally let her collapse onto the floor. And, once she did, he stripped her of her clothes and forced himself on top of her as he told her she would give him a son if it killed her.

Six weeks later, Mei discovered that she was pregnant.

CHAPTER THREE
Escape

Mei wasn't devastated or even really all that surprised. Although she had never missed a single dose of her birth control, deep down, she always knew this was coming. The revelation of her pregnancy did, however, immediately send her into full-fledged panic mode. Her top priority, as it had been since her one and only encounter with the elderly woman who Mei now believed to be a prophetess, had always been the protection of this daughter whom she had been told would somehow be special. Now that the baby girl was on her way, she had to figure out how in the world she was going to keep her away from Sota.

Luckily, she was home alone at the time she learned of her pregnancy. If she hadn't been, her frantic walking in circles would have caused almost anyone to call for an ambulance and a straight-jacket. After sitting still for a few minutes, which was forced by a short dizzy spell, she left the house and spent several hours at the bench overlooking the Yodo River, asking out loud for the return of the elderly woman. She needed guidance. And she needed it badly. But, unfortunately, guidance never came. At least, not in the form of the prophetess.

Forty-eight hours later, the crazies had subsided, and a plan started to develop in her mind. Perhaps, wherever it was coming from, this was the guidance she had been looking for all along. Either way, it was the only plan she had.

The plan began to develop from the realization that if she wanted to escape her current situation, she had already been given the means to pay for it. Sota was so focused on his one-sided competition with his father in the business world that he had placed Mei in charge of all their personal finances. That meant, she had access to every single yen that Sota brought home. Even better, that included all the assets purchased with those yen.

So, a couple of weeks before she needed to, Mei made her quadrennial trip to visit Yamashita in Kamagasaki. But, this time, instead of purchasing birth control pills, she sat him down and laid out a plan that involved changing her identity, cleaning Sota out of every yen that he was worth, buying a plane ticket to America under her new name, and taking every yen she could wire transfer or fit in a suitcase along with her.

Yamashita was astounded at the meticulous and devious plan hatched by the typically shy and seemingly naïve young woman.

It made him smile for the first time in the years they had known each other. He told her that he could help make her plan a success, for a twenty-percent fee. Feeling more confident and audacious than she ever had in her life, Mei got Yamashita to knock his fee down to ten percent. The deal was in place and the execution of the plan had begun.

Over the next four weeks, Mei Tanaka made sure that she saw the most important people in her life, in between trips to a few different banks, charities and Kamagasaki, of course. She never let anyone, other than Yamashita, in on her plan to disappear from Japan forever. So, her family had no idea that they were seeing her for the last time or that what seemed like a typical sayonara actually meant goodbye for good.

The burden of her secrecy was particularly hard on Mei where her parents were concerned. She had spent most of her life trying to please them and she knew this was going to break their hearts. However, the responsibility she felt to protect the child growing inside of her at all costs superseded everything else.

Finally, the day had arrived. Mei got ready, packed her bags, and walked out the door of the house she had lived in with a man she had never loved and had sadly grown to hate. She climbed in the taxi and breathed a sigh of relief while looking out the front windshield as they pulled away.

Forty-Five minutes later, Mei was sitting in the terminal at the Kansai Airport while a local charity moved every stitch of furniture, clothing, dishware and linens out of their house. When Sota got home that night, he wouldn't have so much as a toothbrush waiting for him.

As she finally boarded the plane, she was greeted for the first time as Toki Uchida. It felt good. It was a clean start. She had chosen the name Toki because of its meaning: "time of opportunity." That is exactly what this was for her. And, she was seizing it.

Toki loved Japan and she would miss it. She had done some research and chosen her new home because it would be somewhat familiar. It was also not as far away from Japan as if she had chosen to go all the way to the mainland of America. In fact, it was only 3,850 miles away. Toki would have had to travel an additional 4,900 miles just to get to the coast of California.

She was off to start a new life on another island. This one was called Hawaii. Of course, it was about seven percent the size of Japan. But, it was as close as Toki could get to Japan in America. And, it represented safety for her child. So, it would be enough. She was flying into Hilo and, from there, had no idea where she was going. The freedom she felt as a result, overwhelmed her.

She beamed as she looked out the window while the plane was lifting off the ground. She stared at the water and was thankful that she would have a similar view when she landed in her new home. It was at that moment that she named the daughter that was growing inside of her. The daughter that she had been trying to protect since the elderly woman had prophesied her coming. The daughter she now knew was finally going to be safe. The daughter who was a gift to her and to everyone. And, the daughter she already loved.

Perhaps the voice inside that had been guiding her steps for the last four weeks was the one who named the girl for her. Perhaps it was just the lovely sight of the water out of the airplane window. Whatever it was, her daughter's name became official on that plane ride from Osaka, Japan to Hilo, Hawaii in the United States of America.

The gift growing inside of Toki, would forever be known as Rio.

CHAPTER FOUR
Hilo & Rio

Toki was relieved to find that a woman who worked at one of the rent-a-car counters at the Hilo International Airport spoke Japanese. They had a conversation that convinced Toki that she'd earned some self-indulging. So, she rented a bright red, 1977 convertible Ford Mustang and drove to a four-star inn that the woman had recommended, just outside of Hilo, on twenty-two lush acres of tropical paradise. She spent forty-eight hours being pampered in the spa, staring at the gorgeous waterfalls that fed into the Waiau River, and thanking the strange elderly woman whom she couldn't see but hoped could hear her. She did know, however, that she had never felt better in her entire life.

The inn had an Asian flare and even featured an extensive bamboo garden. She felt right at home. But, on the third day, she woke up and decided that it was time to begin the rest of her life. She needed to explore the island and find a place to call home for herself and the baby girl who would be arriving in a little more than six months.

She fell in love with the area of Kona but quickly realized that the Japanese population was denser back on the other side of the island in Hilo. So, she found a house on a hill that overlooked Hilo Bay. Because she was paying cash, she got a good price for it which gave her a small sense of pride. Toki turned her rental car in and took a taxi to a Ford dealership because she had enjoyed her rental car so much. She bought a 1978 Ford Mustang II King Cobra. This time, Toki chose a beautiful blue color and got the 'T Roof' design. Again, she got a good deal because she paid cash and her sense of pride continued to grow.

Toki settled into the new house and got it ready for Rio. The pregnancy was a relatively typical one. Other than the fact that Rio was very active in the womb, which Toki particularly noticed when she was in the shower, there really were no complications of any significance. The most unusual part of the process was something that Toki chose to do. At the suggestion of her new friend, another Japanese woman and next door neighbor, Nyoko, Toki chose to do a water birth in a private setting near Rainbow Falls on the Wailuku River. The birth process turned out to be an expensive one but it all went smoothly. She was soon home with her daughter and already anxious to find out what was going to make her so special. Besides, of course, the fact that she was already incredibly special to Toki.

By the time all of the bills associated with giving birth to Rio were paid, Toki realized that the money she had taken from her previous life would eventually run out. Fortunately, her friendship with Nyoko, who had two little boys of her own, had quickly blossomed. Nyoko's youngest was only a year older than Rio and she agreed to watch Rio if Toki found a job.

Soon, Toki did exactly that. She took a job in the administration building at the University of Hawaii, helping Japanese students adapt to college life. Toki's English improved greatly in this job because she often found herself forced to translate from English to Japanese and, just as often, from Japanese to English.

It was also at this job that she met Anthony Marlow. He was an astronomer working as a researcher at the University. Anthony sat next to her while they were both eating lunch. And, yes, it was on another bench. Their conversation was immediately easy, fun, and warm. He was the first African-American that she had ever met. And, before long, he became the first man she had ever fallen in love with.

The Marlow family was officially born when Toki and Anthony were married just before Rio's second birthday. It was a good thing, too. Toki needed the help. Rio was a handful from the start and it never stopped. It took three adults to raise that little girl: Toki, Anthony and Nyoko. Each of them felt like it was a full-time job. But, they all loved Rio and Rio loved and truly appreciated all of them.

Even after an early entrance to kindergarten, to which Rio adapted flawlessly, she wouldn't stop throwing herself into new situations. She made daring climbs on playground equipment and found new ways, almost daily, to prove she was just as tough, fast, strong and brave as any of the boys. The most important boy in her life was her little brother, Hani, who was born ten days after her fifth birthday.

Toki was consistently amazed at how different Rio was from both Sota and herself. Emotionally, Rio was an easy child. She was thick-skinned and as friendly as any child in the school. The only problems that arose came primarily when her impermeable attitude permitted activities that were impulsive and occasionally dangerous, like taking Toki's Mustang for a joyride, at age twelve, with seven-year-old Hani riding shotgun. In that instance, she didn't get very far. In fact, she was stopped about forty feet from her driveway when she accidentally put her mom's car through Nyoko's fence. Although she got into a lot of trouble for it at the time, and spent the rest of her summer babysitting and mowing lawns to earn money to repair the fence, Toki gave the sixteen-year-old car to Rio when she got her driver's license. Toki bought herself a 1994 Acura Integra. She got her T-Tops again but, this time, she chose the color white.

Rio was a smart girl and always got good grades in school. However, her swimming coaches had higher praise for her than her teachers did because her bold mouth was occasionally an unwelcome distraction in class. Rio was quick to correct her teachers when they made a mistake because she was focused on the task at hand. However, she was completely at peace in the water and typically quiet as a result. In both settings, she worked as hard as anyone else.

Her hard work paid off when it came time for college. Those good grades and her stamina in the pool earned her a scholarship to the University of Hawaii, where her mother and her step-father both worked. She considered going to a different school but, she already knew the coaches at the University because they had been attending her meets all throughout high school. Ultimately, it was an easy transition and, the thought of her parents not being able to attend any of her meets would have been unbearable.

All in all, Rio had a great, albeit relatively uneventful, childhood. Toki rarely ever thought about the fact that the prophetess had told her how Rio would be special to everyone. Of course, it did occasionally cross her mind and, if it hadn't been for the woman's accuracy about everything else, she might have dismissed it completely. As a result, she still had never told anyone about the prophecy. But, that was all about to change.

CHAPTER FIVE
Major

Rio didn't have the typical long arms, broad shoulders or long torso that the rest of the swimmers on her team had. In fact, she was the smallest person in the pool. Having been a swimmer pretty much her whole life, she had developed a tiny waist and powerful but slender legs. She wasn't the fastest swimmer on the team, either. Therefore, she didn't swim any of the sprints. What made Rio one of the best swimmers on her team, was the fact that it seemed she could swim forever without even slowing down. She didn't have to pace herself like everyone else who swam the distance races did. She simply went all out from the beginning and didn't stop until the race was over.

That had been the case from the time Toki and Anthony put her in a body of water bigger than the bathtub. They had spent a Sunday at the Wailuku River State Park when Rio was two years old. They walked her down the river bank and let her dip her toes in the water. They expected her to yell or laugh, maybe even turn around and run back up the bank. Instead, Rio simply closed her eyes and smiled, as if she was feeling the warmth of the sun for the first time.

When Anthony picked her up and walked further into the water, he held her in front of him and told her to start paddling with her hands and kicking her feet. As he loosened his grip on his step-daughter, she ignored his advice and did a full breast stroke. And then, another one. Suddenly, Anthony was scrambling to grab her as she swam away. Panicked, he and Toki started chasing after Rio but she just swam in a circle around them. They stopped and watched in amazement as their daughter, at two years old and having never taken a swimming lesson, calmly swam around them in about three feet of water.

Toki, of course, was quickly reminded of Rio's consistent reaction to the shower from inside of her womb. She began to wonder, for the first time, if her daughter's affinity for water had anything to do with the prophecy she had received from the elderly woman. But, she continued to keep that to herself. Instead she just started laughing and clapping as she and Anthony looked on in awe.

Rio was enrolled in swimming classes less than twenty-four hours later. Her instructors were as astonished by the child's quick taking to water as her parents had been. Not that it is uncommon to get children into the pool at that age. Some parents have their children in the pool and getting comfortable with a swimming environment before the age of one. However, Rio took so naturally to the water that no one could believe she hadn't previously been taking lessons. Even if she had, she was already well ahead of other kids her age.

They had her competing as early as they could, which was at the age of five. She swam in a variety of events at first. But, as she got older, kids got faster and her consistent winning became, well, less consistent in the sprints. But, no one could beat her in the distance races. So, by the time she was a freshman in high school, the distance races were all that she continued to compete in.

As a sophomore in college she was facing the stiffest competition of her young life. She did well, but she didn't qualify for the Olympic trials the year before. It was tough for her when she came up short but, Rio was a pretty resilient girl. She got right back to training and had just finished up a strong season in March of 1997.

Instead of celebrating her personal best time of 15:38:24 and third place finish in the 1650 Free at the NCAA National Championships, Rio's coach found her in the pool the day after their return from Indianapolis. He squatted down, above the fifty-meter-long and twelve-yard-wide pool, and sat back on his haunches in front of her lane. As Rio swam toward him, she spotted him, touched the wall and put her right arm over the side to hold herself up as she removed her goggles with her left hand.

"Hey coach," she said.

"I'd ask you what you're doing in here but I'd be lying if I pretended to be surprised," he responded before moving on to the order of business. "If I told you I got a call from your academic advisor, would you be able to tell me why?"

"She's on me about choosing a major."

"Right," he agreed. "I'm assuming she explained that it's school policy you have to have a major declared by the end of your sophomore year if you want to participate in the athletic programs your junior year."

Rio nodded in agreement.

"You got that covered?"

"Not yet. But, I will."

"If you want to talk through anything, you know where to find me."

"Thanks, coach."

"Of course. Now, get out of that pool and go have some fun."

"This is fun, coach."

"I mean real fun," he said as he reached a hand down. She grabbed it and he pulled her out of the pool. "Get out of here."

The Gift of Rio

Rio went to the locker room, dried off and changed into street clothes. She was on her way home when she got an idea. She turned off Highway 19 onto Waianuenue Avenue and drove straight to the Wailuku River State Park. She parked the Mustang at the back of the parking lot so she'd be less visible, climbed into the back seat and changed into a dry bathing suit.

Three minutes later, Rio was swimming again. But, this was even better. The only thing that felt more wonderful than being in the pool, was being in water that had no chlorine in it. This was the closest Rio ever got to 'getting high' on a drug. But, this was so much better than Rio could imagine any drug being. Instead of clouding her mind, it gave her clarity. It gave her energy. It made everything feel more spectacular. And, it was exactly what she needed as she pondered her future and prepared to make a major decision.

CHAPTER SIX
Decision

The Marlow family was enjoying a rather typical dinner of casual conversation and a feast of rice, pickled cabbage, mahi mahi and miso soup at the dining room table. But, Rio was about to supercharge the conversation. It had been years since she had so much as asked a question about her biological father. And, when she had brought it up in the past, she had typically done it quietly with only her mom. Therefore, when she finished blurting out the following sentence, the collective shock was severe.

"I think I'm going to talk to my professors and see if I can take my final exams early this year so I can spend a long summer in Japan looking for my biological father."

It was as though God had just hit the pause button on the entire room. Everyone but Rio was frozen with their eyes locked on her. Hani had a piece of mahi mahi resting on a fork, which rested on his lips, as he tried to process what his sister had just said. After all, the subject of his sister having a different biological father than he did hadn't come up in at least ten years.

Anthony finished setting his glass of water down, swallowed, and waited for his wife to speak or Rio to add some additional thoughts to the conversation she had started. He truly loved Rio and thought of her as his own to the point that he rarely thought about the fact that there was another man on the planet who was physically responsible for her existence. So, the idea that she wanted to go and find him wasn't completely shocking to Anthony. But, it still stung a little.

Toki simply folded her hands in her lap and looked at her daughter in bewilderment. She was stunned that Rio had brought this up to anyone but her. And, even if they were the only two in the room, the fact that it was such a drastic, intense statement was both surprising and depressing to Toki. The long pause felt like it lasted minutes but was only a few seconds.

"What?" Rio questioned, honestly stupefied by the reaction.

"Why?" Toki finally asked.

"Why not?" Rio responded with a little bit of attitude.

"Because you don't understand what it is you're asking," Toki stated as her hands and her voice began to tremble. It wasn't because she hadn't argued with Rio before. This was a loving family. But, nearly all families experience a few arguments and fights. Especially during the children's teenage years. This family was no exception. Toki was upset because the thought of Sota learning about Rio was devastating to her.

"First of all," Rio began to retort, "I didn't ask a question. I made a statement. And, second, I think I know exactly what it is that I'm saying."

"I'm sure you do think that. But, why don't you tell me why it is you suddenly want to find Sota?"

"Maybe because of the fact that his name is Sota and you and he were both from Japan is nearly all I know about the man who is half of the reason that I exist. I think it's fair that I want to know where and who I come from."

"That does sound fair," Anthony chimed in, surprising Toki.

"Anthony is your father," Toki stated emphatically.

"Anthony is my dad," Rio agreed. "Nothing is ever going to change that. I love him and he is the man that raised me. But, I'd still like to know a little bit about the man that I share DNA with."

There was a long silence. Toki knew the time had come for the truth. She excused her fifteen-year-old son from the table. Hani argued briefly but then took his plate to his room and finished his dinner there.

Toki told the whole story for the very first time. From the elderly woman to the night she was beaten and raped by her husband, she left nothing out. Rio was devastated and sobbed harder than she could remember ever sobbing before. She felt terrible about what her mom had endured. Even Anthony welled up with tears as he held his wife. He knew Sota had been abusive but, he didn't know anything about the prophetess nor did he know the extent of Sota's abuse. Rio got up from her chair and they all hugged. Of course, Rio had about a hundred questions for her mom. Most of them, Toki simply couldn't answer because she didn't know how to. But, when it was all over, it didn't change Rio's mind. She was about as stubborn as anyone and Toki knew that this was going to happen with or without her blessing.

Rio scooted her chair around the table so she could stay on their side and continue the conversation. "What he did was awful, Mom. I mean, it was about as awful as anything someone can do. So, I'm not making excuses for that. But, in all fairness, he never knew the truth. So, he didn't really have a chance to respond to any of this. He not only didn't know about the woman in the park or the birth control, but to this day, he doesn't even know he has a daughter. I'm old enough to take care of myself now. I want to confront him and give him the chance to respond."

Another moment of silence. This one was even longer than the first.

"You're right," Toki finally spoke. "I didn't trust him. So, I kept you from him. To protect you."

"Of course you did," Anthony chimed in to stick up for his

wife.

"Absolutely," Rio agreed. "I'm not second guessing that at all. I'm thankful you did what you did. You've given me a great life. You both have."

Rio grabbed one of each of their hands in hers. "This isn't about undoing anything. Just the opposite. I'm trying to figure out what the rest of my life is going to look like. In order to do that, I just feel like I need to know the rest of the story that tells me where I come from. Does that make sense?"

"It does," Toki admitted. "But, that doesn't mean it doesn't scare me to pieces."

"I know. But, it'll be okay. I'm sure of it."

Toki invited Hani to come out of his room as she told them where she came from. She told them all about her family and Sota's, giving Rio every bit of information she could think of that would help her daughter go do what she needed to do and then get back home as quickly as possible. And, Rio, of course, took copious notes as if she was in class and the professor was giving out answers to the final exam.

Rio appeared before the academic board and got permission to take her exams early on the grounds that this trip was going to be educational. She agreed to make a presentation when she returned and they were even going to give her elective credit for it. It didn't hurt that her parents were faculty or that she was such a good student and a star on the swim team.

Of course, the board also insisted that she finally choose her major. She picked marine biology and told herself she could change it later if she decided on something else while she was gone. But, at least this appeased the powers that be, for now and gave her academic advisor something to do when it came time to helping her schedule her fall classes.

So, just over two decades after Toki fled Japan to save her daughter's life, Rio was going back to try and figure that life out.

CHAPTER SEVEN
A New Vision

Rio had set out everything she was taking with her the night before. And, she didn't have to be at the airport, which was less than fifteen minutes from home, until about 9:30am. But, she still had to set an alarm because she needed to make sure she had plenty of time to get ready, put everything into her suitcase and backpack, and eat a hearty breakfast. Flying to collegiate swim meets had taught her to eat before she boarded because airplane food was generally not worth eating unless it was truly an emergency.

So, when the alarm went off at 6:30am, Rio's eyes popped open and she gave them a quick rub before springing out of bed. She picked up the outfit she had laid out to wear and took it with her into the bathroom. The shower felt particularly good that morning. Perhaps it was because she knew it would be her last shower at home for a while and she was trying to enjoy it as much as she could without wasting too much time. Or, perhaps it was just a really good shower.

When it was over, per her usual routine, she finished drying off, got dressed, and immediately put her contacts in before doing her makeup. A few minutes into the makeup process, she noticed that she was developing a headache and it felt like her eyes were constricting.

Wondering if she accidentally switched her contacts and put them in the wrong eyes, she held her right hand up and covered her right eye as she stared at her toothbrush. Then she repeated the action on the left side. Neither eye looked the way it normally did. So, she took her contacts out and put them in their case again. Blinking a few times and scrunching her nose, she finally opened her eyes and looked around the room. She was shocked to realize that her vision was suddenly better than she remembered it ever being without wearing glasses or contacts. She decided to leave her contacts out and wait to see if the room grew blurry again. But, instead, as her eyes readjusted, the headache went away and her vision became significantly clearer.

The whole thing was truly confusing. In fact, it seemed to be impossible. But, it was happening and she wasn't about to tell her mother who might use a trip to the optometrist as an excuse to cancel her summer in Japan. So, she finished her makeup, did her hair and packed everything up. She even included her contacts and solution, just in case it turned out that her miraculous optical healing was only temporary.

Rio had never been an over-packer. Still, she went out of her way to be efficient for this trip. She wanted to be light and particularly mobile on this journey because she really didn't know exactly what it would entail.

The truth is, Rio had very little planned. Heading off to an unknown place with virtually no itinerary would terrify most people. It certainly scared Toki, who had tried to convince Rio to let her tag along. But, Rio refused. She didn't want to put her mother through that after hearing about her daring escape decades earlier. And, Rio felt in her heart that this was something she needed to do alone. Besides, she was too excited about the possibility of finding her biological father to worry about any of the potentially negative outcomes.

Of course, the fact that he might reject her had crossed her mind. So had the possibility of not finding him at all. But, she had pretty much dismissed those concerns and focused instead on the positive possibilities. She also knew that her plan was to find the places her mom had described, and in some cases circled exact locations on a map, and then to just start asking questions of the people she found there. But, exactly where their answers would lead was unpredictable. The truth was, as long as those answers ultimately led her from her landing in Osaka, Japan to Sota

Tanaka, Rio really didn't care about anything in between.

She was completely ready waiting, with her carry-on suitcase and a backpack, by the front door at 7:45am. Rio went into the kitchen and helped her mom make her favorite breakfast. They sliced two papayas in half and hollowed out the middles. Then they mixed banana slices, chia seeds, granola, slivered almonds and blueberries into coconut yogurt and poured the mixture into the papayas. This, too, was something Rio would miss while on her quest to find Sota Tanaka.

As they gathered around the table, the different culinary tastes of each family member were evidenced by the type of beverage chosen to go with their papaya boats. Toki had black tea, Anthony had coffee, Hani had orange juice and Rio consumed the only thing she ever drank: water. From the time she was a little girl, nothing had really quenched her thirst like a good old fashioned glass of water. When she was hot, she wanted it as cold as she could get it. And, when she was cold, she would heat it up. But, she never added anything to it. Not so much as a squeeze of lemon. Just plain water was perfect for Rio. And, if it ain't broke, she figured, why fix it?

Conversation was close to non-existent. Rio was trying to downplay her enthusiasm so she didn't make anyone feel bad. Toki was too upset to talk. Anthony stayed mostly quiet because he understood how both Toki and Rio felt and he wasn't sure how to engage one without making the other feel bad. Hani knew he would miss his sister but didn't want to admit it.

So, they all enjoyed their papaya boats and various beverages without more than a few words spoken. The things that were said were primarily small talk about how good breakfast was and how everyone had slept. And, when they were all done and the dishes were clean, it was finally time to take Rio to the airport, say goodbye and send her off to Japan.

CHAPTER EIGHT
Goodbye

The short car ride to the airport started out as quiet as breakfast had been. But, that ended quickly when Toki finally started to break down. She sat in the front passenger-side seat and kept her face forward for fear of truly losing it if she turned around to face Rio. Through tears, she begged her daughter to let her buy a ticket and go with her.

"We've already talked about this," Rio insisted. "I can't put you through that, Momma."

"Letting you go alone isn't any more bearable," Toki contended.

"It's going to be fine. I'll be back in a few months. Maybe sooner. And, I'll call at least once a week."

It briefly went quiet again. The only sound heard over the road noise was Toki's sniffles. Anthony looked over at his wife, then at Rio through the rearview mirror, and then at his wife again before returning his eyes to the road. "That is what we agreed to," he said softly to Toki.

"I know but Sota . . . "

Anthony looked over as Toki lost it. The tears were overpowering her.

"She'll be okay," he offered as comfort. He placed his right hand on her back as he continued to speak and he glanced back and forth between his wife and the road.

"Rio can take care of herself. You know how I know that?"

"How," Toki managed to ask through the tears.

"She's your daughter."

The comforting words helped but the tears didn't stop. They arrived at the airport and Rio insisted that they leave her at the curb rather than coming inside and prolonging the difficult goodbye. As it was, the moment took so much time that a police officer had to tell them to move things along. Clearly, the event was hardest on Toki. But, even Anthony and Hani were fighting back tears. And, although she was excited to go, it wasn't easy for Rio to leave her mother in such emotional distress.

Still, the time had come to do exactly that. Toki slowly made her way back into the car, staring at her daughter as if trying to memorize every square inch of her face, and waving profusely as Rio finally disappeared into the airport. That's when Toki's tear ducts maxed out their workload capacity and flooded her face.

Both Anthony and Hani knew it was going to be a long ride home and an even longer day once they got there. Everyone in the car missed Rio already. But, no one missed her more than Toki.

Rio, on the other hand, felt bad for her mother and immediately missed her family. But, those feelings subsided quickly as she got checked in and started walking toward security. The excitement stirring inside of her overwhelmed the rest of her emotions and soon she was practically skipping as she entered the security line. She put her bags on the conveyer belt and walked through the metal detector. When her enthusiasm boiled over, she tried to start a conversation with a TSA agent by asking if he'd ever been to Japan. The agent sighed as he said he hadn't and Rio was immediately aware that he was annoyed by her. So, she attempted to stifle her delight long enough to get her bags back and start her walk toward the gate.

Her mom's story about the elderly woman prophesying about Rio sprang to her mind. Perhaps, this trip would be an opportunity to learn more about that as well. She didn't know how anything like that could come about. But, she figured that she had a better chance in the very place where the prophecy occurred than she would thousands of miles away from that place.

It was hard to imagine what it all meant, but the thought of it added even more exhilaration to Rio's mood. It didn't take long and she was nearly skipping again. Sure, she was looking forward to the possibility of meeting her biological father. But, more than that, the adventure of the whole thing was really firing her up. She was going to find her family and meet people she had never met. She was going to see places that she had never seen. And, all of it was centered around discovering who and where she had come from. It was almost too exciting to fathom. She was so thrilled that she feared she might burst. Or, at the very least, break out in a song or a scream that could get her some interesting looks.

Fortunately, she managed to contain herself. But, that eagerness carried her all the way to her gate where she couldn't even bring herself to sit down. Instead, she stood just off the walkway and grinned at people as they walked by. She said hello to a few of them and most returned the greeting. Others ignored her. And, some even seemed a bit frightened by her. But, Rio didn't care. Her adventure had begun. That's what mattered. That's what drove her overwhelming enthusiasm.

Suddenly, she noticed an old woman standing across the walkway by a drinking fountain. The woman was staring at her. At first, Rio assumed that the woman was studying her odd zeal as she greeted strangers. But, the longer they stared at one another, the more it began to feel like the woman thought she knew Rio. Since Rio had never seen the woman before, that thought seemed ridiculous. Perhaps Rio just looked like someone she knew.

It didn't dawn on Rio that this could possibly be the same woman who her mother had met in Osaka all those years ago. The very same woman who predicted her pregnancy and declared Rio would be a special gift to everyone. But, that's exactly who it was.

The woman smiled warmly just before a man stepped in front of Rio and stopped, setting a bag down, and lifting a camera to his face that hung on a strap around his neck to take a picture of his wife and two young daughters. Rio tried to see around him but he kept moving, almost in sync with her, as he tried to frame his shot. Finally, he took the picture and the family picked up their bags and kept walking. But when Rio got a clear shot of where the woman had been standing, she was no longer there. Rio looked all around at the different people in the vicinity but the woman had flat out disappeared the same way she had done to Rio's mother some twenty-five years earlier.

CHAPTER NINE
A Fountain Of Surprises

Although Rio didn't know the woman's identity, her strange stare of familiarity and her even more strange disappearance captured Rio's attention. Suddenly, she was as curious as a kitten encountering an empty Kleenex box for the first time. Her eyes darted all over the terminal as she searched for the woman but couldn't find her. Rio bumped into several people as she made her way through the crowd, without truly watching where she was going, to the spot where the woman had previously been standing.

Where could she have gone? Rio's mind was racing with thoughts about the woman. *That old lady can't move that quickly. I've never met an old person spry enough to disappear like that. What just happened? Who was she? And, why did she look like she thought she knew me?*

Eventually, Rio's eyes wandered from the faces and backs of heads in the crowd down to the drinking fountain just to the left of her. She felt thirsty. So, she stepped up to it and bent down as she hit the button to release the water. As she got closer she watched the water start to bend in mid-stream.

Slowly, the water lifted off the stainless-steel basin and the stream turned toward Rio. As her eyes widened, she watched the stream of water straighten out and extend directly into her mouth. Panicking, she released the button and looked around to see if anyone had been watching. No one was looking in her direction. She wasn't sure if she would rather have her anonymity protected or have someone verify that what she thought had just happened did in fact happen, to confirm that she wasn't crazy.

First my contacts and now this, she thought. *What is going on here?*

She looked down at the light gray drinking fountain again. Slowly, she lifted her hand and hit the button one more time. Everything seemed normal. So, she bent down to take another drink. As she leaned in, the water began to bend again. Just like it had before, the water lifted off the basin. The stream turned and extended directly into Rio's mouth. She quickly let go and looked around the same way she had the first time. Once again, she didn't appear to have any witnesses.

Suddenly, a little boy tugged on the back of Rio's shirt. Startled, she turned around and looked down at him.

"Can I get a drink?" the boy asked boldly.

"Of course," she quickly replied and stepped out of his way.

She swiftly surmised that he was approximately eight years old before looking around for a parent. Rio spotted a man standing at the edge of the gate and the walkway. He was watching carefully so, she assumed it was the boy's father. She looked at the boy again and he was struggling to stand tall enough to reach the water with his face. He was pressing down on the button and the water was pouring out as normal.

"Do you need some help?" she asked.

"No," he insisted. "I've got it."

It was clear the boy was never going to get there. He stood on his tiptoes and pushed his lips as high as he could, like a flower straining to reach the sunlight. Rio looked over at the boy's father who shrugged his shoulders as if to say, *the kid insists on doing it himself.* She tilted her head and shrugged her shoulders back at him, acknowledging the truth of his unspoken sentiment.

Rio then sidestepped, folded her arms across her chest, and turned to lean her back on the wall and look down at the water. The boy was still several inches short. His eyes were squeezed tightly shut as he pushed with all of his might. Rio's gaze shifted to the water. She wondered if she could somehow make it bend for him the way it had for her.

Her eyes narrowed as her focus grew more intense. Rio pointed her left index finger at the stream of water. Suddenly, as she lifted her finger, the water began to rise off the basin again.

She slowly pointed her finger toward the boy and watched as the water mimicked her movement. The water started to bend in mid-stream and extend out toward the boy.

When the water hit the boy's lips, his head jerked back because it surprised him. But, as his lips opened, he began to suck as much water in as he could. The slurping sounds were as loud as someone trying to get the last drops out of a soda with a straw. His face got all wet as the water bounced off his chin and cheeks. His shirt displayed the aftermath with water spots as he finally let go of the button and rolled back onto his flat feet. He stared at the fountain for half a second, then looked up at Rio, wide-eyed and sporting a huge grin. He then turned around and ran back to his Dad for high-fives.

"Dad," he yelled. "I did it! I told you I was tall enough!"

Rio chortled as she watched. Her eyes met the boy's father's and she tilted her head and shrugged her shoulders again. This time, it was as if she was saying, *Who knew?* The man reciprocated the gesture and then turned his attention to his son, to whom he offered heaps of congratulatory praise.

Rio finally looked back down at the fountain and began to wonder, once again, what it was that was happening to her. Not needing contacts this morning was certainly very strange. She had never even heard of anything like that happening to someone. But, this water in the drinking fountain incident was even more peculiar. She was physically seeing something take place that seemed like a scientific impossibility. Even more, she felt it happen when the water entered her mouth and quenched her thirst. Then, it appeared that she had willed it to happen to the little boy as well. None of this seemed at all possible. Yet, it had all happened. It wasn't even 10:30am, her journey barely yet begun, and this had already been the strangest day she had ever experienced in her entire life.

As if summoning her to more unfamiliar territory, that's when the boarding call for her flight came over the loudspeaker.

CHAPTER TEN
Take Off

The flying portion of the trip started off uneventfully. The flight from Hilo to Honolulu took less than an hour. Rio then not only changed planes but airlines during her almost two-hour layover. The lengthy break even allowed her time to hit Starbucks and grab a bottle of water and a sandwich to take on the flight. When the break was over and she boarded the next plane, her real adventure began.

Finally, after all the waiting, she was seated by the window, staring out at the runway, about to take off. She was minutes from leaving Hawaii and would be in Osaka in less than nine hours. Her heart was pounding.

Rio had been on airplanes before and, at times, had even traveled great distances for swim meets. But, never, in all of the trips she had taken, had she been as excited as she was at that moment about the trip she was finally embarking on. When the idea for this expedition had hit her while she was swimming in the Wailuku River, she had instantly known it was the right thing to do. Now, barely three weeks later, she was on her way.

As Rio felt the pressure of the engines increase power and then release when the plane finally started to move, her tummy flipped and her heart continued to race but she couldn't keep her eyes off the view out the window. She felt the plane lift and watched the runway disappear. Rio continued to watch as the ground faded further and further away. Soon, it was replaced with the surface of the ocean. If her smile could have gotten any bigger, it would have. It was official. Her next stop was Osaka, Japan.

It wasn't until the captain began to talk over the loudspeaker, to announce that they were almost at cruising altitude, that Rio peeled her gaze away from the window. And, she didn't talk to anyone until the flight attendants came by with snacks and beverages. Rio, of course, just asked for some water.

That's when she finally calmed down a little and began to settle in, stirring her water with her mind and thinking about how cool it could be to take complete control of this new ability she was discovering inside of her. Even though she didn't understand the ability or know where it came from, she figured she might as well make the most of it. That's also about the time she overheard a man behind her and in the aisle seat on the opposite side of the plane complaining about the beer selection. The man said he was going to Japan and he wanted a Japanese beer. The flight attendant offered him Kirin but he complained that he wanted Sapporo. When she told him that they didn't have Sapporo but that Kirin was a Japanese beer that was more than a hundred years old, he said that Sapporo was even older and that's what he wanted.

Rio wondered how much Sapporo he'd already had before getting on the plane as she leaned forward and looked back across the sleeping man sitting next to her to see who the rude passenger was. The obnoxious man looked normal enough but he was getting louder and more agitated.

As Rio sat back in her seat, the flight attendant offered to buy his Kirin for him and the man begrudgingly took it, opened it and filled the plastic cup he was handed with a napkin and two small packages of pretzels. But, he apparently couldn't help himself and continued to mutter obscenities, in between sips from the leftovers in the can. The flight attendants moved their cart past him down the aisle and the woman who had been helping him began talking to another customer.

Rio thought about the fact that water had to be one of the ingredients in beer and she leaned forward again, thinking he deserved a lap full of cold liquid. But, when she did, she noticed the woman next to him crushing up a pill, scooping the powder, and pouring it into her glass of water. Now that her vision was somehow 20/20, or perhaps even better, she looked at the label on the prescription bottle that rested next to the water cup. The woman was stirring the contents of the cup with a plastic spoon on the tray table folded down from the back of the seat in front of her. The drug was called Zolpidem but Rio had no idea what that was. Then she spotted the word insomnia and a sly grin crept up on her face.

The woman with the pills glanced around as if she wanted to make sure no one was watching her. Rio quickly looked away and reached down to her backpack so she could pretend she wasn't looking. While she was down there, she fished out her portable CD player, headphones, and one of the three CD's she had packed for the trip. She put them in her lap and snuck a peek back at the woman. She was crushing up a second pill.

Rio briefly wished she'd been given the gift of telepathy that included all objects, not just water. Then, she'd be able to send the powder straight into the man's beer. Instead, she was going to have to get more creative.

She waited until the woman had dumped the rest of the powder into the water. Then she watched as the man took another swig of his beer and she caused the remaining contents of the can to spill out and dribble down his chin. He let out a curse word and then grabbed the napkin from under his cup.

The commotion caused the woman to let go of her cup of water and look out the window. Rio assumed that it was her way of pretending not to notice so she didn't have to talk to the man. But, while the man was distracted by wiping beer off his chin and the woman was looking out the window, Rio focused in on both cups. She lifted the contents of both out of their plastic containers and gently placed them in the opposite cups. So, the woman suddenly had the beer in front of her and the man had the water, along with the two Zolpidem pills that had been stirred into it.

Finally, the man angrily set his napkin down and, without paying any attention, grabbed his cup. In a frustrated gesture, he lifted the cup up to his lips and took a swig. However, Rio wanted him to down the whole thing before he even realized what he was drinking. So, she sent that water pouring down his throat so swiftly that the man guzzled it all. However, by the time he was done, he was in the middle of a choking and coughing fit.

"What was that?" the man exclaimed as he put his damp napkin to his mouth. He noticed his beer sitting in front of the woman next to him. He looked her up and down as he muttered a few more obscenities, took his beer and tried to drink it in between coughs.

The woman was, of course, every bit as confused as the man was. She looked the tray table over as if she expected it to provide an answer.

Another flight attendant, who had not been unlucky enough to deal with him the first time around, hustled over to see if there was anything she could do to help. He demanded another beer but, this time, he was forced to pay for it.

Rio let out a little chuckle, enjoying the scene as things calmed down. Then, she took the compact disc out of the jewel case in her lap and popped it into the CD player that was resting underneath the case. The disc contained the album *The Score* by The Fugees. Her favorite song on the album was "Killing Me Softly with His Song" but that was track number eight so, she wouldn't get to that one for about a half an hour. She put her headphones on and listened to the *Red Intro* and the song "How Many Mics" before getting to the third track. And it was during this track, "Ready or Not," that she looked back and discovered the obnoxious man a row behind her and across the aisle was sound asleep. The woman next to him was crushing up another pill.

Rio smiled with satisfaction, leaned back in her seat, and looked out the window as she mouthed the words to the chorus: "Ready or not, here I come . . . "

CHAPTER ELEVEN
Serendipity

Rio's tummy flipped for the second time on the plane when the pilot announced that it was time to prepare the cabin for landing. Her enthusiasm was barely containable as she ripped off her headphones and stuffed her portable CD player into her backpack. This was the first time she had noticed the snoring. She glanced back and saw the obnoxious man sound asleep as a flight attendant put his tray table up for him but was careful not to wake him. Rio decided that was best for everyone around him.

She briefly considered the fact that she hadn't dozed off herself. It surprised her. Rio had never been one to sleep beyond the normal seven to eight hours per night, even as a teenager. But, she had typically found the monotony of a plane ride something that caused her to take naps. She chalked it up to the excitement of the expedition and quickly let the thought escape her mind. Instead, she turned her attention to the window and searched for any sign of the land of her ancestors.

It was about 9:30pm back home but they had passed the International Date Line during the flight and it was 10:30am the following day in Osaka. Therefore, daylight was not a problem. At first, however, all she saw was water. But, the cityscape soon came into view. To Rio, it looked like a modern civilization emerging straight out of the ocean. Her tummy flipped for a third and final time. She couldn't wait to begin exploring.

When the plane finally touched down, she completely ignored the obnoxious man who jerked awake behind her. All she could think about was getting off the plane, seeing where she came from and finding the people who made up her long-lost family. The family member she was particularly excited to meet was, of course, her biological father, Sota Tanaka.

The length of time it took for the plane to taxi to the gate, for the ground crew to connect it to the jet bridge, for Rio to retrieve her carry-on suitcase from the overhead compartment and wait for all the people in front of her to get off the plane was only about fifteen minutes. But that fifteen minutes was so excruciating to Rio that it may as well have been fifteen hours. She walked in the dawdling line like a little girl doing the *pee-pee dance.* But, when the opportunity presented itself just outside of the jet bridge, she broke free like a running back in a football game who had picked his lane through the defensive linemen and around the linebackers with the end zone finally in sight.

Rio was walking faster than any of the little old ladies, high-priced businessmen or families headed off on vacations that surrounded her. Had it not been so crowded, she may have flat out sprinted but, that just wasn't possible. Observers probably thought she was late for a flight. The truth was, she just couldn't wait to get out of the airport and decide on her next steps. She probably needed to find a place to stay and some way of getting around. She had read about the excellent public transportation system in Japan and knew that the trains were a popular method of travel. Luckily for her, it was still morning in Osaka and she had plenty of time to get it all figured out.

As she rounded a corner, she tumbled over a guy who was bent down tying his shoe. She let go of her bag on rollers and both she and the young man sprawled out on the floor.

"Oh," Rio exclaimed, "my gosh! I'm so sorry! Are you okay?"

Both scrambled to get to their feet and collect themselves.

"Yeah," the man said with a noticeably American accent as the people passing by changed their course to walk around them but, otherwise, ignored them completely.

Finally, Rio and the young man locked eyes. She was surprised to see the American accent come from someone who looked Japanese. She was even more surprised by the fact that he was so handsome. And, since most men are not all that subtle when they like what they see, she could tell he found her to be appealing, as well.

Rio grabbed her bag and they stepped toward the wall to get out of the way of other foot traffic. Just before they stopped moving, the young man finally managed more words.

"How about you? Are you okay?"

"Fine," Rio answered. "Well, embarrassed but fine."

"You're embarrassed?" the young man asked as if gaining a flirtatious confidence. "I'm the idiot who was tying his shoe in the blind spot of a busy walkway."

"And, I'm the idiot who wasn't watching where she was going."

They shared a grin, followed by a moment of silence. Finally, Rio broke through the romantic tension with the first words that came to her mind.

"Do you feel like maybe we fell asleep on our planes and woke up in the same cheesy rom-com?"

"Well," the young man started to answer, "I haven't been on a plane today but I'm glad to hear you find me attractive."

"What?" Rio exclaimed, finding herself embarrassed again but quickly trying to retrace her words to find out what she said that she shouldn't have.

"I didn't say . . . "

"Sorry," the young man interjected. "I guess I'm making an

assumption. I assume you and I are the leads in this cheesy rom-com and we all know Hollywood never casts unattractive leads. So, I guess I hoped that meant you found me attractive which would help heal my bruised ego from the whole tying the shoe in a busy walkway blind spot incident. It may also help heal your ego from the whole not watching where you're going thing to learn that I find you every bit as attractive as I'm still hoping you find me."

Rio simply smiled. Typically, when she started to like a guy, her experience was weeks of silent glances and a game of *Will They or Won't They* playing out in her mind. This guy had cut through all of that in about a minute and a half. She couldn't help but join the speed dating revolution.

"Consider your ego mended," she heard herself say but could hardly believe it. At the same time, she sensed her grin on her face growing to a point where she felt the corners of her mouth might be stretching beyond their limit. But, they surprised her and grew a little more.

The thought that followed was one that cemented a feeling she'd already been having for several weeks at this point, *Japan is going to be so freaking awesome!*

CHAPTER TWELVE
Unexpected

"Are you hungry?"

"Yeah," Rio found herself honestly answering the young man before even considering the possibility that he might be asking her out. When she finally realized what was happening, she widened her smile and finished her thought. "I am."

"Want to grab an early lunch?"

"I don't know you," Rio teased.

"Getting to know each other was sort of my main motivator for asking you to go to lunch," the young man shot back with a sly grin.

"What's your name?"

"Luke," he answered quickly and extended his hand.

"Rio," she responded as she took his hand to shake it. She held on a split second longer than seemed normal because she really didn't want to let go.

"Better?"

"Better."

"So, how about that lunch?"

"What's good around here?"

"We don't even have to leave the airport," Luke said as he took her bag. "Follow me."

Rio was shocked to see both a McDonald's and a Burger King as they wandered through the airport. Luke was pointing out some of the places he liked including a Chinese place, which Rio was also surprised to see. But, the real kicker was when they passed a Starbucks. Suddenly, Rio didn't feel so far from home. And, the final blow was delivered when Luke walked her into a little restaurant called Kona Kafe.

"Are you serious?" she asked.

"Why?" Luke responded, surprised. "What's wrong?"

"Do you know where I'm from?"

"No. Should I?"

"Of course not. But . . . Do you know where Kona is?"

"Hawaii."

"Right. It's on the opposite side of the same island from where I live. It's, like, an hour and a half from where I grew up."

"No way," Luke said, genuinely thrilled by the coincidence. "That's awesome. I think this place has the best coffee around. And, I can't find Pipikaula anywhere else. I'd never heard of it before but it's awesome and I get it every chance I have. If you're from Hawaii, you probably know exactly what Pipikaula is though, huh?"

Rio nodded her head affirmatively with a grin.

"You want to go somewhere else? There's a great noodle place . . ."

Rio shook her head and stopped his sentence by reassuring him. "Pipikaula sounds really good."

"Are you sure?"

"Positive."

"Good. Because the noodle place doesn't hold a candle to this joint."

The two sat over plates of Pipikaula, which is beef that has been dried and charred like jerky and served with sides of white rice and a Hawaiian tradition called poi. Poi is taro root that has been mashed into a sticky paste. The Pipikaula was also served with a variety of condiments like sesame seeds, kim-chee, garlic powder and honey. Rio didn't have the heart to tell Luke that, although she enjoyed the meal, she'd had better Pipikaula back home. Her guess was, in Hawaii, they stuck to tradition and dried the meat outside until it was chewy before char broiling it but, here, they had probably dried it in an oven. Ultimately, it really didn't matter. The real star of the meal was the conversation.

Rio asked if Luke worked at the airport since he had

mentioned not being on a plane that day, he clearly didn't have to get on one since they were now sharing a meal, and he seemed to know an awful lot about the airport. But, Luke explained that he simply spent a lot of time there. He had been in and out of it several times himself but, even more, he had picked people up and dropped them off there too many times to count. The real surprise came when Rio learned why - Luke was a Christian missionary.

He grew up in the southwestern corner of Torrance, a city in the South Bay region of Los Angeles County, California. The house he lived in for his entire childhood was near a place called Rat Beach. It was wonderful that they had a love for the water and beaches in common. Luke was even a surfer. He was constantly surprising Rio.

He was third generation American and grew up in a Christian home with loving parents. Much to the dismay of his great-grandparents, Luke's grandparents had converted from Buddhism to Christianity at Billy Graham's first crusade in 1949. The crusade was held in a tent they called a canvas cathedral at the corner of Washington and Hill streets south of downtown Los Angeles. Luke considered it a privilege to be born into a family with the Christian foundation already in place. When he learned, as a teenager, that the country of his ancestors was about 35% Buddhist, 4% Shinto, 1% other religions including

Christianity and the other 60% didn't identify with any religion at all, he immediately felt called to go to Japan and share the love of Jesus Christ. But, he was determined to do it all the way. So, he finished high school and moved to Pasadena where he attended Fuller Theological Seminary. He stayed until he completed his Master of Arts in Theology and Ministry. Then, he hooked up with an organization called Christian Youth Outreach International. They put on sports camps around the world for anyone under the age of eighteen who wanted to attend. While there, the kids learned how to be better athletes. And, they also learned that there is a God who loves them. Luke had been working with CYOI for two years now and his passion for it had only grown stronger.

Rio was amazed at his story. She had never met anyone like him. And, Luke was equally fascinated with her story. He had never met anyone like her either. He didn't seem to bat an eye when she admitted that religion had never been a part of her life. She half expected to feel judged but, the judgment never came. In fact, Luke offered to be something of a tour guide and drive her around – even help her find a place to stay. They were amazed when they realized three hours had passed and quickly decided that the adventure they were going to now take together should not be delayed any further. With that, Luke and Rio officially left Hawaii behind and stepped outside into Osaka, Japan.

CHAPTER THIRTEEN
Old Church Van

Rio stopped and stared as Luke approached the silver van with black, red and orange stripes on the side. It was a 1988 Toyota Master Ace Surf that had been lowered on BBS mesh wheels. It had windows all the way around that almost made it look like a space ship in a mid-nineteen-eighties b-movie. The two sets of side windows in the back and the rear window all had curtains hanging in it that, at one time, probably matched the orange stripe on the side but had since faded with years of direct sunlight.

"This is yours?" Rio finally asked, unsure if she should laugh hysterically, show her complete disgust, or run for her life.

"Yeah," Luke stated without thinking anything of it as he opened the rear hatch and placed Rio's bags inside before closing it and turning to face her. "Well, it belongs to the ministry, actually. Why?"

"It's a little creepy, don't you think?"

"Creepy?"

"Definitely. Like, hey kid you want some candy, creepy."

"What? No way."

"Yes way."

"This is the kind of ride rock stars take on tour."

"By that, do you mean to say, this is the kind of ride garage bands take to their first out of town gig because the drummer borrowed it from his uncle who, the day before, was asking kids if they want some candy?"

"Well, thanks a lot. The next time I pick up kids to take them to basketball camp, I'm going to feel like a complete low-life."

"Oh," Rio started with a silly grin that feigned shame, "I'm sorry."

"Sure you are. Maybe you just need to hear the soundtrack."

"The soundtrack?"

"Yeah. Audio Adrenaline plays the van's theme song."

"Audio who?"

"Audio Adrenaline. Christian rock band."

"Never heard of 'em."

Luke walked around to the passenger side of the van, unlocked the door, and opened it for his guest. "Hop in. I'll introduce you."

"Okay. But, if I get in and find a big bag full of candy I'm getting back out and running away as fast as I can."

"Deal."

Rio climbed inside and glanced around at the grey carpeting and matching cloth seats. She didn't see any candy. *Good sign*, she decided as Luke shut the door and walked around to the driver's side.

She briefly thought about how weird it was to be sitting on the left side of the front of the car but not be the driver. But that passed as Luke climbed inside the van, shut his door, started the engine, ejected a compact disc from the stereo and reached across Rio's lap to open the glove box. He pulled out two jewel cases, opened a brown one called *Jesus Freak* by a band named DC Talk, and inserted the disc from the stereo. He then opened the other jewel case and removed the disc inside before closing it again and putting both jewel cases back in the glove box. Rio closed the glove box as Luke put the second disc into the stereo. She noticed that the name of the new album was *Some Kind of Zombie* by the band he had mentioned just a moment ago, Audio Adrenaline.

"Ready?" Luke asked.

"For the Mystery Machine's theme song?" Rio fired back, flirtatiously.

Luke did his best impression of Scooby Doo's laugh which nearly dropped Rio's jaw into her lap.

"Okay," she stated in amazement. "I did not see that

coming."

"I'll take that as a yes," Luke said with a grin as he hit the button on the stereo to bump it up to track number six before hitting play.

It took a moment for the stereo to get the CD going and then catch the right track. But, when it finally did, the first twenty-three seconds of the song were all build-up. It started with an eight second, single electric guitar strum on just one string, drawn out with a slow-moving wow-wow bar. The following fifteen seconds included an up-tempo intro that Rio thought sounded almost like a mash-up of pop, rock, ska, and punk.

But, then the first vocals came in with the lyrics "Fourteen kids in an old church van . . . " and she and Luke started laughing like two old friends.

"Okay," Rio admitted. "I totally get it now."

"Good," Luke stated as if declaring a major victory.

Rio was surprised by how much she liked the music but, even more, by how much she had instantly connected with Luke. The whole thing was so unexpected but so incredibly welcome. A trip she was already thrilled to be taking had now become even more exciting and enjoyable because of this chance-encounter with a stranger in a foreign airport. She smiled to herself as she once again thought about how it felt like a romantic comedy cliché. But, here she was, living it.

"So," Luke began to ask, "where's our first stop?"

The question snapped Rio out of her thought process and forced her to change gears. "Oh," she exclaimed as she reached into her pocket and pulled out a piece of paper, "right. Um . . . I have it circled on this map. My mom said an address wouldn't work like it does back home."

"She's right," Luke agreed. "Most of the streets don't have a name and the buildings aren't numbered sequentially. Totally different system over here. Cities are all divided into Ku and Machi."

"What?" Rio asked as she finished unfolding the map and handed it to Luke while pointing at one of the circled locations on it.

"Um," Luke responded as he took the map, "they're like wards." He looked at the map for a few seconds before commenting. "Yeah, I think we can find this."

With a wink, he tossed the map on the dash, reached his left hand down, shifted into reverse, checked the mirrors and, with a glance over his shoulders, backed out of the parking spot. As the music transitioned into a much more mellow song Luke said was called "Lighthouse," the van rolled out of the airport and onto the Hanshin Expressway, headed south toward the house her mom once lived in with Sota Tanaka. The very same house in which Rio was conceived.

CHAPTER FOURTEEN
Details

Over Pipikaula, Rio had told Luke a lot about herself. She had even shared her reason for being in Japan. Of course, she left out the part about the prophecy and the fact that she had gone to bed the previous night with poor eyesight and awakened that morning with perfect vision and the ability to move water with her mind. But, other than those not-so-minor details, she had pretty much given him an accurate account. He knew that her mother considered her father to be a bad person but, that Rio wanted to find him and decide for herself. Luke thought that made her a brave young woman.

Rio had also learned a lot about Luke. But, now she wanted to pry a little more and find out what made him want to do what he was doing with his life.

"So, how do you know God exists?" she asked boldly.

"Do you think He doesn't?" Luke responded, scrunching his

eyebrows.

"I'm not necessarily saying that," she stated, contemplating.

"Because, I think to know that, you'd have to be God yourself. Which, makes it impossible."

"Whoa. What?"

"I mean, you'd have to simultaneously be everywhere and know everything in order to have the amount of information necessary to truly and emphatically know that God doesn't exist. And, if you were everywhere at once and had total knowledge and awareness, that would make you God. Are you God?"

"Nope. And, that was quite the philosophical smack down you just laid on me. So, thanks for that."

"I didn't mean it that way," Luke said with a chuckle.

"I guess I just don't know for sure one way or the other," Rio admitted. "I'm assuming, as a missionary, you believe pretty firmly that He does exist."

"Correct."

"How?"

"How what? How did I reach that conclusion?"

"Yeah."

"Well, I was raised in a Christian home. But, that doesn't mean I was always truly a Christian. I had my time of doubt before I made a real commitment."

"That makes me feel a little better," Rio said with a grin.

"The things I was being taught in church and the things I was being taught in school didn't always align. That bothered me. I wasn't sure if one was completely true and the other was completely false or, if both had gotten parts right and parts wrong. So, I started doing some deep thinking on my own."

"Is that how you got so philosophical?" Rio teased.

"Maybe," Luke acknowledged with a grin forming on his face. "I did quite a bit of research and a lot of praying. I asked God to, if He was real, show me what the truth was."

"And?"

"And, it started to slowly make more and more sense."

"What did?"

"Well, the first thing that hit me was the question of why is there something rather than nothing. Why does anything exist at all? And, how could it be an accident when all of the details are just so."

"The details?"

"The details. A caterpillar has two hundred and forty-eight individual muscles in its head alone. Each human eye has over two million working parts. There are over four hundred billion stars in our galaxy and something like a hundred and seventy billion galaxies in our universe. Now, obviously, most of that hasn't been explored yet but, so far, the most complex object we can find is the human brain. How could all those details have happened by chance? We're no accident, Rio. And, ultimately, the conclusion I came to was that the Bible offers the best answer."

"But, what if the Bible is wrong?"

"First of all, what if it's not? Second, it is truthful in all areas open to investigation. It's philosophically consistent and all its historical, geographical and scientific claims have already been verified as factual. Even its prophecies, end-time events of course excluded because they haven't happened yet, have all come true. If it holds up in every area we can test it in, why would we assume anything other than that it holds up in the areas we can't test it in, too?"

"You're right. That does make sense. I still don't know though."

"Besides, we know from observational evidence that the universe is expanding and, therefore, had a beginning. That means it clearly isn't eternal. It had to come into existence by way of something else that existed before it. The scientific law of cause and effect also tells us that the effect can't be greater than the cause. So, whatever brought the universe into being is greater than the universe itself. This is true of everything in the physical universe. Nothing exists that is not dependent on something else for its existence. To explain the existence of the dependent, non-eternal universe and everything in it, knowing again that it did have a beginning, there must be an independent and eternal

Creator. And, like I said before, the Bible gives me the most satisfying answer for that. So, the only conclusion I could draw from there was that the Judeo-Christian God revealed in it is very real."

Rio watched him as he talked. If nothing else, she admired his intelligence, passion and certainty. And, she could see how he arrived at the conclusion that he had. Still, she had more questions than answers. Finally, she decided to get after one of the big ones.

"So, that Judeo-Christian God is supposed to be all about love and peace and stuff, right?"

"Yep. He is perfect in love, holiness, goodness, justice, wisdom . . . I could keep going."

"I'm sure. But, let's focus on the part where you say He's perfect in love. Doesn't the existence of suffering and hatred and all forms of evil prove that perfect in love God must not be real?"

"Not at all."

"Well, I can't wait to hear this."

"Good," Luke said with the least annoying smirk Rio had ever seen. "Captive audience."

"No doubt."

"Let me start with a question."

"Okay."

"How do you know what evil is?"

"What do you mean?"

"We can agree that murder is evil, right? Please say yes. Otherwise, I may have to pull this sweet ride over and let you out. For my own safety, of course."

"Have no fear. We can definitely agree that murder is evil."

"Good. But, how do we both know that?"

"We just do."

"Ready for me to get philosophical again?"

"Go for it."

"For us to both know that, a moral standard has to exist beyond us. In other words, without a moral absolute that exists outside of human consciousness, we would never be able to determine right from wrong in any universal sense. Yet anthropology and sociology tell us that there is in fact a universal standard of behavior in all people throughout history regardless of religion or culture. I believe that universal moral code originated with God and He summarized it for us in the Ten Commandments about thirty-five hundred years ago. Unfortunately, there is also sin in our nature. Therefore, when we follow our own standards of behavior, we tend to do evil. But, this is more proof for, not against, the existence of God. Because, if morality were truly relative, if it changed with culture or time, there would be no worldwide continuity. Instead, we have a God who judges perfectly what is right and wrong. He doesn't change.

Therefore, our moral standard doesn't change. He is the law-giver. Evil exists because we are often law-breakers."

Rio continued to listen. It was striking a chord because he was saying things that she hadn't thought about before and it all made sense. But, that didn't make it true. This was going to require a lot more mulling over. She was so deep in thought that she didn't even realize that the car had slowed down and then suddenly came to a complete stop.

"We're here."

CHAPTER FIFTEEN
Stepping Up To The Plate

Rio suddenly felt like her heart was going to burst out of her chest as she looked out the window and realized she had made it. It had all started with a swim in the Wailuku River. That's when the idea for this trip had come to her. And, now, here she was. She was parked in front of the house that her mother had lived in when she was married to Sota Tanaka. The same house in which Rio was conceived. And, the same house her mother had fled when she left Japan for America.

"Oh," she quickly started, "I'm here. I'm actually here."

"Uh-huh," Luke agreed. "Now what?"

"I don't know," Rio admitted as she looked closer and began to doubt that this really was the correct house. "I guess I go up to the door. Although, this doesn't really look like the picture my mom showed me. Are you sure this is it?"

"Pretty sure. Did you bring the picture?"

"No but, this isn't how I remember it."

"Well, it's the spot circled on your map. A lot of the houses in Japan aren't built to last. Some of them are torn down every twenty to thirty years so, it's very possible this is the same location but a completely different house."

"Really?"

"Really. Even if your father still lives here, he may have built a new house on the same lot. Do you know whether or not he does still live here?"

"I have no idea."

"Only one way to find out. Did you bring a gift for him?"

"No. Should I have?"

"I don't know."

"Then why'd you ask me that?"

"Well, it's customary, in Japan, to bring a gift when you visit someone's house. But, I guess that's more for like when you're invited over for a dinner party or something. I don't know. This scenario is pretty much brand new to me, too."

"Like I said, I don't even know for sure if he lives here. And, if he does, I don't know if he'll be home. And, if he is, I don't even know if he'll invite me in. As you can tell, I really don't know anything."

"You're right."

"That's kind of mean," Rio teased.

"No, I mean, you're right that you don't need a gift. You're good. Just go for it."

"Aren't you coming with me?"

"Oh," Luke reacted, genuinely surprised by the invitation. "Sure. Yeah. I'll come with you. Let's go."

They each climbed out of the van and walked to the front of the house. They stopped side-by-side, neither sure exactly how to approach the door. Rio had been so brave and optimistic up to this point. Suddenly, she found herself unsure. But, that wasn't about to stop her.

Rio glanced around at the white wall surrounding the property. It was only a few feet tall and had rounded, gray shingles lining the top of it. The entrance to the property was at least twice as tall as the wall and made from wood. It was covered by a roof that sloped down on either side and was also covered in the same gray shingles.

"Okay," Rio said out loud. She had psyched herself up and Luke followed her through the gated entrance. The property on the other side of the wall had well-manicured green vegetation and the grounds all looked like they had been well taken care of for many years. Rio particularly liked the trees that looked like layers of perfectly rounded puffy green clouds.

Approaching the front door, Rio raised her hand to knock.

"Wait," Luke said, stopping her. "If you're going to knock,

only knock twice.

"What?" Rio asked, sincerely confused.

"In America, we tend to knock three or four times. Here, they only knock twice."

"Seriously?"

"Yep."

"Why are there so many rules?"

Luke simply shrugged his shoulders.

"Bring a gift. Don't bring a gift. They're this particular on the number of knocks on their doors but they don't care about numbering their houses sequentially? Seriously? This is absurd. Are you tricking me right now?"

"No," Luke answered sincerely. "I promise. If you don't want to test the waters, just ring the doorbell."

Rio smiled and, in a display of trust, raised her hand and knocked twice. She was a little surprised when a woman about her mother's age answered the door. She quickly decided that it would make sense for Sota to be married to another woman by now. After all, her mother had remarried a long time ago.

Luke was impressed when he heard Rio properly introduce herself in Japanese by saying "Hajimenmashite, Marlow Rio to moushimasu." He followed Rio's lead and introduced himself as well. After the woman took her turn, Rio realized it was not Sota's wife. In fact, after a few minutes of conversation, they discovered that the woman had never even heard of Sota Tanaka.

Rio and Luke walked away with Rio disappointed but not defeated. It was only the first strike and she still considered herself very much up to bat. They climbed back into the van and Luke immediately started the engine. He quickly changed the stereo to track number six and the song "Blitz" by Audio Adrenaline started to play all over again. This quickly brought delight back to Rio's face.

"Ready to see the outreach?" Luke asked.

"The what?"

"The outreach. The ministry. Where I work."

"I suppose. Although, I should probably figure out where I'm staying tonight and how I'm going to get around tomorrow."

"I've already got you covered."

"How's that?"

"First of all, I'll drive you where you need to go. And, second, we have dorms that no one's using right now because there's no camp. You can stay there."

"Really?"

"Really."

"I was just planning to find a hostel or something."

"Have you seen a Japanese hostel?"

"No."

"You don't want to stay there."

"Why? Is it not safe?"

"I don't think it's any less safe than other hostels. But, the ones I've seen here are like walls of double-decker rooms barely bigger than coffins that look like dryers at a laundromat."

"That's appealing," Rio stated sarcastically.

"Yeah. Not really."

"Will your co-workers be okay with me staying there?"

"Absolutely. We're missionaries. You're my current mission. They'll get it."

"That's amazing."

"I agree. Someone's looking out for you, Rio."

"Yeah, you."

"I'm just a servant," Luke told her as he started to drive. "The One looking out for you is a lot more significant than I am."

CHAPTER SIXTEEN
Spicy Beef

As Luke drove the van into the parking lot of Christian Youth Outreach International, Rio couldn't help but think that the campus looked a lot like a school back home. There were five buildings. The biggest one was used for indoor sports like basketball, ping-pong and gymnastics. There was a second building used for indoor water sports like swimming, diving and water polo. What the staff called the main building was used for administrative purposes and housed the cafeteria. Finally, there were two dorms - one for boys and one for girls. Surrounding those five buildings was a track and several fields used for sports like soccer, baseball and cricket. Rio also spotted some tennis courts. She was very impressed and even remarked to Luke that it all reminded her of an Olympic training facility. Of course, in reality, it wouldn't measure up to those standards. But, for a sports camp, it really was quite extraordinary.

Luke told Rio about how busy it gets when the campers arrive as he led her into the main building. Loud was one of the words he used. It was almost hard to imagine for Rio because it was currently so quiet. However, she had been in enough school cafeterias and on enough playgrounds to know exactly what he meant.

They set Rio's luggage down next to a table in the cafeteria and pulled chairs down from on top of the same table. Sitting down in the chairs, they unpacked the paper bag they had picked up at a local Japanese fast food restaurant on their way in. It contained two dinners. Both were beef bowls, which were basically just beef on rice, because Luke swore it was the best thing on the menu.

Rio teased him about eating nothing but beef since that's what they had for lunch. Once she tasted it, she understood and informed him that she hadn't grown up consuming a lot of beef but that he was quickly turning her into a beef girl. He took it as a compliment, picked the bowl up off the table, and sat back in his chair with a hint of satisfaction and accomplishment showing in his body language.

"Looking kind of proud of yourself over there," Rio pointed out.

"I think what you just told me is that I have really good taste," Luke said in defense. "So, yeah, I take a bit of pride in that."

Rio's face displayed full-on flirtation mode as she responded, "You do and you should, Sporty Spice."

Playing along, Luke jabbed back, "Sporty Spice? From beef and pride to Sporty Spice? I don't see the connection."

"No connection there."

"Clearly."

"But, you're obviously Sporty Spice. Look at what you do for work."

"Oh, okay. Got it. Now it makes some sense. So, which Spice Girl does that make you? You don't seem frightening enough to be Scary Spice."

"Thank you."

"Your hair is black so, you can't be Ginger Spice."

"True."

"That leaves Baby Spice and Posh Spice."

"Neither."

"You have to pick one."

"Then I'm Sporty Spice."

"You can't be Sporty Spice. We already made me Sporty Spice. In fact, you made me Sporty Spice."

"Then we're both Sporty Spice."

"We can't both be Sporty Spice. It's like the Highlander. There can be only one."

"The what?"

"The Highlander. You've never heard of the Highlander?"

"Guess I missed that one. What is it?"

"It's not just one thing. It's like three movies and a TV show."

"Oh. Okay. Guess I missed them all."

"Alright. Let's say there can be more than one Sporty Spice. What's your sport?"

Rio suddenly realized she'd gone the whole day without talking about swimming. She couldn't remember the last time that happened.

"I swim."

"You do?"

Rio nodded.

"Competitively?"

Rio nodded again as she spoke, "I'm on scholarship at the University of Hawaii."

"Oh, wow. Impressive. You'll have to check out our pool."

"I'd love that. What's your sport?"

"Basketball and baseball. I played both in high school. Probably could have played baseball in college. But, I went to seminary instead."

"Also impressive." Luke and Rio shared a flirtatious look that abruptly ended when Rio heard some loud clanging, followed by a squeal. She cocked her head and scrunched her eyebrows. Then she heard what sounded like a repeated thud sound, each followed by something akin to the tearing of paper. She looked at Luke.

"Are you okay?" he asked, with real concern.

She didn't respond at first. Then she heard the clanging sound again and asked, "Do you hear that?"

"I don't hear anything."

Next, she heard a bigger thud, followed by the sound of air being released.

"Is someone here?"

"Maybe in the offices. Why?"

"You really don't hear that? It's so loud."

"Stay here. I'll check it out."

As Luke stood up and walked away, Rio squinted her eyes. She was surprised to realize that his movement was excruciatingly loud. Luke's footsteps sounded like the thud and paper tearing pattern she had been hearing but, even louder. As he disappeared from view, the volume decreased until it balanced out with the first sounds. Then she heard him open a door and walk about twelve more steps before he began to speak to someone. She could hear every word as clear as if it were happening just a few feet away.

That's when Rio realized that what had happened to her

eyesight was now happening to her hearing. Wanting to gain control of it, she looked across the room and out a window. As she focused her eyes on a tree just a few feet outside of the window, the conversation between Luke and a man he called Isaac disappeared and it was replaced by the ribbit sound of a tree frog. Suddenly, the tree frog also came into view as if it were only a couple of feet in front of her face. Rio sat back in her chair, probably looking a lot like Luke had when she admitted he was turning her into a beef girl, when a hand on her shoulder sent her leaping to her feet in alarm.

"Uh," Luke started with a little embarrassment showing through, "Isaac, this is Rio."

CHAPTER SEVENTEEN
Goodknight

Rio quickly collected herself and shook Isaac's hand. "It's nice to meet you," she stated, nervously.

"Likewise," Isaac responded without a hint of skepticism. "Luke tells me you're here looking for your birth father and you need a place to stay. I hope our dorm rooms aren't too cramped for you."

"I'm sure they'll be fine." Rio lit up with enthusiasm as she realized Luke had been right. She was welcome to stay. "Better than fine. I'm sure they'll be fantastic. Thank you, so much."

"It's our pleasure to have you. He also tells me you're quite a swimmer. If you stick around long enough, we might have to put you to work as a coach."

Rio grinned as her eyes darted from Isaac to Luke and then back to Isaac again.

"Well," Isaac said as he extended his hand a second time,

"it's nice to meet you and I'll look forward to seeing you around. Go finish your dinner."

"Thanks again," Rio blurted out.

"Of course," Isaac insisted as he turned and walked away.

Rio and Luke sat down and finished their dinner. Luke beamed as he saw how excited and appreciative she was of the opportunity she had been given to stay in the CYOI girls' dorm. He was even more pleased when she expressed relief and even excitement when he told her that he acted as a Resident Director when the kids came and, therefore, resided year-round on the first floor of the boys' dorm.

When they were finished with their dinner, they threw the containers away and left the main building. Luke escorted Rio to the girls' dorm, unlocked the first door on the right side of the hallway on the first floor, and gave her the key to her dorm room. It looked a lot like the dorm rooms she knew from visiting her friends back at college. Once again, she was thrilled.

They placed her bags inside and began the official tour. Luke showed Rio where all the important places were like the bathroom and the laundry facilities before they left the dorm. He also showed her his room so she could find him if she needed anything. They walked around the campus and even went back to the main building for a more thorough tour. But, Rio's favorite spot was, of course, the building they called the Aquatics Center.

They agreed that a swim was likely an activity they would need to add to the calendar for the following day. However, it had gotten late and Rio wanted to call her mother before bed. So, the last stop on the tour was a pay phone in the lobby of the girls' dorm where the tour had begun. They agreed to meet in that same spot at nine o'clock the next morning. Luke said goodnight and walked out of the building. Both were sad to see the night come to an end but, knowing that they would get to have another day together when they woke up made it all better.

Rio pulled her calling card out of her wallet and picked up the phone to start dialing. Looking at her watch and doing some quick math, she realized her mom wouldn't be at home yet.

Toki was on her feet, behind her desk at the university, gathering her things and was about to start for home when the phone rang. She briefly debated about whether to answer it. Finally, she picked up the phone and answered as she usually would. When she heard her daughter's voice on the other end of the line, her tone quickly transformed into one of relief and excitement as she dropped back down into her chair.

She was thrilled to hear that Rio was safely in Japan and fascinated to learn that the woman who lived in her old house had never heard of Sota Tanaka. She presumed that meant that it had been sold at least twice since she left. Otherwise, she figured that the woman would know the name of the man who sold it.

But, she admitted, the woman's husband may have handled everything and, perhaps, she simply didn't know who they had purchased the house from. Either way, it was interesting for her to hear.

The most fascinating thing that Toki learned from Rio, however, was the story of her meeting this Christian missionary named Luke. She even joked that Rio had been in Japan for one day and had accomplished what Toki hadn't been able to do in a couple decades there - meet her knight in shining armor. She could hear the heart flutters in her daughter's voice when discussing him and how good he had already been to her. It made Toki feel good, too, that her daughter had been given what sounded like a safe place to stay and someone who knew the area to be with her on this journey. That added a sense of comfort for Toki that she didn't have when she dropped Rio off at the airport earlier that morning.

When they hung up the phone, they both felt relieved. Toki could drive home with a smile on her face. Not that all her concerns had disappeared but, most of them had subsided, at least a little bit.

Rio went to her room and got out her toiletries, took them to the bathroom and got ready for bed. By the time she climbed in, her thoughts were back on Luke. It surprised her that she wasn't focused on finding Sota. That, of course, was still the plan.

However, this new man in her life wasn't the man she was looking for when she stepped off the plane. The idea of him had not even occurred to her until she basically ran him over in the airport.

But, her thoughts weren't about how handsome he was, how kind and warm or even how smart he was. Her thoughts were on the things he said about why he was so confident that God was real and how He had revealed Himself in the Holy Bible. What he had to say made a lot of sense but, new questions were beginning to form in her mind. She was already beginning to look forward to having the opportunity to ask them the following day. Until then, she was hoping that it was time to close her eyes and get some shut-eye. But, unfortunately, she wasn't tired at all.

So, instead of drifting off to slumberland, she continued to think about the details that Luke had mentioned as evidence for the existence of God. *We're no accident* she remembered him saying. That made sense to her. All the details that made life work, from as big as the universe to as small as a caterpillar's head or the human eye, it was too specific and too perfect to have just happened by accident. And, as she followed her brain down the rabbit trail, she thought about what was happening with her eyesight, her hearing, and her newfound ability to control water. She thought to herself that this must be part of what the elderly woman had been talking about when she told her mother that she would be a gift to the world. In that moment, she knew there was a plan for her life. She just didn't know what that plan was yet. But, it was comforting to think that a plan did exist. She found herself going back to what Luke had said and reapplying it specifically to herself in her mind, *I'm no accident.*

CHAPTER EIGHTEEN
Before Breakfast

Rio had never been one to sleep her life away, nor had she ever gone a whole night without sleeping a wink only to start her day feeling like she'd just had the best sleep of her life. She was completely ready and waiting in the lobby of the girls' dorm just before 8:30am. That put her at over half an hour early. True, she was excited about what the day had to offer and she was really looking forward to spending it with Luke. However, the main reason Rio had arrived in the lobby so early was simply the fact that she had never gone to sleep and, therefore, had nothing else to do.

She wished she'd had the keys to the pool because she would have loved to go for a swim. But, that wasn't possible. Instead, she had to settle for an extra-long shower in which she had spent some time playing with her new abilities. She had stood under the shower head and redirected the water spray all over the sixteen-square-foot stall. The biggest kick came when she had telepathically spread the water out so it thinly sprayed everywhere and became like a mist after which she quickly funneled it into a steady stream like it was bursting out of a wide-open hose. She was practically famous for taking long showers but, this may have been her longest one yet.

With the lengthy shower having been over for more than an hour, Rio found herself waiting for Luke's arrival and time seemed to be nearly standing still. Luckily, Luke was excited about spending the day with her as well. So, she didn't have to wait too long. Luke arrived about ten minutes early and, he wasn't about to tell Rio but, truthfully, he could have been there about ten or fifteen minutes before that. Of course, they greeted each other ardently and immediately started walking toward the van. Excitement was certainly in the air.

"How'd you sleep?" Luke asked, sincerely.

"I didn't," Rio answered, honestly.

"At all?"

"At all."

"Why not? Was everything okay with your room?"

"Everything was great," she interrupted to reassure him. "I just never got tired."

"You must be exhausted then."

"I'm really not."

"Wow," Luke genuinely responded.

"I know. I'll probably hit a wall later."

"Yeah, I would think so. What'd you do all night?"

"Mostly laid in bed with my thoughts."

"Thoughts about finding your father?"

"That was part of it," Rio responded as they arrived at the van and Luke unlocked the passenger side door for her. She climbed in and reached across the driver's seat to unlock his door as he closed hers and walked around to his side. Rio sat back in the passenger seat and looked out the front windshield, realizing for the first time just how close they were to a lush, green mountain.

"That's gorgeous," she exclaimed as Luke climbed in and closed the door behind him.

"Mount Gozaisho. Not bad, huh?"

"Not bad at all," she agreed.

Rio finally peeled her eyes away from the beautiful view and pointed at another circle on the map as she informed him, "That's our destination for today, by the way."

"Okay," Luke said as he started to look it over. "Heading a little further south and a lot further east today, I see."

The distance wasn't exactly a surprise to Rio since she could see that by looking at the map but, she did calculate in her mind that Luke's statement meant this was more than ninety minutes in the car each way since that was about how long it took them to get to CYOI from her mother's old house the previous night. She realized that it was a good thing that she enjoyed the company with whom that time would be spent.

"Yeah, I think we can find this," Luke finally said. "So, what else?"

"What else, what?"

"You said finding your father was part of what you laid awake thinking about," Luke said as he set the map down and put the keys in the ignition to start the van. "What else did you think about?"

"Quite a few things," Rio answered, reflectively. She looked out of the passenger side window as the van started to move.

"If you don't feel like talking about it, you don't have to."

"Well," Rio started with a bit of hesitation before finally going for it. "I was thinking about the conversation we had about God and the Bible."

"Oh, okay."

"How can you be so confident that your religion is the right one? I mean, isn't it possible that all roads lead to the same place?"

"First of all, in spite of the old saying about Rome, that's not how roads work. Second, there are hundreds of religions out there and they can't all be true because they contradict each other."

"Okay, that's fair. So, how do you know?"

"Well, like I said yesterday, the Bible is accurate in every way that it can be tested."

"I know you did say that it was philosophically consistent and that its scientific, historical and geographical claims had been proven factual."

"And, prophecy."

"Right. But, not to sound dumb . . . "

"You don't sound dumb, Rio. This is heavy stuff that deserves a lot of questions."

"Thank you," Rio said, looking at him appreciatively. "But, what does all of that really mean?"

"Well, in large part, the Bible is a history book. It provides us with all kinds of information, including the customs, languages, ethics, religions and cultures of many ancient civilizations. And, when you compare what it says on those subjects with other sources, the Bible is proven to be accurate, reliable, and factual every single time. Secular archaeologists frequently use it to determine the location of their digs and, when they do, they consistently prove that reliability all over again. The last hundred years of archaeology have been fantastic for proof of the accuracy of the Bible. Thousands of finds in the Middle East have supported the biblical record. Places and events once thought by many to be legendary and mythological have instead been proven to be factual by archaeological digs."

"Like what?"

"Like the city of Jericho and the Hittite civilization. The five cities in Genesis and even the destruction of Sodom and Gomorrah. Like the fact that Israel's ancestry is derived from Mesopotamia and all the world's languages come from a common place of origin. Jewish captivity and their entrance to Jerusalem through a tunnel during the reign of David. All of which is taught in the Old Testament. But, the New Testament has been proven every bit as factual. Particularly the book of Acts which we now know had to be written within thirty years of the life, death and resurrection of Jesus Christ. The Gospel of Luke was written even earlier, by the same author, which means eyewitnesses would have still been alive to refute anything inaccurate or exaggerated."

"I don't know anything about any of that, let alone what's questionable and what's not."

"The point is that it was all considered questionable a hundred years ago and archaeology has proven that the Bible got it right thousands of years earlier."

"Huh," Rio pondered. "Wow."

"Yeah. There hasn't been an archaeological discovery yet that disproves anything in the Bible. Add to that the fact that there is no other religious document that provides thousands of prophecies regarding a whole host of subjects and then watches history fulfill those prophecies with total accuracy and I find it impossible not to believe the Bible."

Luke continued talking but Rio's mind began to drift. Her thoughts were on the things that Luke was explaining at first but, then they turned into what was happening with her. Of course, that included what she was doing there in Japan but those thoughts were also about the things that were going on with her physiologically. Ultimately, she started testing her vision abilities and trying to discover just how far off in the distance she could now see.

"I've got a bunch of books I can give you with tons of this kind of information if you're interested in reading them," Luke went on but finally stopped when he realized that he wasn't getting any kind of response and hadn't for quite some time. He looked over at Rio and noticed that she was staring out the window with great intensity.

"Rio?" he asked. "Did I bore you to sleep by going on and on?"

Still no response.

"I'll take that as a yes. Makes sense after you didn't sleep last night. I'll try not to be offended."

After noticing that her eyes were still open, Luke looked past

Rio and out at the green field on the side of the road to see if he could tell what had Rio so transfixed. There was nothing there. He looked further away at the water off the coastline.

They were travelling south on Route 23 just outside of Yokkaichi and Rio appeared to be staring out at Ise Bay. Luke could understand why. It was beautiful to look at. *Not unlike the person doing the looking,* he admitted to himself. But, it was more than that. Rio seemed to be concentrating, as if she was trying to figure something out. He thought he could see a dot way in the distance. Maybe a boat or something. But, it was too far away. That couldn't be it.

"Rio? Did I lose you?"

Finally, Rio responded but it wasn't at all what Luke expected. "Get down there, now!"

"What? Where?"

"There!" she yelled, pointing to the coast on their left. "He's drowning!"

CHAPTER NINETEEN
A Fisher Of Men

Luke, with heart racing, steered the van off the highway and onto a dirt road that wound its way toward the coastline as he peppered Rio with questions. "Who's drowning? Who do you see? Where is he?"

"The man by the boat!"

"What boat?"

"The boat out there!" she said, frantically pointing.

"I don't see anything. How can you see that far?"

Rio ignored the question as she continued insisting, "Just get down to the water."

"Then what?"

"Then I showcase the competitive swimming skills I told you about."

Luke glanced at Rio, surprised by her response and further surprised by the fact that she had begun to disrobe. The combination shocked him into silence as he sped down the bumpy dirt road and made an abrupt stop a few feet away from the water. By the time he did, Rio was already opening her door.

She leapt out and sprinted into the water. Luke couldn't help but notice that she was only wearing her bra and panties. He told himself it was no different than a bikini as he climbed out of his side of the van and began praying for her safety.

Rio swam as fast as she ever had in any competition. Had she not been so focused on getting to the man by the boat, she would have taken notice of how good the cool water felt on her skin. Or, she may have noticed how choppy the waters were. Instead, she simply powered through, with a tunnel-vision-like approach, to try and save the life of someone she had never even met before.

Luke stood in front of the van, shocked by how quickly Rio was out of view. This, of course, made him very nervous. *Lord,* he continued to pray, *protect her. Keep her safe. And, save this man as well. Please, send your angels to bring them both safely to shore.*

That was the moment Luke noticed a woman standing about a hundred and fifty feet away. She was watching Rio just like he was. Or, was she watching the man on the boat? Could she be waiting for him to come in? Had she been there the whole time? Where did she come from? Luke didn't see any car or bicycle around her and he thought she looked too old to have walked from anywhere of significant distance. But, there she was, just standing, alone, watching Rio and she took no notice of him.

Who cares? He thought. Rio and the man she was trying to save were all that mattered right now. He turned his attention back to the water, even though he couldn't see Rio, and continued to pray.

Rio finally reached the boat but the man was nowhere to be seen. She dove under the water and looked around, ultimately spotting his lifeless body, about thirty feet away, as it sank directly below her. Swimming in a hard, torpedo-like dive, she raced toward the man as fast as she possibly could. Her hands shoved the water to her sides as she reached in front of her face and then spread her arms out and back to her sides to pull her body toward the bottom of the ocean with all her strength. Finally, she reached forward and grabbed the man's shirt.

Pulling the limp body with her, she kicked her feet like a dolphin tail. It was a similar motion to the one she used when she turned at the pool wall in the middle of a race, right after kicking off the wall but before resurfacing for air. Had the man been conscious, he probably would have thought he was being rescued by a mermaid. Unfortunately, he was unable to make that mistake.

When Rio finally reached the surface, she gasped for air and pulled the man on top of her, his back resting on her chest. She noticed that he didn't breathe and quickly decided that she could be back on land more quickly than she could lift the soaking wet, heavy man up into his boat to perform CPR. In fact, she doubted that she was strong enough to get him into the boat at all, even if she had, had more time. She immediately started to swim backwards with one arm while the other held the man in place. She kicked her feet as hard as she could but the man was really slowing her down. *God,* she found herself praying for the first time in her life, *if you're up there, please speed this up and help me save this man's life.*

Finally, Luke could see Rio. She wasn't more than a hundred feet out. Without even thinking about it, he ran into the water to meet her. As soon as he arrived at Rio's side, he lifted the man up onto his back and rushed to the shoreline where he laid the man down in the sand.

Rio followed Luke and watched as he immediately began to perform CPR. She couldn't help but think about the fact that she felt like she had time-travelled on the way back to shore. Or, somehow, the distance out had been longer than the distance in. Perhaps, her very first prayer had been answered. If so, this man must be meant to live.

She calmly watched Luke go back and forth seven times between breathing into his mouth and pumping on his chest. But, it seemed, to Rio, like no progress was being made. Rio dropped slowly to her knees beside the man, opposite from Luke. She extended a hand and touched Luke's chest to gently stop his actions.

"What?" Luke exclaimed. "I'm not done. We might still be able to save him."

"I know," she peacefully replied as she placed her hand a few inches above the man's mouth and closed her eyes.

"What are you doing?" Luke asked.

Suddenly, water erupted out of the man's mouth like it was being shot out of a geyser. It hit Rio's hand and sprayed out around the man's head.

Luke sat back on his haunches and just stared in awe. He wouldn't believe it if he wasn't seeing it with his own eyes. She was telepathically pulling the water out of the man's lungs.

As the water stopped spewing, Rio placed her hand on the man's chest and pumped it five times. She then breathed into his mouth before starting to pump his chest again. On the twelfth pump of Rio's second round, the man sat up and gasped for air.

Luke continued to stare in total astonishment as the man caught his breath and then finally spoke.

"Arigatō, Rio."

CHAPTER TWENTY
Another Realm

Luke listened as Rio and the man had a conversation in which he introduced himself as Daichi, a life-long fisherman who couldn't swim. He had never been in the water above his waist before today. More importantly, he told Rio that he had in fact died and that, while dead, he had a conversation with an angel who informed him that it simply wasn't his time to go home yet. In fact, Daichi was told that a young woman by the name of Rio was going to be the one who brought him back.

Barely able to take his eyes off Rio and Daichi, Luke suddenly remembered the woman he'd seen watching and wondered what she thought of all of this. He spun around and searched with his eyes but the woman was no longer anywhere to be seen.

There goes the theory that she knew the drowning man, he thought. *Still, why would anyone leave in the middle of such an exciting event?*

Deciding to ponder that mystery later, Luke turned his

119

attention back to the miracle in front of him with his mind still racing.

Rio offered to give Daichi a ride to a pay phone so he could call a friend that he said would be willing to bring his boat down there and help him go back out into the bay so he could retrieve his fishing vessel. The three of them walked to the van and Rio introduced Luke. They exchanged pleasantries but, Luke was otherwise silent. Rio kept glancing at him awkwardly. She knew a conversation was coming and that, the longer she had Daichi around, the longer she could put it off.

On the ride back north, headed into Yokkaichi in search of a pay phone, Rio was putting her dry clothes back on over her wet undergarments when she mentioned that Luke worked near Mount Gozaisho at Christian Youth Outreach International and Daichi's face lit up. He explained that his son had attended camp there less than a year prior and had come to know Jesus on the final night of his stay. He also told them his son's salvation had spread through the family and that he was proud to call himself a follower of Jesus as well. It turned out the man he was going to call was not only a friend but his pastor who held a church service in his house.

For a moment, it was all too overwhelming for Luke. He had literally run into this stranger in the airport. Sure, he was instantly attracted to her but he had also felt that helping her was the right thing to do. So, he was driving her around and had even given her a place to stay. But now, she had seen an accident that was taking place too far away for any normal human being to see. Then she had performed a miracle right in front of his eyes and saved this man's life. Finally, it turned out that the man's son had become a Christian at one of CYOI's camps and had led that very man to the Lord. So much mystery and coincidence that none of it could be coincidence at all.

At first, it was too much, even for a man of such great faith. But, Luke gradually let it sink in that the man Rio saved, in a nation where only a fraction of one percent of the population shared that faith with him, was a practically brand new follower of Jesus Christ. His mood slowly lightened and his smile progressively brightened.

God is really something else, he thought to himself.

Not that he understood any of it yet. There were too many questions to count. Why Rio didn't seem at all surprised by any of it was at the top of the list. A little further down was the elderly woman on the beach who was watching the whole thing and then seemed to vanish into thin air as soon as it was over. But, he also knew some of that mystery was simply the God factor. The rest, he would be talking to Rio about as soon as they found Daichi a pay phone.

Luke drove the van off Route 23 and onto a city street. He

quickly spotted a pay phone. Rio briefly took notice of its bright green color as Luke pulled up close to let Daichi step out. Immediately, Luke looked at Rio with a big grin on his face like he was waiting for an explanation. Rio was quiet and had a difficult time making eye contact. Finally, Luke had to break the tension.

"So, that was really somethin', huh?"

Rio chuckled a bit as she agreed, "Yeah."

"You seem like maybe this isn't the first time," Luke pried.

"Oh," Rio piped up to explain. "No, this is the first time anything major like this has happened."

"What does that mean? Were there smaller incidents or something before this?"

"There was no sign of anything until I woke up yesterday," she stated with some uncertainty.

"Another coincidence that can't be a coincidence."

"What?"

"Nothing. What, specifically, have you noticed?"

"Well, I had to wear contacts before."

"And, now you have eyes like an eagle."

"I guess so."

"What about the whole telepathy thing?"

"The what?"

"I don't know what else to call it," Luke quickly admitted.

"But, somehow, you pulled water out of Daichi's lungs without actually touching him."

"Yeah, I first noticed I could move water when I was at a drinking fountain at the airport in Hilo."

"So, it's just water. You can't move other things?"

"No. I think it's just water."

"Interesting. Do you think you could pull the water out of my clothes? I wasn't smart enough to strip down. Feel a bit like I'm still swimming here. Kind of wish this sweet ride had leather seats, too."

The proverbial light bulb went off in Rio's mind. Why hadn't she thought of that sooner? She waved her right hand in front of Luke and held her left hand in front of her own body. Water began to travel out of their garments and the cloth seats, forming a sphere of water that hovered in the air between them. Rio then moved her left hand across her body and pulled the water out of the back seat where Daichi had been sitting and the water left his seat, entering the same sphere. By the time all the water had been collected it looked like a floating, translucent softball.

"Window," Rio calmly said.

"What?" Luke asked, truly confused.

"Can you please roll your window down?"

"Oh, yeah." Luke quickly did as he was instructed and Rio sent the sphere of water out through the window, finally dropping it on the ground. It popped like a water balloon. Astonished, Luke looked at Rio with wide eyes and a huge grin on his face.

"You're not scared of me?" Rio's question was sincere. She didn't want Luke to run and hide from her but she wouldn't have blamed him if he had.

"Scared? No. I'm a Bible-thumpin', faith lovin' man of God who just witnessed his first miracle. Scratch that. First two miracles. I'm not scared. I'm excited!"

"You are?"

"Absolutely."

"You sure?"

"Definitely."

"Because," Rio poked, "a few minutes ago you looked like you'd seen a ghost."

"I had just seen something nearly unexplainable," Luke defended. "Give a guy a moment to process the divine."

"I don't know about divine."

"Rio, God has given you a unique gift. Which might be one of my all-time biggest understatements. And, you just used that unique gift to save a man's life who told you an angel spoke to him about you. If that's not divine, then I'm in the wrong line of work."

Luke's response was hard to argue with and his use of the

word "gift" caused Rio's thoughts to begin running wild. She remembered her mom telling her about the elderly woman and using that same word. She may have explained further but Daichi came back from the pay phone and told them that he needed a ride to the dock where he was going to meet his pastor. Of course, they agreed to take him and within seconds they were on their way. Rio looked over at Luke and thanked God, whom she hadn't even believed in twenty-four hours earlier, that she had found him.

"Maybe after we drop Daichi off," she suggested as she leaned over and spoke quietly, "we can grab some breakfast or lunch or whatever time it is, grab some food and process this some more."

Luke agreed without words. He just nodded and smiled at the amazing young woman riding shotgun next to him.

CHAPTER TWENTY-ONE
Processing

Luke and Rio dropped Daichi off, exchanged pleasantries with his pastor friend, and then stopped at the first decent looking restaurant they passed on their way back to Route 23. The short drive was quiet but friendly and included several mutual glances and smiles.

Over an early lunch that finally included something besides beef, Rio explained everything about her life that she considered pertinent to the current circumstances. She knew in her gut that she could trust Luke. It was a good thing, too. Because, after what he had just witnessed, she was well-aware of the fact that she didn't have any choice in the matter.

So, as they shared a plate of Tempura and a chicken and egg rice bowl, Rio hit the reset button on the "get to know you" conversation that had begun over Pipikaula back at the airport the day before. This time, she left nothing out. She told him about the horrible way in which she was conceived, reiterated her mother's bravery in fleeing to Hawaii, informed him about each event while discovering her new abilities, and even explained every detail of the elderly woman prophesying that Rio would be born and that she would be a gift, not only to her mom but, to everyone.

After getting a great deal of amusement at the obnoxious airplane passenger and the sleeping pills incident, it was Luke who connected the dots on the elderly woman map. He pointed out that such a woman was at the beach that day which made Rio think of the woman by the drinking fountain in the Hilo airport. When they described the woman that each had seen, they were convinced that they had seen the same woman. That led them to believe they had possibly also seen the same woman who first spoke to Toki. Of course, Toki didn't even exist back then. At that time, Toki was a far meeker young woman named Mei.

Once again, Luke was riveted by Rio's story. Even more so, the second time around, now that he was being given all the details that had been left out during the first run through. He mentioned a verse from the Bible. Luke told Rio that Psalm 139 stated "you knitted me together in my mother's womb. I praise you, for I am fearfully and wonderfully made." He explained that the Psalm was written by King David as an affirmation of God's omnipresence but that the verse he was citing applied beautifully to her own life. Her story made it clear, in his opinion, that God had planned her life, and everything that was currently taking place in it, long before she had been conceived. Pre-ordained, he called it. He told her that he agreed that the way in which she was conceived was awful. But, it didn't change the fact that her conception had great purpose. In fact, he would go so far as to tell her that he believed God's plan for her life long-preceded her mother meeting the elderly woman on the bench that day. And, he felt truly honored to be a part of that plan.

Luke's words were comforting to Rio. She was encouraged by his faith, even if she didn't know exactly where she stood with her own, and she was thankful for his friendship beyond anything she could express at that moment. In fact, she found herself wondering how she would have survived this trip without him. Perhaps Luke was right and God had been looking out for her all along.

Rio insisted on paying for lunch to thank Luke for all that he had done, and was continuing to do to support her on this journey. Of course, Luke told her that wasn't necessary. But, ultimately, Rio won the friendly and flirtatious argument.

Leaving the restaurant, Luke had a sudden thought. He stopped in front of the van and looked at Rio as he spoke, "I know we're trying to get down to Shingu today but, even though it would be in the opposite direction, maybe we should try and find that bench."

The idea gave Rio pause. She was torn. The whole point of this trip to Japan was to find her father. Or, at least, that's how it started out. And, finding Sota Tanaka was still a high priority for her. But, when things began to physiologically change for her the day she left, those changes immediately began re-shaping the nature of their trip, too. Having just saved a man's life and the idea that the woman who prophesied all of it had possibly shown up both at the Hilo airport and again at Ise Bay, her priorities were in fact shifting. Finding her father was still very important. But, it might no longer be more important than finding out what was currently happening to her. Particularly, if this was such a big deal as to have been, as Luke had put it, pre-ordained by God Himself.

"What are the chances that we can do both?" Rio finally asked Luke.

"Well," Luke started to respond as he thought about it, calculating the distance and time, "I suppose, if we made the trip a big loop and did the bench on the way back, it's possible. Kind of depends on how much time we spend in Shingu."

"And, we won't know the answer to that until we get there."

"Right."

After another moment of thought, Rio finally made a decision: "I say we stick to the game plan and head for Shingu.

We can try to squeeze the bench in on the way back."

"Deal," Luke eagerly agreed. "Let's get going."

"Let's.

They climbed into the van and Luke popped in a new CD as he began to drive.

"I have a new theme song for you," he explained as he drove the van back onto Route 23. When the music started, it was a song called "Flood" by a band named Jars of Clay and Rio immediately recognized it from the introductory music.

"Hey," she exclaimed with enthusiasm, "I actually recognize this one."

As Dan Haseltine's voice kicked in, the first word sung was rain and he said it twice in a row. Rio instantly got the connection to water and they both started laughing.

"Perfect!"

CHAPTER TWENTY-TWO
Shingu

Luke and Rio had been on Route 42 longer than on any other road they had traveled that day. When they finally got off that highway, they backtracked slightly northeast on Route 168 and then took Route 44 south into Shingu.

Rio was instantly taken with all the bright colors in the architecture of the shrines and the beautiful gate to Jofuku Park. Other than the gorgeous orange, curved rooftops, red seemed to be the predominant color. But, the reds were flanked with greens, blues, yellows, and purples. She also noticed the scary looking gargoyles and the amazing amount of detail work that went into the colorful structures as well as the immense dimensional feel that all of the different angles and layers gave to the configurations.

The van rolled to a stop in a parking space across the street from Jofuku Park. Luke turned the engine off, pulled the keys out of the ignition, and took his foot off the brake.

"So," he started to ask with a heavy flair of skepticism, "we're just going to start walking up to strangers and asking them if they know the Tanaka family?"

"I guess so," Rio responded, letting Luke in on her uncertainty.

"How about we start over there?"

Rio's eyes shifted to look where Luke was pointing. "Why there?"

"Sign says they serve tea of tendaiuyaku. Never had it before. Never actually even heard of it. Some hot tea sounds good to me. How about you?"

"I prefer water," Rio said with a grin.

"Of course you do," Luke said with a laugh.

"I suppose I could try something new. It's as good a place to start as any."

With that, they climbed out of the van and walked over to the small café with the street sign advertising the little-known tea. The building was mostly covered in white tiles and naturally brown wood paneling but also had areas where the grey concrete underneath was showing. The two steps that led to the front door were covered in smaller white tiles and had a metal railing on one side. The glass door and the three window panes on the front of the café were all covered in neon-colored writing that advertised what potential customers could expect to find inside. The windows had wooden planters underneath them, with plants that looked like they could use some attention, and a large air conditioning unit sticking out of the front of the building above them. There was also a wooden, framed glass case, next to the front door, that displayed the café's menu and a gaudy, light-blue awning with yellow Japanese characters all over it, above that same door. Nothing seemed to match. And, yet, somehow the place still seemed inviting.

Luke opened the door and let Rio walk in ahead of him. He then told the young hostess that they weren't there to eat but they wanted to try the tea of tendaiuyaku and hopefully ask someone who was familiar with the area a few questions. The young lady ushered them to their seats at a finished but unstained, wooden table and said that she'd have her grandmother stop by, commenting that no one knew the area better than she did.

The hostess returned just a moment later and introduced her grandmother as Ichiko. Luke returned the favor by standing, bowing and introducing both he and Rio. Rio followed his lead by standing and bowing before asking Ichiko if she would mind sitting with them. The hostess pulled a chair over for her grandmother before telling them she would return shortly, with tea.

Ichiko spoke with a warmth and kindness. She was friendly

but formal, inviting but respectful. She began by asking if they had ever had tea of tendaiuyaku. When she learned that they hadn't, she continued by telling them about the tea they were going to drink.

They were surprised when the explanation started with the namesake of the park across the street. She told them that Jofuku had been ordered, by Emperor Shi Huang-Ti of China's Xin Dynasty in the third century B.C., to go to an eastern island, find the mountain of Horai and bring back a legendary elixir of immortality. Jofuku set sail with three thousand men, women and children. When they finally arrived in Shingu, they found a medicine tree called Tendaiuyaku that offered relief for stomach and pain issues that had arisen on the hard voyage.

Jofuku, and his three thousand fellow travelers, fell in love with the warm climate, the beautiful landscape, and the kind people of Shingu. Unfortunately for Emperor Shi Huang-Ti, none of these explorers ever returned to China. They made Japan their permanent home and imported Chinese culture, technology and skills of agriculture, fisheries, weaving and paper making to the area.

The hostess arrived with tea for all three of them and Ichiko explained that tea of tendaiuyaku is the elixir of life made from the very medicine tree that Jofuku had discovered when he arrived in Shingu twenty-two hundred years earlier and was still used to treat pain and stomach issues to that day. She further explained that Jofuku remained a symbol of the friendship between Japan and China.

As they sipped their tea, Rio and Luke each tried to hide their shock over how pungent the flavor was. Soon, Luke's eyes were watering, his nose was running and beads of sweat began to form on his forehead. Rio noticed this and understood exactly why he looked the way he did and why he was sniffling and wiping his eyes and brow. She was suffering the same unpleasant taste in her mouth but showed none of the physical side effects from it.

Rio asked Ichiko about her own personal history and Ichiko shared that her family had lived in Shingu going back for many generations. It was home, always had been, and always would be. Rio appreciated that answer. She liked the idea of putting down roots and having a history that was known and honored. That was a lot of what had drawn her to Japan in the first place.

Ichiko started to giggle. At first, neither Rio nor Luke understood where the giggle was coming from. Finally, Ichiko informed them that it had taken her almost seventy years to build up a tolerance so she could sip tea of tendaiuyaku politely. She told them a story about when her mother had given it to her as a child and she had been reprimanded for immediately spitting it out. Luke and Rio had never felt so much like tourists in all their lives. But, Ichiko's laughter was contagious and soon they were all laughing with water in their eyes for an entirely different reason.

As the laughter subsided, Rio decided it was time to ask if Ichiko knew anything about her father or the Tanaka family.

CHAPTER TWENTY-THREE
Family Feud

"Do the names Sota Tanaka or Mei Akagawa sound at all familiar to you?" Rio asked the question without expecting the perplexed look she got back from Ichiko.

"They do," Ichiko acknowledged, rather quickly, despite the look she had on her face. "Those are names I haven't heard in a long time. But, they're names that stay in the memory if you're from around here."

"Why's that?"

"They created quite a stir in Shingu a couple of decades ago. The question I'd like to know the answer to is, how do you know those names?"

"I'm their child," Rio responded.

"That's not possible," Ichiko insisted.

Luke was quiet but silently thanked God that he knew Japanese since the entire conversation between Ichiko and Rio was taking place in the language. He had realized that Rio spoke some Japanese when they met the woman who was now living on her parents' old property. But, he was now discovering that, while her Japanese wasn't perfect and there were several words she struggled with, Rio's Japanese was better than his own.

"It's not only possible," Rio countered, "it's the truth."

"Sota Tanaka and Mei Akagawa never had a child," Ichiko maintained.

"My mother left the country, and my father, shortly after learning that she was pregnant with me."

Ichiko was silent, at first, as she contemplated the possibility that Rio was telling the truth. "I suppose you're about the right age," she finally admitted. "Where did you grow up?"

"America," Rio answered with a bit of hesitation. She glanced at Luke, knowing that he already had the particulars. But, then she looked back at Ichiko as she continued. "I don't think my mother would want me getting much more specific than that. Do you know if I still have any family members in the area?"

"Sota Tanaka and Mei Akagawa certainly do. So, if you are who you clearly think you are, then yes."

"Can you tell me where to find them?"

"I think opening old wounds is a bad idea."

"You mean, because my mom left."

"It goes deeper than that, young woman."

"What do you mean?"

"The Tanaka Corporation was founded by Sota's father who had left Shingu for riches that he felt he could only find up north in Osaka. But, the roots of both the Tanaka and Akagawa families here in Shingu go back many generations. It was Sota's father who talked Mei's father into relocating and going to work at the Tanaka Corporation once it became successful. Many years later, the bond of the two families was cemented when Sota married Mei. When she left, everything changed."

"I had no idea."

"How could you? Something tells me, although your mother knew the positive impact her marriage had on her family, she couldn't possibly know the negative impact of her leaving. Not without staying in contact with someone in the Akagawa family."

"She didn't."

"I wouldn't imagine she did."

"She was right to leave though," Rio said in her mother's defense.

Ichiko looked surprised and possibly even a little offended by Rio's remark.

"How so?"

Rio thought for a minute. It wasn't Ichiko's fault she didn't have the whole story. Her mother had left without telling anyone what Sota had done to her or how loveless the marriage was, even before he had gotten so drunk and abusive. No one knew her mother's side of the story at all. And, Rio silently decided, she wasn't there to change that. It wasn't Rio's story to tell.

"Never mind," she finally said. "You say everything changed. What exactly do you mean by that?"

"From what I understand," Ichiko started in a very somber tone, "Sota lost his mind. He searched everywhere for Mei. And, when he couldn't find her, he disappeared in shame. Accusations of adultery, abandonment, even murder, flew forth. Both families blamed each other although neither had any evidence to back up their claims. No one has heard from Sota since probably about the time you were born. Most assume he took his own life. Either way, the Tanakas and the Akagawas haven't spoken to each other since."

Luke and Rio both sat back in their seats. Rio hadn't thought a whole lot about the aftermath of her mother's decision. Only the part where her father didn't know she existed. Luke couldn't believe the story he was hearing. It was like he was watching a real-life Japanese soap opera. And, he found it to be completely fascinating. Rio, on the other hand, mostly felt sadness. Of course, she already felt bad for her mother. But, now she found herself feeling deeply saddened by what her family, who she didn't know at all and had never even met, had gone through. It all happened because of what her father had done.

Maybe her mother was right and her father was someone to get away and stay away from. Perhaps he was a horrible man that she was better off not knowing. Or, maybe he was a man who felt as trapped as her mother had in a marriage he hadn't wanted. Perhaps he dealt with it by getting drunk and taking his anger out on his wife who he resented. Even if that were true, it didn't excuse it. But, it could, possibly, explain the motivation behind the horrible thing he had done and the awful chain reaction it had caused.

Rio couldn't help herself. She wanted to know more. She needed to know more. And, the only way to keep learning was to keep searching. So, she looked Ichiko in the eyes and made her pitch.

"I know you said that it's better not to re-open old wounds. But, I have a right to know my family. I have a right to know where I come from. Regardless of the past, I want to know the people I'm related to who are still here. Clearly, my mom's disappearance, and the events that led up to it, caused the Tanakas and the Akagawas to cut ties with one another. But, maybe that makes me exactly the person to bring them back together again."

CHAPTER TWENTY-FOUR
The Akagawas

Leaving the café, Rio now knew exactly where to find members of her family on both her mother's and father's sides. For that, she was thrilled. Of course, she was also overwhelmed by the sad news of how her family had been torn apart by the events leading up to her birth. The worst part of all of it was the, apparently wide-held, theory that Sota may have committed suicide a long time ago. While the possibility of suicide was only theoretical, it was all pretty upsetting and made approaching her family an even scarier proposition than it had already been.

What if they don't want to talk to me? she couldn't help but wonder. *What if they hate my mom and, by extension, hate me, too? If they do, this quest just became much more intimidating.*

"So," Luke interrupted her thought process as he began to ask, "where to now?"

Rio stopped walking and looked at Luke as she spoke, "I

can't stop now."

"I'd be stunned if you did," Luke said with delight.

"I think I have a better chance of being welcomed by the Akagawas," she said, finally answering his original question. "Let's start there."

"Let's," Luke enthusiastically agreed.

Rio shot back an artificial look of horror and they resumed their walk toward the van.

"You know," Luke started to say as he tried to comfort his new friend, "if you need a day to process what you just learned, that'd be okay. We could always go find that bench and then come back here tomorrow."

"You really want to find that bench."

"That's not it," Luke told her with a small chuckle. "I'm in no rush. I just want you to know you can take your time if you need to."

"Thanks," Rio said appreciatively. "Don't you have work you should be doing or something? You can't just keep running me all over Japan."

"It's a down time anyway," Luke told her, working up the nerve to confess something he feared would make Rio feel bad even though he didn't want it to. "I was actually supposed to be heading back to the airport tomorrow to hop on a plane to go see my family but, I cancelled my trip early this morning. So, I was already scheduled to be absent for a while."

"What? Why'd you cancel?"

"I want to see this thing through with you."

"Why? You just met me."

"True. But, I also know it's the right thing to do."

"How?"

"Discernment."

"What's that mean? Like, God's telling you, or something?" Rio's layer of skepticism was detectable in her voice but, it was a lot thinner than it would have been just days earlier.

"Not exactly. Well, sort of. Maybe. I guess. It's hard to explain. I just know that our meeting has a purpose and if I went home to see my family right now I'd be abandoning that purpose. I can't . . . I won't do that."

Rio surprised Luke, just a few feet from the van, by stopping again. This time, she threw her arms around him and hugged him tightly.

"I can't imagine doing this without you." She let go and looked him in the eyes. "Thank you."

"Of course," Luke responded. Both felt butterflies, enjoying the innocent hug even more than they might have imagined. But, they each tried to hide that feeling, too. It showed, subtly, in the slight increase of their smiles.

"With all that's happening right now," Rio told Luke, "I

think meeting you is the biggest miracle so far. And, that's saying something."

"Yeah, it is saying something. But, I couldn't agree more."

"Let's go meet my family."

"Let's."

Within minutes, Rio was knocking, only twice, of course, on her grandparents' front door. She and Luke were greeted by a frail, old woman who was short in stature and sported a full head of white hair. When Rio introduced herself, the woman met her with severe skepticism. She kept furrowing her brow and shaking her head, refusing to believe that Mei Akagawa had a daughter.

It wasn't until Rio produced a picture of she and her mother that the woman's cold demeanor began to warm. She looked, repeatedly, back and forth between Rio and the picture. Tears began to form in her eyes and, without warning, the woman reached forward and embraced Rio as she began to sob. Rio suddenly realized that she, for the first time in her life, was embracing one of her grandparents.

As Rio caught the contagion of her grandmother's tears, she and Luke were invited to come inside for a visit. The old woman, who eventually introduced herself as Emi, made tea, which tasted a lot better than the tea of tendaiuyaku they had shared with Ichiko less than an hour earlier. Rio's faith in drinks, other than pure water, was quickly restored.

Emi had gone from cold and suspicious to warm and welcoming. She wanted to know all about Mei, her departure and what she had been up to in the more than twenty years since they had last spoken. Unfortunately, Rio felt that there was only so much she could say. A lot of the story, after all, was once again not hers to tell. She did, however, promise to pass Emi's contact information along to her mother and suggest that she finally make a long overdue phone call. She also let her grandmother know that her daughter was in good health and happily married to a man she truly loved.

It was clear that all the news Rio was willing to share, was not only appreciated by Emi but, truly comforted her. Conversely, when Rio turned the conversation to questions for Emi, it was as if a dark cloud settled over the room. The last couple of decades had not been kind to the Akagawa family. And now, to add fuel to the fire, Rio learned something she briefly wondered why Ichiko had not informed her about. She must have known but ultimately decided, much like Rio had about Mei, that it was not her story to tell. Rio learned that her grandfather had been diagnosed with cancer of the jaw more than a year earlier. The cancer had likely come from decades of smoking a pipe and Eito Akagawa succumbed to the disease and passed away only three months before Rio's arrival in Japan.

The joy of meeting her grandmother diminished slightly with

the realization that the opportunity to meet her grandfather was already gone. Rio knew that not every story has a perfectly happy ending. If the suicide theory about her father proved to be true, this one could even be devastating. However, she was still determined to put all of the pieces of the puzzle together and find out exactly where on the happiness spectrum this story would end up.

CHAPTER TWENTY-FIVE
The Tanakas

Luke walked side-by-side with Rio as they left the Akagawa house. Rio was already dreading the fact that she had to tell her mother that the father she hadn't spoken to or seen in more than two decades was gone and with him the chance for reconciliation. However, the excitement of having finally connected with an important part of her ancestry was nearly palpable in the air that surrounded her. She had left her grandmother with warm hugs, happy tears, the promise to keep in touch, and an invitation to return with some advanced notice that would allow Emi to gather some more family members for a significantly larger reunion.

The walk started with a final wave goodbye between Rio and Emi, continued in silence for a moment as they distanced themselves further from the van, and ended less than half a mile from the Akagawa residence. The conversation that was taking place when they passed, on their left, a one-story white stucco house with brownish red wooden trim and a matching terracotta roof that made it look like it could have just as easily been in Italy, was mostly small talk.

They walked the cobblestone street that had been nearly overtaken by weeds and turned right to approach the Tanaka residence. It was a two-story yellow stucco house with gray wooden trim and another terracotta roof that had been painted a dark green many years ago.

The residents of the Tanaka house were not, as Rio was warned by Ichiko, Rio's grandparents. Those people had never moved back from Osaka. The couple who lived in the house were Rio's cousins. However, they refused to talk to her. It was a man who answered. He never introduced himself and wouldn't listen to anything Rio had to say. The mention of family names only seemed to make him angrier. He told them to get off his property and, ultimately, slammed the door in Luke and Rio's faces.

"Two sides of the family," Rio started as she looked up at Luke before turning to walk away, "two very different responses."

"I'll say," Luke agreed.

"Kind of fits the narrative as far as where my mom comes from versus what I know of my dad and where he comes from," she acknowledged as they re-entered the weed covered cobblestone street.

"Make you less anxious to find him?"

"Nope."

Luke chuckled, getting exactly the answer he had expected. He suddenly noticed a man, who was about twice their age, working in the garden behind the white house they had passed a few minutes earlier.

"Maybe we should ask this guy if he knows your family."

Rio looked at the man, then at Luke again as she asked, "Why would he know anything?"

"I don't know," Luke admitted. "Ichiko did."

"Good point."

They continued walking and stopped in the street, at the edge of the property, about fifteen feet away from the man. Each of them bowed respectfully as Rio announced their presence by introducing them in Japanese. She continued to speak as the man stood up and approached them.

"I'm searching for information about my parents. They were originally from here but, neither of them have lived here for a long time. I'm particularly interested in my father, Sota Tanaka."

The man's blank stare changed quickly. He was suddenly very interested in what Rio was saying.

"Do you know that name?" she asked.

"I do," the man responded sadly.

"That's great," Rio exclaimed.

"He never had a daughter. He never had any children. Who do you think your mother is?"

"My mother is Mei Awkagawa," Rio insisted.

"Impossible," the man dismissed Rio with a wave of the hand as he turned around to go back to work.

"Not impossible," Rio assured him. "Fact."

"Mei Awkagawa disappeared over twenty years ago. Sota Tanaka disappeared shortly after that. They never had a child. You're wasting your time searching for ghosts who are of no relation to you."

"I don't know about Sota Tanaka, but Mei Awkagawa is no ghost. She's still alive."

This caught the man's attention. He turned around to face Rio and Luke again. Slowly walking back toward them, he asked, "How do you know?"

"I saw her yesterday. And, almost every day of my life before that. She was pregnant with me when she disappeared. Sota Tanaka is my father. I've never seen him. Never spoken to him. But, biologically speaking, Sota Tanaka is absolutely my father."

Everything about the man's demeanor changed as Rio spoke. He became softer and his eyes began to move around and blink as if they were trying to keep up with his brain. Suddenly, he spoke.

"Wait here."

The Gift of Rio

The man disappeared into his house for several minutes before returning with two old photographs. One was a black and white photo of a couple of young boys.

"That's me on the left, your father on the right."

Rio's eyes lit up and her mouth opened slightly as if she was going to say something but nothing came out.

"And this one," he said as he slid another photograph on top of the first one, "I'm on the right, your father is the one on the left. He was my best friend then."

Rio stared at the faded, color photograph of a couple of young men. They were probably no older than Rio was at that moment. It was the first time she had seen what her father looked like. She couldn't believe she was finally staring at a picture of Sota Tanaka. Granted, if he was alive he was much older now but, this gave her an idea of who she would see if, and when, she finally found him.

She noticed that the picture of the two kids showed a couple of carefree children. But, the picture of the two young men showed that the man they were now talking to was still a happy young person while her father looked as if he had already become more stoic. She wondered what had happened between the two events and how it may have affected, or even led to his actions the night she was conceived.

She realized in that moment that, so far, answers only seemed to beget more questions. But, still, she was thrilled to finally be finding some answers. That fact spurred her on. And, she couldn't wait to find out what answers would come next.

CHAPTER TWENTY-SIX
New Direction

Almost as excited as Rio was, Luke did most of the talking directly following a goodbye with their new friend who they eventually found out was named Yoshito. And, before their final goodbye, they had promised to tell Sota, if and when they finally found him, how much Yoshito longed to see his old friend again. The meeting had started a bit cold but had ended up incredibly warm. The same was true of their meeting with Emi, and Rio wondered if the trend would continue.

The best part of the encounter was that Yoshito had given them a lead and let them keep the pictures he had shown them. As it turned out, Yoshito may have been the only person from Sota's past to speak to him after he disappeared. He said he had never told anyone else about their conversation because Sota had made him promise not to.

Yoshito told them that Sota had called several months after

his disappearance and told him that he was in Kyoto. He wanted his friend to know that he was safe. He told him that he had searched everywhere for Mei, even after the authorities had given up. But, that he ultimately had to give up, too. Since then, he had disappeared on purpose and he wasn't coming back until he knew he could be a better man.

Yoshito said that his friend sounded full of grief, possibly even guilty of something, but that he never said what it was that had troubled him so much. However, Yoshito knew that Mei's disappearance had been the epicenter of the whole explosion and understandably so. Yoshito said he was certain that there was more to it than anyone but Sota knew about. He had even feared that Sota killed Mei. He hoped, if this was the case, that it had been an accident. But, he had worried that he would never know. So, he was greatly relieved when Rio told him that Mei was still alive, well, and living in America.

On their way back to the van, the focus of their discussion was on what to do with all the new information that Luke and Rio had learned. It had gotten late in the day and it was clear that their next step was to drive back to CYOI and spend the night before going to look for the bench and then moving on to Kyoto in the morning. Luke explained that Kyoto was almost directly west of CYOI and, if they were to drive straight there, it would be less than a two-hour car ride. However, if they went to the bench first, it would be a couple of hours to get there and then a little over an hour to go to Kyoto from the bench.

Rio listened and nodded. She appreciated Luke's support and enthusiasm. But, she couldn't help feeling a little flabbergasted by everything. Her emotions felt like they were in the middle of a spin cycle.

Before today, she didn't understand the devastation that her mother's disappearance had left behind. It was a decision her mother had made on Rio's behalf. Probably even more so than for herself. She had been trying to protect herself and her unborn daughter from Sota. But, it seemed as if her father had later changed. Or, at least, he wanted to. This was all, of course, according to his best friend, Yoshito. However, he may not have even realized that he needed to change if Mei hadn't made the decision that she had made. There was no way to know. What Rio was now sure of, was that her mother's decision had a destructive ripple effect on a lot of people. And, Rio could only hope that the ripple effect hadn't left her father so disturbed by what he had done that he had taken his own life.

Rio was suffering from a bit of confusion. She was unsure whether she should be mad at her mother. But, how could she be? What she did was brave. Or, was it selfish? Many of her thoughts contradicted each other. She stayed mostly quiet as she tried to reconcile what she knew before leaving Hilo with what she had learned since arriving in Japan.

Ultimately, with what had happened to Mei and the life that Rio had enjoyed because of the resulting decision her mother made to change her name to Toki and flee Japan, Rio concluded that she couldn't be mad. She was sorry that the decision left behind a trail of wreckage but, it was still a brave decision and Rio was thankful that her mother had made it. Rio had just been confronted, for the first time, with both sides of the story.

Side one came a few months earlier with her mother. And, today, with Ichiko, Emi and finally Yoshito giving her the other side of it all. So, of course her emotions were all over the place. But, when all was said and done, she loved and appreciated her mother and the bravery she had displayed when she learned that Rio had begun to grow inside of her. That mattered more than everything else. It had to.

As they climbed into the van and started to drive back to CYOI, her mind magnified the enormity of her family events by adding to it the events that were happening with her personally. Briefly, her eyes welled up with tears as she became overwhelmed. But, suddenly, as if he knew exactly what to say to shift her thoughts in a different direction, Luke cut through the thickness of imprisoning thoughts and pulled her back to safety.

"Well," he thought out loud, "I think you'll have a hard time denying the likelihood of a divine plan on your life now."

"What?" she asked as she looked at him, bewildered. "What do you mean?"

"Think about it," Luke insisted. "You might be able to argue that finding Ichiko was a wonderful coincidence but, you can't honestly tell me the same about Yoshito. I mean, your father's best friend just happens to be working in the garden behind his house when we walk by from getting straight up rejected by your father's family? Come on, Rio. You have to see the hand of divine providence in that."

"Well," Rio started as she pondered the event in a way she hadn't yet, "it makes sense that he was there because he lives there. We were only a block away from the house Sota grew up in. So, obviously, Yoshito still lives where he grew up."

"True," Luke agreed before launching into his argument, "but he just happened to be outside when we walked by. Plus, he still had pictures of himself and Sota that he had saved all these years but was willing to give to us. And, it just happens to turn out that he was also probably the last person around here to speak to Sota."

"Yeah, it's pretty amazing."

"It's flat out awesome."

"I agree."

"About that hand of divine providence?"

"I won't disagree with that," Rio said as they shared an

affectionate look.

"I'll take it. That's progress."

CHAPTER TWENTY-SEVEN
The Word Is Spreading

The ride back to CYOI was the quietest one Luke and Rio had experienced together. Rio was clearly deep in thought and Luke knew she'd had an emotionally eventful day. So, he decided not to press. Instead, he introduced her to a new music artist and just let the music cover the road noise and fill the space any quiet moments left.

The new artist was a man named Rich Mullins. In the small amount of conversation, the two had during the car ride, Luke told Rio that Rich Mullins had written some of his favorite Christian songs of the last two decades and that he found the man to be equally as inspirational as his music. He explained that Mullins had moved to a Navajo reservation in New Mexico a couple of years earlier to teach music to children. He kept the amount of the average American salary from the profits of his tours and album sales in any given year and the rest went to charity.

Rio found the story inspirational too. In fact, she listened to the words of his songs and they meant more to her because of what she had learned about the man who wrote them. Still, her mind drifted in and out of paying attention. Of course, she continued to think about the events of the day. But, additionally, she began to wonder if what was happening to her, with the newfound ability to control water, had ever happened to anyone else. She decided that, if it had, she would have heard about it and, therefore, it likely hadn't. It was a lonely conclusion to draw.

Somehow, as she drifted back in and heard Rich Mullins singing, she felt comforted. She particularly liked a song called "Brother's Keeper." The song was about caring for people, rather than judging them, regardless of their weaknesses or their strengths. She peeked at Luke as he quietly sang along with the song and, suddenly, she didn't feel lonely anymore.

Luke had quickly become a very good friend to Rio. And, she couldn't help but wonder if there was something there beyond a friendship. He was certainly attractive in the physical sense. That was one of the first things she had noticed about him when they met in the airport. But, he was even more attractive to her now because of who he was and how he had treated her. A lot of that, from what he had told her, came from his deep-seated Christian beliefs. His devotion to those beliefs was attractive, too. And, although she wouldn't admit it to Luke, his devotion to his Christian beliefs made Christianity more attractive to her as well.

Both Rio and Luke were tired by the time they got back to CYOI. They had stopped for another quick bite to eat, which helped, but it wasn't enough to completely rejuvenate them. For Rio, it was primarily an emotional exhaustion. For Luke, it was more physical and mental. The hypnotic effect of the road, after a full day of driving, exaggerated the tired feeling even more and it was a pretty quick goodnight once they got back.

The only thing that slowed it down a little bit was that Luke asked Rio to stop by his room so he could give her a key to get into the pool so she could take a swim in the morning before they left for the bench and Kyoto. While she was there, he also offered to loan her a couple of books to read. Based on Luke's recommendations, she chose *Science Speaks* by Peter Stoner and *Evidence That Demands A Verdict* by Josh McDowell.

After giving Luke a hug and another warm thanks, Rio took the books back to her room and set them on the bed. She wondered if she should call her mother but didn't feel like rehashing all that she had learned that day. Plus, she knew her mother wasn't expecting another call so soon. Instead, she gathered some pajamas and toiletries and walked down the hall to the bathroom where she took a shower. The water was refreshing and invigorating. Almost instantly, Rio felt revitalized and briefly considered staying in the shower all night. But, she knew that was a silly thought and decided she'd keep it to about twenty minutes and then get out and prepare for bed.

That twenty minutes quickly turned into thirty, however, as she found herself wanting to experiment with her gift the way she had in the shower that morning. It was quite possibly the only place she could be certain that no one was watching. This time, she played with the whole water-sphere technique that she had discovered when drying out the clothes and seats in the van. She took the water coming out of the shower head and turned it into another translucent softball, then smashed it against the wall. Suddenly, she started doing the same thing over and over, rapid fire, until she had smashed almost a hundred balls of water on three different walls in less than a minute and a half. A grin crept over her face as she realized that she felt a little like a warrior. It was fun and empowering. She had gone from emotionally exhausted to feeling totally fired up. But, with the shower complete, it was time to turn her attention to a calmer exercise. Rio was looking forward to reading the books that she had borrowed from Luke.

Having decided to check in with Isaac before hitting the sack, Luke walked over to the main building to find out if Isaac was still in his office. Sure enough, Isaac immediately greeted him.

"There he is."

"Yeah," Luke started, "I thought I'd better check in with you and let you know I decided not to fly home."

"I wondered if that might be the case."

"You did?"

"I did. What's the latest with Rio?"

Luke's eyes widened and he exhaled. "That's a long story. Fascinating but long."

"Have a seat," Isaac offered with a hand gesture.

Luke sat but didn't speak. Much like Rio had decided about her mother's story earlier in the day, Luke felt that Rio's story wasn't his own and, therefore, it wasn't his to tell. Just because Rio had told him everything didn't mean he should pass the information along.

"You know," Isaac said as he caught on to the reason for Luke's hesitation, "you don't have to tell me anything. I won't ask you to betray her trust."

"Thank you," Luke said, sincerely. "I can tell you this much. She's American and she's here looking for her father who she's never met."

"So, pretty much what I already knew."

"That, and the fact that I feel led to help her."

"Kind of already knew that, too. But, when you say led, do you mean by God or, by the fact that she's an attractive young lady?"

"The honest answer is both. She's not just attractive to the eye though, Isaac. She's a really cool person, too."

Isaac smiled. His young friend was clearly smitten. But, it was time to raise the real issue he wanted to ask Luke about.

"This afternoon, I heard from a guy whose son went to one of our camps a while back. He tells me you were with, what he called a young female miracle worker, and that she saved him from drowning in Ise Bay earlier in the morning."

Isaac paused. He could see that he had Luke's full attention and that essentially answered his next question.

"Curious," Isaac started, "wouldn't you agree?"

"Curious," Luke stated with very little commitment.

"You know what he's talking about?"

Luke stared at Isaac for what felt like minutes before finally responding, "Matthew, chapter sixteen, verse twenty."

From memory, Isaac quoted the verse that Luke was referencing, "Then he warned his disciples not to tell anyone that he was the Christ."

Luke continued to stare blankly at Isaac but his mouth remained closed.

"You know," Isaac started, "there's only one messiah . . . "

"Yes," Luke interrupted as Isaac cracked a knowing grin. "Of course, I know that. That's not the point I'm looking for you to draw from that verse."

Isaac nodded his head as he stated, "I get it. Enough said."

CHAPTER TWENTY-EIGHT
Old Testament

Once again, Rio spent the entire night without sleeping. Instead, she read both books that she had borrowed from Luke and her mind was now whirling with profound information. Instead of focusing on that, however, she wanted to clear her mind and she was going to do that by going for a swim.

She let herself into the indoor watersports building and, after just two wrong turns, found her way to the women's locker room that Luke had pointed out on her tour when they first arrived at CYOI. She changed into her bathing suit and stuffed everything but her towel into a locker before heading out toward the pool.

As she stepped into the pool area, she noticed a few things that had not struck her on the initial walk-through she had quickly made with Luke. There were similarities to her training center back home but she also took note of a few differences. The diving platforms were lower, the pool had eight lanes instead of ten and, of course, there were no banners with team names, mascots or a list of the team's accomplishments hanging on the walls. Rio also quickly noticed that she was not alone. There was a woman swimming laps in lane eight. On the opposite end of the pool from Rio, was a young girl Rio assumed was the woman's daughter. She was jumping into the water and then immediately climbing back out to do it again. Rio decided that she looked to be about eight years old, comfortable in the water, but far more interested in jumping in and out of the pool than swimming.

After quietly setting her towel down on a bench just in front of the wall, Rio stepped up to the starting platform on lane one. She stretched a little, climbed up onto the platform, reached forward and grabbed the edge of it with both hands. She squatted twice and then launched herself forward, diving in to swim the length of the pool. The water felt soothing and peaceful as Rio glided beneath the surface. She kicked her feet in a synchronized rhythm until it was time to breach and begin a breast stroke. The process was as natural as breathing for Rio. She was completely at home in the water. It had always comforted, galvanized and pacified her. Today was no exception.

As Rio dipped below the surface again, somersaulted her body and kicked off the pool wall, she heard a sound that caught her attention. The constant sound of a light motor from the water filtration system was no surprise to her. However, this sounded like something had strained that motor or possibly clogged the suction of the water the motor was designed to take in.

Just as she had previously, Rio kicked her feet in a synchronized rhythm until it was time to breach and restart her breast stroke. Every time her head turned and her ear went back into the water, she heard the noise again. But, it wasn't until she was nearly back at the end of the pool from which she had started that she heard a loud scream. Rio stopped and turned to find the woman she had noticed earlier rushing toward the wall of her lane on the opposite end of the pool and going under the water. Rio immediately ducked underwater herself and focused her vision until she could see what was going on clearly, as if it were happening directly in front of her.

The little girl was standing on the bottom of the pool with her back to the wall. She was flailing her arms and trying to move her head but she was obviously stuck. Somehow, she had managed to get her long black hair caught in an induction inlet and the suction power was pulling at the back of her head. The mother was trying to free her but wasn't having any success. It was at that moment that Rio realized if she didn't do something, the little girl was going to drown. Rio and the woman breached the surface at the same time and the woman instantaneously began screaming for help.

Rio quickly responded, "Go get a pair of scissors!"

"You," the woman shouted back. "I'm not leaving my baby!"

Rio briefly thought about the fact that she was the closer one to the locker room, which was the most likely place to find scissors but she had to be there to make sure the girl didn't drown and she didn't have the time to explain. Nor did she think that the hysterical mother was likely to have a rational conversation during such a crisis.

So, instead of trying to argue, Rio stopped kicking her feet and moving her hands. As she slowly sunk, she turned her palms upward and the water began to pull to the sides in front of her. Soon, Rio wasn't in water at all. Her feet were touching the ground and the water had begun to form two walls, one on each side of Rio's body, about four feet apart. The walls of water went straight up in the air and slowly extended diagonally across the pool toward the woman and her little girl.

When the break in the water reached them, the girl gasped for air and wiped her face. She and her mom both looked at Rio through the pathway in front of them and then up past the lane dividers, running from one wall of water into the next, at the miraculous sight of the water being held back for them. The little girl's fear dissolved and was replaced with peace. She smiled at Rio while her mother continued to stare, completely stunned by the whole event. Finally, she looked at her daughter and remembered Rio's suggestion that scissors would be needed to free her daughter from the motor's grasp.

The woman frantically climbed out, sprinted around the pool and into the locker room, praying out loud the entire way. Desperately searching for scissors, she finally found a glass container full of combs in barbicide. Amongst the combs was one pair of scissors. She pulled the metal top that raised the contents up from the bottom, grabbed the scissors and sprinted back out of the locker room.

When she reached the pool area, she was relieved to find that everything looked the same as it had when she left. Realizing she could take a quicker route to her daughter than she had on the way to the locker room, she jumped into the water and then quickly stepped through a water wall and into the clear path Rio had created. She had to duck under each lane divider but hustled as fast as she could.

Finally approaching her daughter, she was shocked at how calm her little girl was. She reached behind her daughter's head and cut the hair that was trapping her. With her daughter finally free, the woman picked the little girl up and gave her a big hug.

"Are you alright?" she asked.

"Yep," her daughter responded.

"Thank God."

The woman lifted her daughter out of the pool and set her on the ground above it. She then pulled herself out and turned to face Rio as she sat on the concrete, picked her daughter up again, placed her in her lap, and squeezed her tightly.

Rio finally let go of the water and, all at once, it came crashing back down into the pool.

CHAPTER TWENTY-NINE
Witnesses

Jacoba, as Rio had learned the woman was called, couldn't decide who to hug more: her daughter or Rio. She went back and forth between the two, thanking Rio profusely and embracing the child she nearly lost. Tears had started to fall just before Isaac had walked into the room, only moments after the water had re-filled the pool. Rio quickly discovered that Isaac and Jacoba were husband and wife. She also learned that their daughter, the girl whose life Rio had just saved, was named Zahava. Isaac, however, kept calling her Zee.

Luke was the last to arrive on the scene. Both he and Isaac were shocked to learn about the events of the early morning. Isaac was just stopping by to see his wife and daughter before going to his office to get some work done and Luke was up and ready early, figuring he'd find Rio in the pool before they left on the new adventures the day was sure to hold. Little did he know the adventures had already begun.

Zee never shed a tear. She had, however, taken quite a liking to her savior and wanted to go right back into the pool. But, only if Rio would go with her. Of course, Rio obliged.

While the two girls were swimming, splashing and laughing together, Luke, Isaac and Jacoba had a conversation about what had taken place just moments earlier. The word miracle was used several times, mostly by Jacoba. Both Isaac and Jacoba reassured Luke that Rio's secret was safe with them. Of course, it was. Rio had just saved their daughter's life. And, in doing so, exposed herself. That was a major risk that demanded a great amount of loyalty.

They discussed the many potential downsides to people learning about Rio's gift. Not only would the resulting fame mean that she would likely find herself constantly hounded for the rest of her life but, even worse, she could find herself spending that life living as someone's rat in a lab somewhere. It was clear to them why Rio wished to keep this a secret for however long she was able.

Eventually, the conversation subsided and Isaac asked if he could pray with everyone. Rio and Zee climbed out of the pool and dried off with their towels. The five of them gathered in a circle and held hands as Isaac began thanking God for sending Rio into their lives and the fact that they got to leave there this morning with little Zee needing nothing more than a haircut to even things out.

Luke peeked out of his left eye and saw Rio with her eyes closed, listening and involved. He smiled briefly, then closed his eye, feeling guilty for breaking his own concentration.

Isaac continued praying. He asked God to protect Luke and Rio as they went in search for Rio's biological father. To prepare the way and give them guidance. To lead them and to use them for the glory of the Kingdom of God.

Rio noticed that, as he was wrapping up his prayer, Isaac praised the name of God the Father but also mentioned that he was praying these things in the name of God's Son, Jesus Christ. She made a mental note of the confusion over the duality of persons in that prayer, wondering if it was one God or two that they believed in. From what she had read last night, it was just one. It was a bit puzzling and she decided she would ask Luke about it later. She thanked Isaac for his prayer and hugged him before everyone started making their way toward the locker rooms.

Isaac and Luke exited through the men's locker room and went out to the hallway on the other side of it. Jacoba and Zee dried off and said a difficult goodbye to Rio on their way through the women's locker room. Rio stayed behind, showered and quickly got ready for the day. Luke was waiting for her when she came out. Isaac's family was long gone by then and Luke greeted Rio with a big grin.

"So," he began to ask, feigning both ignorance and casual triviality, "what's up?"

"Not much," Rio teased back.

"What've you been up to?"

"Nothin'," Rio gave Luke a gentle push and they both started laughing.

"Big morning," Luke said, now speaking sincerely as they began to walk toward the building's exit. "Two in a row, actually."

"Yeah, unexpected to say the least."

"I'm sorry I missed this one."

"I'll try to let you know ahead of time from now on," Rio quipped.

"Thanks," Luke said with a chuckle. He thought a moment before adding, "You know, that's kind of their second miracle with Zee."

"It is?"

"Yeah, it's really just a miracle she's here at all."

"Why's that?"

"Well, our staff gets together once a week for an early morning devotional and Isaac shared a few months back that about a year after they were married, doctors told Jacoba she couldn't have children. She was devastated. Isaac prayed every day for almost three years that God would see fit to bless her with a child. One day, He finally said yes. Isaac joked that he thought he had nagged God until He caved in. But, ultimately, he realized that sometimes God just makes things that we take for granted difficult so that we have no other choice but to rely on Him until He can bless us and we'll unmistakably know exactly where that blessing came from. Zee is, without a doubt, that blessing for them. Maybe he just wanted to remind them of that this morning. And, he used you to do it."

The thought of God using her in that way gave Rio pause. It didn't make sense to her that He would use someone like her at all. Until recently, she hadn't given Him much consideration. But, that was all changing now. Perhaps, that too, was part of His plan.

"You ready to go find that bench? Or, are you wanting to go out to Kyoto first?"

Rio remained quiet for a moment. But, the new questions from Luke had sent her mind spinning off onto a different course. Now, she was deep in thought, trying to prioritize the day, as they exited the building and started their walk toward the van. Finally, the thoughts all started to meld together and she gave Luke his answer.

"This morning was a pretty strong reminder that my time of anonymity might be running short."

"I talked to Isaac and Jacoba. You don't have to worry about them blabbing to anyone or anything."

"I believe that. I do. But, I don't know what the days that lie ahead hold. Heck, I don't know what the rest of today holds. And, if I'm in a situation like I was this morning, where I have the chance to save a life, I'm going to take it. I don't care who's watching."

Luke smiled, tears forming in his eyes as he told her, "God knew that about you before He even started knitting you together in your mother's womb. That's why He chose you."

CHAPTER THIRTY
Seeker Of Truth

As the van pulled out of the CYOI parking lot, Rio was deep in thought again. But, this time, she wanted to invite Luke in to be a part of it. She just didn't know where to start. Then, suddenly, as if he could read her mind, Luke created a verbal bridge.

"So," he began to ask, "did you get any reading done last night?"

"Yeah," she responded. "A lot, actually."

"Interesting stuff, huh?"

"Very." Rio swallowed. She was about to take a giant leap. She had reached some conclusions but, now it was time to admit them out loud.

"I had never given God a lot of thought until I met you. If anything, I would have said He was a myth that a lot of people believed in but not all in the same way. Jesus, too. But, I know that's not true anymore."

Luke listened intently as Rio continued talking.

"Not just because of what's happening to me or the fact that the books you gave me to read prove it to be true in every way that something like that can be proven. Although, they do. They make me believe that the Bible is as true as any history book. Maybe even more so because it's been put to the test more than any other book of any kind. And, that means God is real. That means Jesus is, not only real but, exactly who He claims to be. When you realize that the likelihood of any person fulfilling just eight of the prophecies about the coming Messiah, written hundreds and in some cases even thousands of years before Jesus was born, is roughly the same as a huge meteorite landing on your house, then you read that Jesus fulfilled all three hundred and fifty-three of those Old Testament prophecies . . . Well, I think in order not to believe you'd have to make a decision to flat out ignore the truth."

Luke smiled and his eyes filled with tears again.

"That's what I want to read next, by the way. I want to read those Old Testament prophecies for myself. Then I want to read how Jesus fulfilled them. So, if it's alright with you, I'd like to borrow a Bible next."

"Of course," Luke responded with quick enthusiasm. "You mean, after you finish the books you borrowed last night? Or, right away."

"Both."

"What do you mean?"

"I mean, I did finish."

"Which one?"

"Both."

Luke nearly ran off the road as he asked, "You read both of those books in their entirety last night?"

"Yeah. I didn't sleep again. Tonight, I want to read the Bible."

"Okay . . . Now, you said it wasn't just the books or your abilities that make you believe. What else is it?"

"You," Rio answered without hesitation. "You make me believe, Luke. Because you believe so deeply that it pours out of who you are. And, I know you to be true, good, and honest. I know very little about what the Bible teaches but, I have gotten to know you and someone who believes that deeply must represent what's in that book. Therefore, I look at you and I know it's authentic. I know that, not only is God real, but He's someone I want to meet and get to know. I've never known anyone like you, Luke. But, getting to know you has made me also want to get to know the one who has made you the way you are. So, tonight I want to read the Bible."

"I'm lucky if I can get through it twice in one year. You'll probably get through the whole thing in one night."

Both chuckling, Rio looked over and noticed that Luke was wiping tears off his cheeks.

"Why are you crying?"

"There's not a higher compliment that anyone can be paid than the one you just gave me."

"Well," Rio joked, "don't let it go to your head."

Luke started laughing as he told her, "I'll try not to."

"Now, before we start strategizing about the day, I do have a quick question that's kind of on topic."

"Shoot."

"When Isaac was praying earlier, he mentioned both God the Father and His Son, Jesus Christ. It got me thinking, and I know reading the Bible will probably help clear this up too but, how is one God multiple beings?"

"Wow. That might be a quick question but it's not a quick answer."

"Oh. Okay."

"The quickest analogy I can think of, which you already have a special relationship with, is water."

"Yes, I'm quite familiar with water."

"Good. Then you know it can be liquid, solid or vapor. But, it's always still water."

"Oh, ice and gas. Yeah. Right."

"That's kind of the same thing with God. In all three forms, the chemical composition of water never changes. Father, Son, and Holy Spirit are all still God. But, unlike water, God is all three at the same time."

"Got it. That's kind of awesome."

"It is, isn't it?"

The conversation continued pretty much the whole way to Kyoto and, therefore, they never came up with much of a strategy for the day before their arrival. So, when they got there, they parked the van and started walking around as they discussed their next steps. They tried to put themselves in Sota's shoes and asked where he would go. Ideas like bars, homeless shelters and brothels were tossed around. However, they kept returning to the fact that Yoshito said Sota wanted to return a better man.

Luke got hungry so, they stopped and ate. But, otherwise, they walked around, until mid-afternoon, showing Sota's picture and asking people if he looked familiar. They were close to giving up and going to look for the bench instead, and Rio had even remarked about wishing her newfound gifts included psychic abilities, when someone finally recognized Sota.

An older man, who appeared to be homeless, looked long and hard at the picture. Speaking in Japanese, of course, the man pointed to Sota and exclaimed, "I remember."

Both Luke and Rio, who were barely even paying attention

by this point, did double-takes between the man and each other. "You remember?" Rio asked in English before correcting herself and repeating the question in Japanese.

"Yes. Long time ago. Many years."

"Yes. It probably would have been many years ago. Did you know him?"

"For a short time."

"Where did he go?"

The man pointed at Mount Kurama.

"He . . . He went up there? Into the mountains?"

The man nodded before speaking again. "Never returned."

Rio stood in stunned silence as the man walked away. Luke stared at her. It was the first time he'd seen her look defeated. She backed into the concrete wall of a building, slid down it, and sat on the pavement like a scene out of a movie.

"What are you doing?" Luke asked.

"I don't know. What if he went up there and committed suicide like so many people think he did. If he's dead then I don't know why I'm even here."

"Maybe you being here has nothing to do with Sota. And, maybe it has everything to do with Sota. We don't know. But, God brought you here for a reason and you're finding God on this trip. Not only is that a purpose . . . it's not just something, it's everything, Rio. Now, get up. Let's go."

"Go where?"

"To find your father."

CHAPTER THIRTY-ONE
Fanning The Flame

"We can't just march up into the mountains without knowing where we're going," Rio nearly shouted as she chased Luke down the street, dodging passersby as she went.

"You finally have some direction," Luke stated sincerely. "And, you don't want to take it?"

"Some strange guy pointing at a mountain barely qualifies as direction," Rio insisted, hurrying as she attempted to keep up with Luke.

"Are you kidding?" Luke asked as he finally stopped, almost causing Rio to run into him. "You came all this way to find your father. We just found the man who may have been the last person to see him alive. We know, generally, where he was heading. You have been indomitable in your quest up to this point. And, this is where you want to call it quits?"

Rio didn't answer right away. Luke made it sound simple and

made her sudden hesitation seem a bit ridiculous. He was right. But, so was she.

"I never said I wanted to quit. I just want to hit the pause button so we can come up with an actual game plan rather than going off half-cocked. What I don't want to do, is head up into the mountains a couple of hours before dark just to spend the night getting lost with no one to find us but wild animals who are hungry and see us as food. Please, tell me I'm making sense."

"You're making sense," Luke admitted. "Maybe I was being a bit rash."

"A bit," Rio teased.

"Now I'm the wild animal who wants food," Luke said with a smile.

"That's more like it," Rio said as she returned the playful look. "Dinner's on me. I saw a place a few blocks back that looked really good."

Now it was Rio in front as they reversed direction and started walking. She quickly led him to a tucked away okonomiyaki restaurant that Luke didn't even remember passing. When he saw what kind of restaurant it was, his eyes lit up.

"Have you had okonomiyaki before?" Luke asked with enthusiasm.

"No," Rio admitted. "It just looked good. Is it?"

"It's awesome."

"What is it?"

"A savory pancake with all kinds of yummy ingredients. I didn't even know they had an okonomiyaki restaurant in Kyoto. You mostly find them in Kansi and Hiroshima. Come on. This is going to be a real treat."

Luke opened the door and Rio went inside. They were both quickly intoxicated with the delicious smell. Rio was excited to try something new and Luke was equally excited to have something he had enjoyed before and was certain it would be delicious.

The restaurant was small. It only had two tables. Each had four seats and all eight of them were full. Luckily, there was also a counter with six additional seats and the two closest to the grill were empty. Rio and Luke sat at the counter and were immediately greeted by the very sweet husband and wife owners, Kazuo and Cho, who made their suggestions to the new customers. Rio and Luke decided to try the yakisoba with pork in addition to two different kinds of okonomiyaki: tomato and modern, the latter of which was served with fried noodles.

It only took a few bites for Rio to decide this was her favorite meal in Japan so far. The food, which was fantastic, was, of course, a major factor in that decision. But, so was the warmth and kindness of Kazuo and Cho. And, possibly most important, was the feeling that she and Luke were growing closer and closer with each moment they spent together.

Rio had wondered, before this moment, if their relationship could possibly go beyond a friendship. Either way, she was already thankful for what they had. The bond between them continued to grow stronger. And, at the very least, she knew they would always remain friends. But, the wonder had begun to turn to hope as her own feelings grew more romantic. Somehow, it seemed that Luke was becoming even more physically attractive the more she had gotten to know him. It was almost as if the depth behind his dark brown eyes had increased as she had learned more about who he was. As she saw further inside, behind those ocular windows, the beauty of his soul had extended itself to reach the outer shell.

She found herself wanting to ask him if he felt the same way about her. But, the fear of embarrassment is a strong barrier and she couldn't bring herself to do it. So, they made small talk for a while. They both appreciated the food they were eating and Luke told her about other restaurants he wanted to take her to. Planning things in the future just brought her back to how much she had grown to like him. In that moment, she wanted to stay in Japan forever. But, they were on a specific mission and, ultimately, in between bites of deliciousness, the conversation shifted to focus on a plan for trying to find Sota in the mountains at the edge of Kyoto.

"How about this?" Luke asked, "Why don't we go back to CYOI and hunt down some camping gear, get totally outfitted, get some much-needed sleep, and hit the mountain first thing in the morning? Then, we stay there until we've either found Sota or feel satisfied that we've exhausted the possibility that he's up there."

"I wish I was more confident about the whole sleep thing," Rio quipped. "At this point, I've nearly given up hope."

"Yeah, I don't know how you're still standing."

"Well, currently I'm not. I'm seated, next to you, at the counter of what I think just might be the most delectable restaurant in Japan."

"You know what I mean."

"I do. And, I don't know how I'm still functioning either. In fact, I feel completely fine. But, back to the plan. Other than the sleep part, I'm all in."

"Good. I think that turned out to be easier than we set it up to be."

"Agreed."

As Rio and Luke shared a smile, another customer exited the restaurant and a strong, cold gust of wind blasted into the room through the doorway. It caused Rio to shiver, as her hair waived and the cool air caressed her skin. Unfortunately, the same breeze blew past the counter and caused the open flame between a stovetop in the kitchen and the pot resting on the grate above it, to fan out. When it did, the tie at the front of Cho's apron instantly caught fire as she stirred the contents of the pot, completely unaware.

CHAPTER THIRTY-TWO
Heroes

"Chilly," Rio stated casually as she shrugged her shoulders, shook her head and exhaled before taking another bite of yakisoba with pork.

"I know," Luke agreed as he felt the effects of the breeze that had just swept through the restaurant. "Where did that come from? I don't remember it being quite that cold out . . . "

The conversation was interrupted by Cho's startled gasp as she finally realized her apron was on fire. Rio and Luke both turned and, with eyes widening, watched Cho try to untie her apron. Of course, that was impossible because the tie was the very part of the apron that was on fire. She grabbed a rag and tried to pat the fire down but, the rag had previously been used to wipe up grease and quickly went up in flames. Cho let out another yelp as she released the rag in fear and it dropped to the ground, completely engulfed by the fire. Meanwhile, the fire on her apron continued to spread. Cho looked down her torso, in absolute helpless terror, and waved her arms as if she could somehow create enough wind to blow it out, like the futile motion a person makes when they eat something too spicy.

Kazuo rushed over from the back of the kitchen and started frantically stomping the rag with his feet while simultaneously trying desperately to pat the fire out on his wife's apron with his bare hands.

Cho was now in a complete panic as the fire on her apron had spread well beyond just the tie. It had started to crawl across both the strings around her waist and the body of the apron itself.

Luke jumped up and reached over the counter. He stretched forward and used the tips of his fingers to scoot a full pitcher of water that was almost out of reach. Finally, he could turn the handle toward him. He grabbed the pitcher, pulled it in near his chest and then lunged it forward. The water shot out of the pitcher and tore through the air at Cho.

Rio watched with hyper-focus. It almost felt, to her, like she was seeing the water fly in slow motion. Rio could tell it was going to miss so she redirected the water with her mind and caused it to spread enough to completely cover the fire. Thankfully, it was instantly snuffed out and everyone looked on in amazement. They were shocked at first and eyes darted back and forth between Cho and Luke as everyone tried to process what had just happened. Naturally, everyone assumed that Luke had accurately splashed Cho with the water from the pitcher and there was no reason to think that Rio had been involved at all or that anything miraculous had taken place. So, it was only a matter of seconds before everyone began to breathe sighs of relief.

The other customers in the restaurant started to clap and cheer enthusiastically. And, after hugging his wife, Kazuo joined in the clapping as he and Cho immediately began thanking Luke. For a few minutes, Luke got to feel like a true hero. In appreciation, Kazuo and Cho wouldn't let him or Rio pay for their meals. As the door closed behind them, and they started their trek back to the van, Luke spoke quietly to Rio.

"You made sure that water put the fire out, didn't you?"

"I might have helped a little," Rio admitted with a smile as they walked side-by-side. "But, you're the one that really saved the day."

"Teamwork," Luke said as he put his right arm around Rio's back without even thinking about it. When he realized what he had done, he almost retracted it. But, before he could even react, Luke felt Rio tilt her head to the left and rest it gently on the front of his shoulder.

"Teamwork," she agreed.

It was a glimpse of what being a romantic couple could feel like. And, they both thought it felt amazing. Luke and Rio held that position all the way back to the van and, although they didn't admit it out loud, both were sad to end it when they arrived. It was a physically small and completely innocent step forward in their relationship. But, in their hearts, it was a giant leap. They both knew it too. Not a single word had to be spoken about it. And, not a single word was.

Luke opened Rio's door and closed it behind her once she was seated inside the van. He walked around the back and climbed in on his side, wearing a grin that couldn't have been slapped off his face by a four-hundred-pound gorilla. He started the van and pulled out of the parking space. It was quiet for a few minutes as the journey back to CYOI began.

While Luke's mind remained on Rio, Rio's mind began to drift to all the crazy events that had taken place since she landed in Japan. Luke glanced over and noticed that her own grin had faded. She looked more pensive than she had just a moment earlier.

"What are you thinking about?" he asked.

"Oh, several things."

"Like?"

"Like, well . . . I'm starting to think I'm bad luck."

"What?" Luke asked, sincerely taken aback. "What do you mean, bad luck?"

"I mean, everywhere I go, people seem to be . . . they seem

to be almost dying. Daichi, Zee, Cho . . . Could I somehow be putting these people in danger?"

"I guess you could choose to look at it that way."

"How would you look at it?"

"Pretty much the opposite," Luke insisted. "I think it's far more likely that those things were all going to happen whether you were there or not and that God guided you to those places, at those times, so that you could help those people. And, you did. You saved their lives."

Rio looked over at Luke and her grin returned. "Actually, you saved Cho."

"Not without your help, I didn't."

"Teamwork."

Luke nodded his head in agreement and shared a smile with the woman who he couldn't help but admit to himself he was falling for.

"Teamwork."

CHAPTER THIRTY-THREE
Supplies

Rio was standing in the doorway of the massive storage closet as Luke found the items he was looking for and, one-by-one, handed them to her. She was setting the items on the ground in the hallway and had just placed the second sleeping bag down when Isaac approached.

"There she is," Isaac said as he walked up and hugged Rio.

"Hey," Rio responded. "How's Zee?"

"Great. She keeps talking about you. I think you have a new fan. Correction. I think you have several. Jacoba hasn't stopped thanking the Lord for you and, to be honest, neither have I. As far as I'm concerned, the best things to ever happen to me are the Holy Trinity, my wife and daughter, now you, and the Dallas Cowboys are a distant fourth."

Rio nearly blushed as she smiled and gave a small chuckle at the inclusion of an NFL football team on Isaac's list.

Luke, on the other hand, furrowed his brow as he feigned insult.

"No offense taken," he insisted. "Also, go Chargers."

After a shared chuckle, Isaac glanced around the storage closet and asked, "What are you guys up to?"

Luke stepped out of the closet with a long, rectangular box and set it down next to a couple of backpacks. "We're going hiking and camping tomorrow," he told Isaac.

"Where?"

"We found someone who remembered Rio's father and said he last saw him right before Sota headed into the mountains just outside of Kyoto."

"Wow. That's progress."

"Yeah," Luke agreed.

"Which mountain? Atago, Hiei, Kurama?"

"Whichever one is to the northeast of the city."

"Sounds like Mount Kurama. Pretty area. In fact, there's a beautiful monastery up near the top."

"A monastery?" Rio asked.

"Yeah," Luke started to explain, "a monastery is a building where . . . "

"I know what a monastery is," Rio interrupted. "Smarty-pants . . . But, that could explain why Sota never came back down off the mountain. If Yoshito is right and Sota wanted to stay away until he could return a better man, then maybe he's been at that monastery all these years."

"It is possible," Luke said while he pondered the thought out loud. "Huh. Interesting. Like he's serving out a self-imposed penance for his sins."

"Exactly," Rio agreed. "Which could be indefinite. Maybe he's waiting until he feels like he's redeemed himself."

"That's a life sentence. We're all sinners. Even when the church is called the righteous, what that really means is we're repentant sinners. We're only redeemed because a truly righteous God made it so. If he went up there trying to redeem himself, he's either given up by now or, he's still up there."

Rio found hope in this new possibility and could hardly contain her excitement. The trio stood outside of the storage room and talked for about ten more minutes before finally deciding to load the equipment up in the van. Isaac helped them and the conversation continued. He was a wealth of information and happy to share because he was so fascinated by Rio and her family. He even took them to the cafeteria and found some sandwich materials as well as a few canned goods and a skillet they could take with them so they would have food to eat on their journey.

Afterwards, Luke and Rio said goodnight to Isaac and then Luke took Rio back to his room so she could borrow a Bible. Rio was surprised at how many different versions of the Bible he had. She noticed a King James version, a New King James, a 21st Century King James, an American Standard, a New American Standard, a New International, a New Revised Standard and something called *The Message* but that one, apparently, only included the New Testament.

"Why are there so many different versions?" Rio finally asked.

"They're really just different translations of essentially the same thing," Luke offered. He could see that she wanted more so, he continued.

"The Old Testament is the Jewish Tanakh which was written primarily in Hebrew and a little Aramaic before eventually being translated into Greek. The New Testament was all written in Greek. Then, everything was translated into Latin. The writings we have in the New Testament were officially accepted by the church about sixteen hundred years ago. Since then, the Old Testament has been translated into about five hundred languages and the New Testament is more than double that."

"I sure hope one of them is English because if you hand me a Bible written in Latin I'll be handing it right back to you."

"You're safe. I have a Greek Bible and a Japanese Bible but the rest are all in English."

"Why do you have more than one English Bible?"

"Because of language issues, we're still arguing over what the best translation of every detail is. And, in some cases, just trying to make it as easy to understand as possible by putting it into current terms including some translations that even use modern slang."

"I did not realize it was so complicated."

"Well, think about how different we talk today versus a couple of hundred years ago. For example, that King James Bible right there, that translation is almost four hundred years old."

Rio's eyes grew wide as Luke continued.

"That book isn't. The printing is closer to four years old."

"Which one is your favorite?"

Luke drew a deep breath and let out an extended exhale as he thought about it. It wasn't an easy choice. But, finally he spoke.

"I have a profound reverence for that King James version. But, the one I probably read the most is the New Revised Standard."

"Is that the one you think I should read?"

"Not necessarily. You can pick whichever one you want."

"I don't know the difference."

"Let me ask you this. Do you want to read it in the traditional order, or in chronological order?"

"By chronological, you mean the order that events happened in, right?"

"Right."

"Then why isn't the traditional order chronological?"

"When the Bible was originally assembled, they grouped the writings mostly by type of literature. In the Old Testament, you've got the historical books, then the poetry, then the prophecy. In the New Testament, it's kind of the same thing. You've got the historical, then the letters written to churches, and last, you've got prophecy again. The chronological Bible I have, which is N.I.V., just puts it all in the order events actually happened in."

"I think I'd rather have that. It sounds less confusing."

"Probably right," Luke said as he removed the chronological Bible from his shelf and handed it to her. "Don't let all of that overwhelm you. You're right, it is complicated. Of course, it is. It's sixty-six different texts, written in a variety of literary styles by more than thirty authors from extremely diverse backgrounds, over the course of more than fifteen hundred years. Plus, it's the inspired Word of God and a record of His relationship with us. How could it possibly be simple? But, the most important thing is, despite all that, it's completely unified with one clear and consistent message."

"Which is what?"

"God is gracious, merciful and patient. But, he's also just. He hates sin but He loves us. All of us. And, because He loves us,

He gave us Jesus Christ as His redemption for humanity."

As Rio pondered the weight of Luke's statement, she reminded herself that he told her not to let it all overwhelm her. It certainly had that potential. But, instead, Rio found herself growing even more excited to start reading.

CHAPTER THIRTY-FOUR
Waterfalls

After saying goodnight to Luke, which seemed to take a little longer each night, Rio watched Luke walk back toward the boys' dorm before exchanging a final wave and turning to head toward her room. She noticed the payphone in the lobby and felt a small wave of guilt rush over her. Rio knew she should call her mom and update her but, she also knew that it was going to be a long conversation. There was a lot of new information to divulge. But, more importantly, she knew that it was going to be difficult to explain everything without causing her mother to feel some guilt of her own. She figured that wave would be closer to a giant sea swell and it just felt easier to avoid the call for another day or two. She reasoned that her mom wasn't expecting her call yet and that meant she would get to take her shower and curl up in bed, that much sooner, with the Bible that she had just borrowed from Luke.

That's exactly what she did. About the time that she was wrapping up the book of Exodus, Rio realized that almost six hours of reading had passed. She slid the bookmark in place and closed the Bible, taking note of the fact that she was about ten percent of the way through the book. She chuckled to herself at the thought of Luke joking that she would probably read the whole thing in one night.

Rio got up and gathered her things. She walked over to the indoor watersports building, let herself in, and went for an early morning swim. This time, she had the place to herself. The water felt peaceful, as it always did, even when she was just taking a simple shower. Still, Rio couldn't help but miss the almost perfect feeling she got every time she went swimming in the Wailuku River back home. That was an utterly tranquil experience every single time and she looked forward to doing it again soon. But, not until she finished what she set out to do in Japan. Besides, while the idea of going home was still appealing, the thought of leaving Luke was becoming an increasingly difficult one to face.

To that point, the only thing that motivated her to get out of the pool on this particular morning was knowing that she was about to see Luke and then the two of them would head up to Mount Kurama to try and find Sota. In fact, this was the first morning since she'd arrived that she was ready and waiting outside of the boys' dorm when Luke walked out.

"Let me guess," Luke started as he opened the door and stepped outside, "you didn't sleep a wink and you read the entire Bible."

"You're both right and wrong," Rio said with a brief chuckle. "I didn't sleep but I only read Genesis, Job, Exodus and there were some bits of Chronicles sprinkled in there."

"Oh, is that all?"

"That's it."

"You must be slowing down," he teased.

"I must be," Rio agreed with a sarcastic but flirtatious grin on her face.

"So," Luke began to inquire, "any thoughts on what you've read so far?"

"Well, like I said, I'm not that deep into it."

"Genesis, Exodus and Job . . . That's a pretty sizeable chunk of reading for one night."

"True. And, there was a lot to it. I see what you mean, already, about God being patient. I find myself getting mad that people won't just do what they're supposed to."

Luke nodded in agreement.

"But," Rio continued, "then I remember, that's me, too. I don't always do what I know I'm supposed to do either."

"It sure seems to me like you've got a head start on a lot of people in that department, Rio. But, you're right. When you get to Paul's letters in the New Testament you'll read where he says that we all fall short. And, that's why Jesus did what He did for us."

"Because or despite?"

"Because. The law of the Old Testament proved that we couldn't be righteous on our own. So, God loved us enough to intervene. Under the law, a pure sacrifice had to be made as atonement for our sins. It was what made it possible to have a relationship with God. Jesus was that final and ultimate, pure sacrifice."

Luke could see Rio pondering his statements. He appreciated how deeply she was thinking it all over. But, he didn't want to overwhelm her to the point where she found it easier to stick her head in the sand. So, he decided to move the conversation along and allow it to develop organically as she read further into the Bible.

"You'll get to that soon enough. The more I think about it, the more I realize reading it in chronological order like you're doing is the right call."

As they arrived at the van, the conversation shifted. They loaded their bags in and decided to consolidate the new stuff with the things they had loaded the previous night into the backpacks once they reached Kyoto. After climbing in and taking their seats, Luke took another look at a map Isaac had given them the night before. He circled the approximate location of the monastery he had told them about when he confirmed for them that, while there were roads on Mount Kurama, none of them got you very close to where they wanted to go. So, they had all agreed the best approach was to park the van in Kyoto, take the train up to the village of Kurama, and start their hike from there. Isaac had been kind enough to take the time to show them everything on the map and then give it to them to take on their journey.

After re-familiarizing himself with the map, Luke put the key in the ignition and started the engine. Rio immediately reached forward and ejected the CD. This took Luke aback.

"You got something else in mind?" Luke asked Rio.

"I do," she quickly answered as she took the CD from the player and put it in its case.

"What have you got?"

"I was inspired by that rain song you played so, I brought my own."

"Let's hear it then."

"Coming right up," Rio said as she started to dig it out. "Now, don't judge me too harshly. I only brought three CD's with me from home."

"Well, if you only brought three, then the three you chose will say a lot about you."

"Oh," she started to say as she looked over at him with a

furrowed brow, "don't say that. That's too much pressure."

"Okay, I take it back. Forget I said that. No pressure at all."

"Alright," she said with hesitation before hiding the CD case as she took the disc out and slid it into the player. She bumped it up to track number eight, hit play and was shocked when Luke started bobbing his head to the intro as he threw the van into reverse and backed out of his parking space.

"Just like you knew the rain song, which is called 'Flood' by the way, I know this one."

"You do?"

"Of course, I know 'Waterfalls' by TLC. I haven't been living on the moon."

"I don't know why I'm surprised but I totally am."

"You're surprised because you thought I only listened to Christian music."

"Yeah, I guess I did."

"As a Christian," Luke told her, "I try not to be of the world. But, I still live in it."

Luke began to sing along with the first verse and Rio quickly joined him. The journey to Mount Kurama was officially under way and neither of them was sure about exactly what they would find when they got there.

CHAPTER THIRTY-FIVE
Kurama

In talking to Isaac, the night before, Rio had learned that Mount Kurama is one of the more famous locales in Japan. It holds a lot of significance for the country and culture, both in its folklore and its history. From personal observation, she also found it to be breathtakingly picturesque.

Rio was taking in the beauty of the mountain from the train window as she and Luke rode the Eizan Electric Railway into Kurama. They wore their fully loaded backpacks and Luke carried a long cylinder-shaped bag with everything inside he needed to pitch a tent. A smile crept up out of the corners of his mouth as he watched the woman he had developed some ever-growing romantic feelings for. She was staring at God's creation from inside of man's.

Awestruck. That's the best word Luke could think of to describe the look on Rio's face as she watched the suburban houses disappear. They were replaced with every shade of green Rio could imagine. She noticed the gorgeous maple trees but found the old cedar trees particularly majestic.

Suddenly, the train entered a thick fog and, although the overall vision was severely hampered by it, everything became just a little bit more magical. The wonder on Rio's face was pure joy for Luke who preferred the view he was taking in to the one that Rio was so enamored with. They were both wearing smiles that nearly stretched from one ear to the other when the train came to a stop.

Luke and Rio followed the crowd out of the train car and stepped onto the covered platform at Kurama Station. They continued to follow the small mob and stepped out into a parking lot where Rio noticed a statue of a bright red, angry-looking face that had to be more than nine feet in height and sported a disproportionate nose that was easily as long as the statue was tall.

"What is that scary looking thing?" Rio exclaimed as she stopped and stared at it.

"Tengu," Luke said matter-of-factly as he stopped to wait for her. "You'll see a lot of those around here."

"Who's Tengu?"

"More like, what's Tengu?"

"Okay, what's Tengu?"

"Mythological demons that haunt the mountain forests. Especially on Kurama. If I remember right, this is supposed to be where the Tengu king lives. I'm sure Isaac could tell you a lot more about that though."

"Doesn't that scare the heck out of you?"

"Not at all. Why would it?"

"We're talking about spending the night out here."

"So."

"So? What if the myth is based on something real?"

"I know I'm on the right side. History's already been written. My God wins. Keep reading that Bible. You'll get it."

Luke started walking again.

"Still scary," Rio said as she hurried to catch up with Luke. "I hope you packed a lot of toilet paper."

They approached a large, stone staircase that was lined with red lamps and stopped. Above the staircase was the gate to Kurama-dera Temple. The whole thing gave off a dramatic, almost eerie feeling.

"It almost seems like we've stepped back in time," Rio said.

"Well," Luke began to answer, "I think it is about eight-hundred years old."

"Wow. Really?"

"Yep. Come on, let's keep moving."

Luke led Rio around to the back of the temple. The

abundance of cherry blossoms, about a month past their peak bloom, allowed Rio to quickly leave the eerie feeling at the front of the temple. Luke found the hiking trail Isaac had marked on the map. It took them through the forest and past several other temple structures. The climb became steep as they headed further up the mountain but the scenic surroundings made the trip too enjoyable to complain. Everywhere they looked was another batch of gigantic pines, a small stream or, at one point, a whole section of above ground cedar roots. It was unlike anything Rio had seen in Hawaii and she was appreciative of the whole experience.

About forty-five minutes into the hike, they reached a trail that split off from the main path. Luke pulled out the map Isaac had given them and decided that it was where they had been told to break off.

"This way . . . " he said out loud with a hint of indecision in his voice.

"You sure?"

"As sure as I can be since I've never been here or where we're going before."

"I trust you," Rio assured him. "You've got Boy Scout written all over you."

"Well," he began to playfully respond, "that's odd."

"What? That you've got words all over you?"

"That, too. But, I was referring specifically to the Boy Scout comment."

"Why's that odd?"

"Because I was never a Boy Scout. My family never did any kind of camping at all. My mom's idea of roughing it is two weeks without a mani-pedi."

Rio giggled.

"Seriously. Not that she's some self-involved, rich snob. She's not at all. She's one of the kindest, most compassionate and generous people I've ever known. A great example for me of what it means to be a Christian. Both of my parents are. Two very different people and two different angles on the same thing. My dad is a fair-minded, hard worker and a real people person. The kind of guy everyone enjoys being around. A jokester. He's got a great sense of humor, which sometimes embarrasses my mom. But, she also loves him for it."

"They sound great," Rio said sincerely.

"They are."

"Do you miss them? Being so far from home?"

"Of course. I call every other week or so. And, I get home at least once a year."

"Wait," Rio said as she stopped walking and looked at him, wide-eyed. "Are you missing your one trip home a year right now?"

"No. Well, kinda-sorta . . . I guess so. But, don't worry about that."

"Don't worry about it? I feel terrible."

"Don't. You shouldn't. I want to be here. I chose to be here."

"Still."

"That makes it sound like a bigger deal than it is. The real big deal is here, what we're doing. This is beyond once in a life-time, Rio. If I hadn't stayed, I'd be missing out on one of the most important things to ever happen in my life. I chose to be here because I'd rather be here. It's an honor to be here. To share this with you."

"Luke, if you hadn't stayed, I don't know where I'd be right now."

"Oh, come on . . . I'm sure God would've sent someone else to help."

"No, really. I mean it."

"So do I, Rio. You're too important. Whatever He's got planned for you, it's big."

CHAPTER THIRTY-SIX
Buddha Belly

"You're the best parts of them," Rio said as she started walking again.

"What?" Luke asked as he began to walk as well.

"I've obviously never even met them but, I'd be willing to bet just about anything that you're the best parts of each of your parents."

"I don't know about that," Luke said, trying to brush the praise off.

"You're pretty great," Rio persisted.

"You're right," Luke joked. "I am pretty great."

"I'm serious," Rio said as she playfully smacked Luke in the arm. "Just take the compliment."

"Thank you," Luke said sincerely. "That's a very nice thing to say."

"You're welcome," Rio said warmly. "It's the truth. I'm not

sure I know anyone else who would be on this journey with me right now."

"Oh, I'm sure you could find plenty of people who would do this with you."

"I completely disagree. It's a sacrifice. Most people are too self-centered to give up their time like this."

"You're a pretty easy person to want to spend time with, Rio. It's not much of a sacrifice. Really."

"Whether you'll admit it or not, you're giving up a lot to be here right now. I appreciate it and I admire the kind of person who is willing to do that."

"Enough to reward me?" Luke asked.

Rio's tummy fluttered as she anticipated the request of a kiss. "Depends on what you have in mind."

"Well, the sandwiches are in your bag, so . . . "

"Oh," Rio let out in surprise as she stopped, peeled her backpack off, and tried to hide her disappointment. "Yeah, let's eat."

Rio dug out two sandwiches and handed them to Luke as she put her bag back in order, zipped it up and strapped it back on. Taking a sandwich from him as they began to walk again, Rio decided to change the subject in a continued attempt to hide the fact that she was secretly wishing that Luke would kiss her.

"I know I gave you a hard time about acting like I wouldn't

know what a monastery was but the truth is . . . "

"Uh-oh," Luke interrupted with a big smirk on his face as he unwrapped his ham sandwich.

"I know, this is kind of hard to admit. Before you jump to any conclusions though, I generally know what a monastery is. But, it seems like that word gets tossed around sort of interchangeably with temple and shrine. I'm not sure I understand the difference between the three and I kind of feel like I should before we get to this place."

"Fair enough," Luke said sincerely as he let go of the teasing and swallowed his food before continuing. "I wouldn't exactly say this is my area of expertise but, let me break down what I do know. Or, what I think I know. Hopefully, I can get all of this at least close to right."

"Okay."

"First, a shrine is where they practice Shinto."

"Oh, that's what both of my parents' families were."

"Temples are where Buddhism is practiced. But, here in Japan, the two religions have kind of merged over the centuries and most of the people here tend to practice elements of both."

"Really?" Rio asked as she finally took the first bite of her sandwich.

"Think of it like this," Luke started explaining, "Buddhism was introduced here from China and Korea something like twelve or thirteen hundred years ago. Since then, the Japanese people have adopted it but haven't let go of Shinto. So, Shinto has become the Japanese religion as it pertains to earthly things. People commonly go to shrines to pray for their success in business or for a happy life. But, Buddhism is considered the more spiritual side of religion. People go to temples to pray for their ancestors. So, a wedding might be held at a shrine and a funeral at a temple."

"Interesting," Rio said as she pondered all the new information. "Where do monasteries fit into all of this?"

"A monastery is really just a religious building where a community of monks from one of any number of religions live under strict religious vows."

"That's what I thought."

"Sure you did," Luke jabbed Rio with a friendly tease.

"I did," Rio insisted.

"I believe you."

"Which religion is the one we're going to?"

"Buddhist. Which means it's technically called a vihara. Monastery is the English term and it's way more common globally to call it that. But, the monks here will call it a vihara."

"What are the differences between Christianity and Buddhism?"

"That's a long list."

"How about the highlights?"

"One of the few common grounds is that they both sprang out of other religions. Christianity from Judaism and Buddhism from Hinduism."

"Oh, so Buddhists believe in many gods? I kind of thought Buddha was their god."

"No, Buddha just means 'enlightened one' and he was the guy who started it all. His name wasn't even Buddha. Originally, he was known as Siddhartha Guatama. No one called him Buddha until he left his wife and son in search of a release from this world of suffering. Six years after disappearing, he resurfaced saying he had received the four noble truths while meditating."

"What are those?"

"Life is suffering, suffering is caused by desire, the ending of desire eliminates suffering, and you end desire by following 'The Middle Way'."

"And, how do you do that?"

"By having the right view, resolve, speech, action, livelihood, effort, concentration and ecstasy."

"Wow. I thought you said this wasn't your area of expertise."

"It's not. But, I did have to learn the basics so I could talk to the kids that come to our camp. This is what they come from. The craziest part of all of this, and this is what usually blows these kids' minds, is that Buddha had a Hindu background but he was basically an atheist. He didn't want to start a religion. Quite the opposite. He believed Hinduism had turned into the worship of all these false idols and that was what was holding people captive to a life of suffering. He was right about that. But, where I would say he went wrong was, while they did need to turn away from worshipping their false idols, what they needed to do instead, was worship the one and only true God. Instead, they took his teachings and thrust all their false idols back into the mix. All you have to do is look around here at all of these temples and shrines. They're littered with false idols. He'd be intensely disappointed with what people have done with his teachings."

"Sounds familiar," Rio responded ponderously.

"You mean the way the Jews turned to false idols? Like in the desert?"

"Yep."

"Someone just read the book of Exodus," Luke teased. "You're getting it. Keep reading. That's a consistent issue. People often want to create their own gods to fit their own selfish desires. What they're really doing is making a god out of themselves. That's pride. The root of all sin. Then, when they don't get their way, they want to blame God for the ills of their world or the world at large but, true enlightenment comes when you realize God's not the problem, He's the answer. Unfortunately, people and their acceptance and embracing of pride and sin are the real problem."

Rio listened intently as she finished her sandwich. She treasured these deep conversations with Luke. She felt like they were a window into his soul and the view continued to get more beautiful every time they talked. Rio also appreciated the fact that she was learning so much about things that she had never considered in her life but now seemed so important. These were the things that truly transformed people. They were timeless falsehoods and truths that had shaped the world. And, knowing the truth was always fascinating to Rio.

What she didn't know was how close they were to their destination. She was only moments away from seeing her first Buddhist monastery. Perhaps even more fascinating to Rio would have been knowing that with each step she took, she was getting closer to discovering the truth about the fate of Sota Tanaka.

CHAPTER THIRTY-SEVEN
Invitation

As Luke and Rio rounded a corner of the trail they were on, flanked on either side by thick groupings of maple trees, all signs pointed to the monastery being close by. Suddenly, the trail was lined with stones and railings made of bamboo trees. As the elevation of the path grew steeper, it also included steps made of cedar wood sanded into perfect cylinders and pounded into the dirt before being locked into place with two smaller cedar wood spikes in the front of each end.

"Looks like we're close," Luke announced.

Rio's heart sped up as they began climbing the stairs on the windy path. The stairs had varying sizes of dirt platforms from three to eight feet that made any real sense of rhythm in their stride impossible. She was tired from the long hike but Rio's leg movement sped up to match her heart rate.

"Maybe we should look for a spot to set up camp," Luke said

as he tried to keep up with Rio.

"We can't stop now," Rio fired back.

"I'm just thinking the sun will be going down in a couple of hours and we don't want to have to set up in the dark. Maybe we should pitch the tent and then go looking for someone to talk to."

"I can't wait," Rio exclaimed. "Can't we at least get a look at the place first?"

"Sure. If I don't have a heart attack first. I swear you've got the stamina of a wild stallion."

"I'm sorry," Rio said as she finally slowed down to a more typical pace. "I'm just excited."

"I know," Luke agreed. "Me, too. But, I'd like to get up there and not be worried that I'm going to throw up on a monk."

Rio started giggling as she stopped altogether. She handed him her canteen and he took a big drink of water. He handed it back to her and she did the same.

"Better?" she asked him.

"Better. Thanks."

They started their climb again, this time at a pace they could both handle, and ultimately arrived at another staircase. This one was all cement, lined on both sides with rocks of all shapes and sizes, and huge cedar trees, all of it covered in moss that displayed itself in varying shades of green. The new staircase was extensive and the vertical angle of it seemed less staircase and more ladder. It led straight up to a tall, ornate building with a white picket fence in front of it that almost seemed out of place.

"Does this qualify as a look," Luke began to ask even though he already knew the answer, "or, are we about to climb another insanely long and steep staircase?"

Rio looked at him and smirked before she started moving, now even more quickly than she had when Luke complained of being close to a heart attack. This time, he breathed a deep sigh and then followed but at his own pace. By the time Luke reached the top, Rio was gone. He spun in both directions and finally spotted her about fifty yards away, already making a new friend who couldn't have been much older than them.

Luke approached and heard Rio doing all the talking. Her words were flying out of her mouth as fast as her feet had just been moving. This was particularly impressive to Luke since the words were all Japanese. The short, round, bald man was quietly nodding and when Luke stopped next to Rio, the man bowed and walked away.

"Hey," Rio started to say as she turned toward Luke, "slow-poke."

"Cute," Luke responded to Rio between deep breaths.

"Thanks," Rio teased, knowing full well that Luke was referring to her comment on his tardiness and not to the way she looked.

"No, I meant . . . Either way. Who's your new friend?" Luke asked, changing the subject.

"I never got his name. In fact, he never said anything at all."

"He's probably taken a vow of silence."

"Oh," Rio said as her eyes widened, "I hadn't thought of that. No wonder he's such a good listener. I can think of a few people back home that might want to consider taking a vow like that."

"I hear ya."

Luke and Rio finally looked around at the beautiful architecture of the gorgeous building that they were standing in front of. There were three main floors to the building but there were towers that went up four more floors in each corner and every layer had beautiful, slanted roofs with pointed edges. There was a lot less color than most of the other religious buildings they had previously seen. This building was primarily white with dark red trim and a dark green roof.

"Beautiful," Luke commented.

"Yeah," Rio agreed. "I wonder how they got all of the materials back here to build this thing?"

"Monks are nothing if not patient."

"Good point."

Finally, the man returned. He brought another man with

him. This one was much older. He was also tall, skinny, and had long, white, braided hair with a beard that matched. Rio immediately thought he looked like he could have stepped out of one of the old Kung-Fu movies her step-dad, Anthony, used to watch back home.

"Let's hope this one talks," Rio whispered to Luke as they were approaching.

The tall man immediately introduced himself as Gorou and his fellow monk as Orochi. He confirmed Orochi's vow of silence and then dismissed Orochi to return to the gardening that he had been doing when Rio first approached him. Gorou then began addressing Luke and Rio and they were immediately taken with what a different demeanor the man had. He wasn't exactly cold but, he certainly wasn't warm. There was nothing mean-spirited about him but he wasn't offering genuine kindness. Later that night, in bed, Rio would decide that if she had been forced to describe it in a word, she would choose hollow.

Rio explained her predicament to Gorou and showed him the decades-old picture of Sota and Yoshito. She could tell right away that he recognized Sota but he didn't say one way or the other. Instead, he simply invited them to come inside.

CHAPTER THIRTY-EIGHT
Buddhist Hospitality

Unfortunately, Rio did not get all of the answers that she was seeking. She did, however, confirm that Sota had lived at the monastery for many years. As a matter of fact, his time there had been divided over two separate periods. In between those periods, he had done a stint at a Shinto shrine in Shizuoka on the Suruga Bay called the Kunōzan Tōshō-gū Shrine. Gorou also stated that, he thought he remembered Sota had spent very short periods of time at both the Kurama-dera Temple back where they had gotten off the train and the Kifune Shrine just east of Mount Kurama.

Although she remembered Luke saying that the Shinto and Buddhist religions had essentially merged into shared space within the Japanese culture, Rio couldn't help but think that Sota's inconsistency and possibly even restlessness and indecisiveness seemed like he was a man without focus. Or, perhaps, a man in search of something he had not yet been able to find. At least, not by the last time Gorou remembered hearing anything about him. Rio appreciated the new information but, couldn't help feeling a bit disappointed at the fact that, as they continued to find answers, those answers seemed to raise more questions, and a conclusion to the mystery of Sota Tanaka still seemed to be out of sight.

Gorou invited Luke and Rio to stay for a meal and some sleep before departing in the morning. Rio's instinct was to graciously turn the offer down out of fear that Gorou felt obligated to make the proposal. However, Luke quickly stepped in and accepted to keep Gorou from being unintentionally insulted.

After setting their bags in their rooms, they had dinner with the monks. It was the quietest meal Rio had ever eaten in a room full of people. There was more slurping and click-clack of dishes and chop-sticks than speaking. The meal included three small bowls. None of which Rio thought looked particularly flavorful. One bowl contained rice, another had a variety of pickled vegetables that included a heavy amount of bamboo shoots and had a distinctly ginger flavor, and the third was full of cold squash soup with wasabi mustard greens. Rio was surprised by how delicious all the food was and by how consistently salty the dishes were.

Shortly after dinner, Rio said goodnight to Luke and then settled into her room to read more of the Holy Bible. Neither she nor Luke was surprised by the fact that monks go to bed early. So, that gave her extra time to read. She read the next six books, some of which were significantly shorter than others, as well as bits of 1 Chronicles, a small number of the Psalms and most of 1 Samuel before Luke knocked on her door and she realized the morning had gone from dawning to daylight.

"Good morning," Luke said as Rio opened the door and realized he was completely ready to go.

"Good morning," Rio responded as Luke noticed the Bible in her hands.

"You hooked yet?"

"What?" Rio asked before realizing he was referring to her Bible reading. "Oh, yeah. It's far more interesting than I ever thought it would be. There are times when I'm reading names of people and tribes like Nimrod, Phineas, the Edomites, and the Witch of Endor, or places like Hamath, Canaan, and Gath and I could swear I'm reading the Lord of the Rings."

"I can see that," Luke said with a chuckle.

"Of course, that could also be because everyone seems to be the son of . . . Like, I can't imagine being called Rio, daughter of Toki. What a mouthful."

"No kidding," Luke agreed. "No wonder we've simplified it

over time. Looks like you're pretty deep into that dense piece of historical literature."

"Yeah," Rio agreed. "Speaking of a mouthful. No wonder most people just call it the Bible."

"That's my way of emphasizing the point that you're not whipping through some little piece of fluff. That's a heavy read."

"Oh. True. Well, I'm at least a quarter of the way."

"I love that book but I can't fathom reading it in under a week. You're on track to do exactly that. Phenomenal."

"It helps that I've given up sleeping."

"Also incredible. Nothing ordinary about you. That's for sure."

"You think you're impressed now?"

"I know I am."

"Wait until you see how fast I get ready."

"Let's see it."

It took Rio all of two minutes to throw her hair back in a ponytail, put her shoes on and tie them, put the Bible in her backpack, and return to the doorway where she stood facing Luke. She jokingly gave him a cocky shrug of the shoulders as if asking him how impressed he was.

"You certainly know how to break stereotypes," Luke offered.

"You ain't seen nothing yet," she responded.

"I can't even wait."

Rio let the door close behind her as she followed Luke out of the monastery. They said goodbye to Gorou after thanking him profusely for his hospitality and kindness. Rio appreciated all he had done for them but couldn't help wondering where the helpfulness was coming from since she still sensed an emptiness when he spoke.

They walked down the steep, mossy, concrete staircase and then the large dirt platforms framed by sanded cedar wood cylinders before entering the part of the trail lined with stones and railings made of bamboo trees. It was there that Rio began to feel a little light-headed. At first, she kept it to herself. But, as the indications of civilization disappeared and they found themselves on the portion of the trail where there was no sign of human existence, other than the trail itself, the feeling that something was wrong with her became too overwhelming to bear alone. Rio was forced to stop walking. She bent forward, placing her hands on her knees.

"Luke," she said with an abnormal amount of breath behind the word.

Luke turned around just in time to see Rio fall backwards and land on her backpack as she began wheezing.

"Rio!" he yelled as he dropped the tent and rushed to her side, stripping off his backpack.

"What happened? What's wrong?"

"I . . . don't . . . know."

CHAPTER THIRTY-NINE
Mysterious Ways

Luke did the one thing he could. He exercised the only power he had in an otherwise helpless situation. He started to pray.

"Heavenly Father," he began, "I praise you and thank you for trusting me enough to bring this amazing young woman into my life. I know you have great plans for her and I am honored to be a part of that no matter how big or small. She's under attack right now and I don't believe it is your will that her journey end here and now. So, please, heal her by your power and for your glory. Raise her up to do your will. It is in the name of your Son, Jesus Christ, I pray this. Amen."

Luke watched and waited but nothing changed. He looked up at the sky, then back at Rio who was wheezing so badly that she couldn't speak.

"It's going to be okay," Luke told her. "God will heal you."

Looking up at the sky again, waiting expectantly for a

response from God, Luke suddenly spotted something peculiar. It was a tiny bit of movement and it was getting closer and larger. Finally, it was close enough that he knew what it was right before it hit him square between the eyes: a single rain drop. *Well, that's kind of rude,* Luke thought as the impact caused him to shut his eyes. When he opened them again it was as if the single rain drop had led the way and his battalion was behind him. Headed straight for the both of he and Rio was a sky full of rain.

Within seconds, Luke and Rio were getting drenched. Luke considered lifting Rio up and taking her under a tree so that she could be more comfortable while they continued to wait on God. But, as quickly as the weather had turned from dry to a torrential downpour, Luke realized that the rain was God's answer to his prayer. He looked down at Rio and saw that her wheezing had already subsided.

Luke stood up and backed away to let Rio get the full onslaught of God's blessed healing. After only a few steps, he realized that he had walked completely out of the rain and that what he was witnessing was a tiny cloud burst, big enough only to surround Rio and completely soak her in the restorative waters sent straight from heaven.

Tears formed in Luke's eyes as he stared at the miracle occurring in front of him. It took a few seconds for him to be able to glance away but, finally, he looked back up at the sky and praised God for the incredible blessing that he and Rio were experiencing.

When Luke's gaze returned to Rio, she was standing up with her arms stretched out and her palms turned open to receive as much of the rain as she could. Her eyes were wide open as well and she was wearing one of the biggest smiles Luke had seen on her face so far. Her beaming face was a trigger for his own and he continued to thank and praise the Lord.

In an instant, the rain stopped. Luke was very wet but, Rio appeared as though she had worn her clothes swimming. They looked at each other, still sporting wide smiles, each of which could have lit up a room.

"Can you believe that just happened?" Luke asked like a little kid who had just stepped off a sleigh ride above his hometown with Santa and Rudolf.

"I guess I just needed water," Rio said as her mouth finally closed without her smile fading and her eyes widened even more.

"You guess you just needed water?" Luke asked as he began to laugh loudly. "And the same God who parted the sea for Moses and the Israelites sent a healing rain specially designated for you. You guess you just needed water. Do you have any idea how significant that is?"

"I think I do," Rio said as tears started to form in her eyes, as well. She meant it, too. The reality of God and his purpose for her life was setting in and the weight of it was substantial.

"Never in my life have I seen something that blew my mind like that just did. And, I've seen some crazy stuff since I met you. Plus, I fully expected God to answer my prayers. But, not like that. That was straight up, crazy, insane! I know the old cliché about the Lord working in mysterious ways but, that was phenomenal. I-I can't believe that just happened . . . One minute you look like you're going to die and the next, you're standing there like Tim Robbins when he finally escapes from prison in *The Shawshank Redemption*. Just unbelievable . . . "

"I know this is going to sound trivial after what we just experienced," Rio started, "but, you saw *The Shawshank Redemption*?"

"Yes," Luke exclaimed. "I know 'Waterfalls' by TLC and I saw *The Shawshank Redemption*. I'm a Christian. Not a monk."

"But, wasn't that rated R?"

"Again . . . "

"Christian. Not a monk. Got it."

"How are you not blown away right now?"

"I am. I'm just . . . I'm also feeling very humbled at the moment. Like you said when you were praying, it's become quite clear that God has a plan for what is happening to me. That's humbling. And, a little scary."

"Understandably so," Luke said as he stepped forward and

gently embraced Rio. "I'm with you. For all of it."

Luke started to release his hug but Rio squeezed tighter.

"Thank you," she said, sincerely.

Although she enjoyed Luke's hug from a romantic point of view, she truly appreciated the friendship and the comfort of it at that moment.

"Of course," Luke agreed as they finally let go. "And, right back at you."

They shared a knowing look of warmth and mutual appreciation and then gathered their things to start the hike down the mountain again. The fact that something momentous was going on with Rio was not new information but, somehow, it all felt different now. The direct intervention of the divine had just taken place and that changed everything. Finding Sota Tanaka was still the earthly mission. However, there was no longer any doubt in either of their minds that the God of both heaven and earth had a mission of His own for them. Causing their brains to race at an even quicker rate were the fresh reminder that His ways were not theirs and the growing suspicion that they would soon learn what that mission was.

CHAPTER FORTY
Kurama Onsen

"I guess we now know why you haven't needed sleep lately," Luke said matter-of-factly as they continued their hike back to the train at Kurama station.

"We do?" Rio asked with a hint of skepticism.

"I think God just showed us."

"You mean the rain?"

"I mean water in general. Everyone else on the planet needs sleep to rejuvenate the body. But, you haven't slept since you got here and yet, you've been fine. At least, until just a few minutes ago. So, what have you done differently in the last twenty-four hours or so?"

"No shower, no pool . . ."

"There you go. So, when your body wore out, God sent the rain because He knew that's what you needed."

"Like the manna and quail that He gave the Israelites in the desert," Rio said out loud as she made the connection.

"Exodus sixteen," Luke said in agreement as he grinned with pride for Rio. "That's exactly right. How cool is that?"

The corners of Rio's mouth turned up as she acknowledged the exciting, albeit humbling, cool-factor of what had just taken place. "It is pretty amazing."

"Yeah, it is. Most amazing thing I've ever seen."

They continued to hike all the way back to the Kurama-dera Temple, stopping only briefly for sandwiches and a bathroom break. Rio was not a fan of the outdoor bathroom experience but the length of the hike left her with no alternative. This had been the case the day before as well so, it came as no surprise on the trip back.

The conversation on the hike ranged from childhood memories to the Bible and even included Luke telling Rio about a well-known hot spring at the bottom of the mountain that he felt she should experience before they finally left Kurama. Of course, the subject of Rio's abilities came up several times as well. They agreed that there was no use trying to grasp God's plan for those abilities but took comfort in the fact that they now considered it undeniable that a plan did exist.

Both Luke and Rio continued enjoying the process of getting to know one another. Because they were spending so much concentrated time together, that process was happening at an unusually rapid pace. In some cases, that can be a good thing. In other cases, it might not be. For Luke and Rio, it was very good. The more they learned about one another, the deeper into the relationship pool they each found themselves wanting to dive.

When they arrived at the Kurama-dera Temple, Luke reminded Rio to bow before talking to people and to speak quietly, particularly if they entered the shrine hall, out of respect for the Buddhist practitioners who would likely be prostrating in silence. He further suggested that she avoid walking in front of any such practitioners, stepping over any dharma materials, and try to avoid allowing her feet to point at the altar. Finally, he told her that if she found herself wanting to yawn, cough or laugh, that she should cover her mouth with her hand. When she told him that was a lot to remember, he assured her that she would be fine and they went inside.

There were no mishaps or major gaffes but, unfortunately, there were also no new leads. They were unable to find a single person who had any memory of Sota Tanaka whatsoever.

Since the day was winding down, Luke suggested that they find a place to camp and offered to set up the tent while Rio went to the hot spring. Rio agreed and they hiked about twenty minutes away from the temple before finding a suitable camp ground where they believed they would be left undisturbed overnight.

With the site selected, Luke escorted Rio to the hot spring. Along the way, he explained that the Japanese word for hot spring was onsen. As good as Rio's grasp on the Japanese language was, this was a word she hadn't learned. He also informed her that the onsen was at a specific type of traditional Japanese inn called a ryokan and she would be renting access to a "women only" outdoor tub full of warm water from the natural hot spring. All of this was a surprise to Rio and she found herself getting a little nervous. As she thought about it, an idea sprang to mind and she suggested getting a room at the inn instead of camping out.

"I know I said I wasn't a monk but I can't do that," Luke insisted, taken aback.

"I'm not suggesting any funny business," Rio quickly stated in defense. "We only need one bed because I won't sleep. So, it really wouldn't be any different than the tent. It would just be a lot more comfortable and easier for me to read. Plus, we might be able to get a decent meal instead of heating up a can of baked beans over a campfire. I have a feeling, with the way this journey is going, we'll get our chance to do that another night."

Realizing that the room probably came with access to the onsen, Luke rationalized that it would almost pay for itself. And, a night in a comfortable bed did sound a lot better than a sleeping bag on the hard ground. *I'm my mother's son,* he thought to himself before responding to Rio with his main concern.

"I know you're not suggesting any funny business, as you so delicately put it, but it's not just about my not wanting to commit a sin. God also tells us in His word to avoid the appearance of sin so, while we wouldn't be doing anything, I can't allow it to look like we might be doing something. Does that make sense?"

Rio nodded affirmatively and thought for a second before asking a question.

"Is the tent different because it's in the woods and no one would see it?"

"God would see it so, no. I was actually going to surprise you with your own tent when you got back. There're two of them in this bag," Luke said with a smirk on his face like a man who'd been planning a surprise party that had just been spoiled.

"Oh," Rio said, genuinely surprised.

"I'll tell you what, let's get two rooms. I'll pay for it."

"No, I can't let you do that."

"I want to. The room sounds nice. Although, I wish I hadn't been carrying this bag around with me the last two days."

"Better safe than sorry?" Rio asked with a purposely fake grin.

"Sure," Luke teased. "Let's go have a nice night. I think we've earned it."

"Agreed," Rio said with a very real smile.

They checked in and took their things to their rooms. They were right on the river which offered complete serenity. Each of them beamed as they realized that this was the right decision. Luke explained he was going to check out the restaurant while she bathed in the onsen so that he could have dinner figured out by the time Rio had finished relaxing. She tried to insist that he deserved the relaxation, too. But, he couldn't be swayed. He told her that it would be good for her since the water rejuvenated her body and that he would get a lot of the same results from a meal and a good night's sleep.

They walked back to the lobby together but then split up. Rio walked to the women's locker room, changed out of her clothes and stored everything in a locker before walking out to the women's side of the onsen. She felt awkward and nervous being naked, outdoors, and anticipating a bunch of strangers. However, she was relieved when she entered the onsen to discover that she had the place to herself. Reasoning that everyone else must have been eating dinner, she was thrilled to take advantage of the unexpected privacy.

As she climbed into the warm water that rapidly relieved her from the cool, crisp air, she looked up at the gorgeous hills and beautiful trees. She immediately began to relax and feel the peace wash over her. It was the best she had felt on the entire trip.

But, what she couldn't possibly know was how much better

the evening would soon become. Although the fragrance had yet to hit her senses, romance was in the air.

CHAPTER FORTY-ONE
The Ryokan

It was difficult for Rio to peel herself out of the onsen but, dinner with Luke was a pretty strong motivator. So, after about an hour of soaking in the warm water and taking in the beautiful surroundings, Rio got dressed and went back to the adjacent rooms. She didn't even bother going into her own room but, instead, immediately knocked on Luke's door.

"Right on time," he said as he opened it.

"Oh, yeah?" Rio asked with a curious smile on her face.

"Yeah, come on in."

Rio walked inside and quickly noticed that everything had been set up to have dinner in Luke's room where they could enjoy the view and the sound of rustling water. They sat and talked for hours as the warm and friendly staff brought course after course until neither of them could eat any more food. They spent a lot of the evening laughing together and enjoying one another.

Although it wasn't officially a date, it felt like the best date either of them had ever had and neither of them wanted it to end.

Eventually, however, it had to. And, when it did, Luke and Rio lingered in the doorway as they had a difficult time saying goodnight. In fact, at one point, there was a long pause in the conversation and it was clearly obvious that they both wanted to kiss each other. It felt as if their lips were magnetized and a strong force was drawing them toward a connection. But, eventually, Luke broke the romantic tension by saying they could pick things up over breakfast in the morning and then lamenting that he might not be hungry again by then. Rio agreed and went into her room a bit disappointed but, not enough to spoil the evening. If anything, it only made her anticipate the next morning that much more.

Luke didn't go to sleep right away. He got ready for bed but his mind was racing and all his thoughts were about the miraculous young woman who had just left his room. He realized that in spite of the short amount of time that he had known Rio, she had impacted his life in such a way that he could no longer imagine it without her.

Strangely enough, Rio was having the exact same realization about Luke in the room next door. It was causing her to wonder if she really wanted to find Sota Tanaka after all. If she did, it would soon be time to return to Hilo. That was a thought that terrified her. She loved home in all the ways she could think of but, getting to know Luke had changed her perspective on everything. Was it possible that she could decide to stay in Japan? Or, would Luke ever consider moving to Hawaii? That seemed silly. He was in Japan to fulfill a calling on his life and he was clearly committed to that above everything else. It was part of what attracted Rio to him in the first place. Perhaps, she would have to go home for two years and finish school. Then she could return to Japan. Maybe she could get a job teaching swim lessons at CYOI or join one of those programs in America where they send college educated young people to teach English abroad. But, Rio wondered if she and Luke could survive those first two years apart? Two years seemed like a painful eternity.

Rio quickly realized that she had gotten way ahead of herself. *We haven't even kissed yet*, she thought. *Heck* we *haven't even admitted out loud that we have romantic feelings for each other.*

Of course, those mutual feelings had become obvious and, the truth was, no conversation was necessary for confirmation. Either way, Rio had managed to put the proverbial cart before the horse and she told herself not to worry about the future until it became a real and present problem. Instead, she decided to distract herself by continuing her Bible reading.

With the window open and the constant sound of rustling water in the background, Rio read until early morning when she decided to start her day with another dip in the onsen. The warm water felt so good on her skin and, once again, she was thrilled to be able to experience it alone. It was sad to think she and Luke would be checking out soon but, that only made her want to take it all in and truly enjoy the moment even more. Her mind did drift a bit though. She thought about all the things that she had read in the Bible over the previous three nights. It appeared, based on where she left her bookmark, that she was not quite half way but had already learned a great deal about God and His chosen people in the nation of Israel. Rio had especially enjoyed the books of Joshua and Ruth. She had also relished the stories of Joseph, Moses and David. But, so far, she loved reading the Psalms the most. They contained such beautiful words and were so full of emotional expression. They portrayed their writer's fear, hope, frustration and the reverence for, and worship of, God.

One verse, the thirteenth verse of Psalm 139 had particularly impressed her in this last reading because Luke had nearly quoted it to her, without her realizing it, the day she had saved little Zee's life in the pool back at CYOI. The verse said, "For you created my inmost being; you knit me together in my mother's womb." Luke was trying to tell her that God created her, knew everything about her, and had chosen her for a specific purpose. And, she finally believed that it was true.

Ultimately, Rio had to pull herself out of the onsen and get ready to meet up with Luke. The timing was perfect because other women started to pour into the locker room as she was getting ready to leave. Rio went to her room to pack up and finish putting herself together, during which she found herself trying a little harder to make sure that she looked cute. Little did she know, in Luke's mind, she couldn't look anything but cute.

When Luke knocked on Rio's door, he never expected that she would be completely ready to go. She even had her backpack on.

"Surprise," he started, "I am ready to eat again. One more meal in the room before we check out?"

"Definitely," Rio said with a huge smile.

Neither of them ate a ton of food at breakfast that morning. It was obvious that the meal was more about the fact that they didn't want to leave. Unfortunately, they couldn't put the inevitable off forever. The mission was still to find Sota Tanaka. While the brief reprieve was, by all counts, magical, it was clearly time to return to the mission at hand. And, once they had managed to complete that mission, they would be forced to face the consequences of their success together. Little did they know, their journey's biggest surprises still lay ahead.

CHAPTER FORTY-TWO
Shinto

It took Luke and Rio a little more than an hour to hike down to the Kifune Shrine. Rio was amused to learn that the area was called Kibune and couldn't understand why the town was spelled with a "b" but the Shrine, which was otherwise spelled the same exact way, was spelled with an "f" instead. Luke had no explanation to offer and agreed that it was kind of strange.

On their way, they had a long discussion about the Shinto religion. It fascinated Rio because it was the religion of her ancestors, including her parents. Her mother, however, had left it behind with everything else when she fled from Sota.

In addition to what they had talked about previously, when discussing the differences between Buddhism and Shinto, Rio learned that Shinto practitioners worship at the 80,000 public shrines in Japan, small home shrines called kamidana, or in natural places called mori, which are said to have an unusually sacred spirit about them. They worship a multitude of gods called kami. Luke further explained that Shinto practitioners believe the kami can manifest their essence in just about any form. They believe that people, mountains, waterfalls, animals, rivers, trees and even rocks can possess the nature of kami. The practitioners, therefore, find themselves worshipping nature and man-made idols that represent the kami. Of course, this immediately caused Rio to think about the man-made idols, often in the form of a golden calf, referenced in the Bible. She couldn't help but feel sad about how offensive the Bible said that was to God.

Rio also considered how much she appreciated nature but, the thought of worshipping it didn't make a lot of sense to her. She remembered reading in the Bible on the first night about how God gave mankind dominion over nature and that made a lot more sense to her because mankind shows dominion over it every time a man or woman does something as basic as eating and drinking. They even show that same dominion over it when they use it to build homes to live in, offices to work in, cars to drive, or even those same man-made idols that people then bow down to.

Why would you worship something below you on the food chain? she wondered. *And, why worship creation instead of the Creator?* It seemed cut and dried to her but, she accepted the fact that it was obviously something that had managed to confuse people since the beginning of time.

As they approached the fifteen-hundred-year-old shrine, on the banks of the Kibune River and just upstream from the Yodo and Kamo Rivers, they faced another long and steep stone staircase. It was divided by a red metal railing in the middle and flanked on both sides by red lanterns with black roof tops positioned every two steps. The site seemed to be covered in a green canopy from the tall maple trees that surrounded the grounds. But, the red color theme that started with the lanterns and railing on the stairs continued throughout the property with the fencing. This was also true with the large and imposing gates, which matched the lanterns with their black roofs, through which Luke and Rio entered each new area. Nearly everything else seemed to be wood in its natural coloring which was primarily a light brown.

The property was separated into three shrines: the main shrine; the site of the original main shrine; and an associated shrine dedicated to the god of marriage. Both Luke and Rio were particularly interested to learn that the main shrine was dedicated to the god of water and rain and believed to be the protector of those at sea. Legend had it that a goddess named Tamayori-hime had traveled in a yellow boat from Osaka all the way up the river into the mountains north of Kyoto. Kifune Shrine had been built at the site where her boat journey had come to an end. They were told that there was a huge rock about a kilometer up the valley that is said to be where the goddess' boat is buried.

Unfortunately, that was the full scope of interesting information obtained at the Kifune Shrine. Just like at the Kurama-dera Temple, they were unable to find anyone who knew Sota Tanaka's whereabouts. They were, however, able to find one man who remembered him and knew that he had moved on but couldn't remember where to. He thought it was a temple rather than a shrine but, that was the extent of what he could pull out of the recesses of his memory.

Also, just like at the Kurama-dera Temple, the place was crowded with tourists and practitioners. A lot of the people were participating in something called "mizu-uranai." They received fortune slips at the conferment building, then dipped them into the spring water, which they considered holy, flowing from Mt. Kibune, and the water revealed characters on the slips that told them their fortunes.

Others were purchasing paper at the main shrine and writing wishes on them and then tying them to trees outside of the shrines. It was said that the gods would then determine their destinies regarding things like romance, job hunting, higher education, friendships and health. Luke and Rio decided not to participate in either of the main activities.

Rio's favorite spot was crowded, too. It was a little red

bridge, just beyond one of the big red gates, that crossed over the middle of a small river's four-stage waterfall and it was astonishingly beautiful. Had it not been so crowded, Rio imagined it may have been almost as serene as the warm onsen in which she had started her morning that day. The sound of the water trickling by and the stunning visual of all the amazing, green vegetation gave the two places a similar, albeit intangible, feeling of peace.

If I was going to worship nature, Rio thought to herself, *this is where I would do it.*

Rio glanced next to her, at a little boy standing beside a man who was taking a picture of a woman on the opposite side of the bridge. She assumed that the two adults were the little boy's parents. The boy stepped behind his father, backs to one another, to peek at the water through the bridge as the man waited for other tourists to clear the way so he could snap his photo.

Rio looked the other direction to share a smile with Luke, then turned just in time to see the boy climb up to the top of the railing as his father took a step backward. Their backsides collided and inadvertently knocked the boy off the bridge. The mother screamed and the father spun around as Rio watched the boy begin the more than twenty-foot plunge toward the shallow water. Her eyes widened as the horror of what was taking place set in and she immediately knew that she had to stop it.

Unfortunately, there was virtually no time to decide if, or how, that was going to be possible.

CHAPTER FORTY-THREE
Quick Exit

Without thinking, Rio swung her right arm backward and then, in a scooping motion, raised her right hand, palm open to the sky, straight up in the air. Summoning the water below, it looked as if an arm made of water burst out of the river and shot upward, with an open hand, to catch the boy just before he reached the end of his fall.

It was no longer just Luke, Rio and the boy's parents who were watching, pointing, screaming, crying . . . The crowded bridge instantly turned into an audience. And, several people were looking back and forth between the river and Rio, making the connection.

The arm made of water gently rose all the way to the bridge and handed the boy off to his parents, who stood in total shock.

"Tamayori-hime?" Rio heard a man gasp, wondering if he was seeing the manifestation of the goddess who had supposedly traveled to the region in her yellow boat and now protected people at sea.

As quickly as it had appeared, the arm and hand made of water disintegrated into millions of droplets, rained down into the river and disappeared.

"We have to get out of here," Luke whispered to Rio.

Rio looked around and saw that most people were staring at the boy and his parents, who were fawning over him. But, a few people were looking at her inquisitively.

"Yep," she agreed.

Luke grabbed Rio's hand and they started backing their way out of the crowd. They moved slowly at first but, people continued to stare, point and talk. The more they did, the larger the group looking at them instead of the boy and his parents became. Luke panicked that too many people were seeing Rio's face.

"Let's go," he said and they both turned around to face the gate.

Running as fast as they could with their bags in tow, Luke and Rio hustled out of the Kifune Shrine and raced back up the path that they had previously come down. When they finally realized that no one had followed them, they stopped to catch their breath. The break didn't last long and they walked as quickly as they could back to the train station so they could return to

Kyoto and get the van.

They were very quiet on the train and Rio kept her head down just in case there was anyone on board who had been at the shrine and witnessed the event with the boy. Luke and Rio barely said a word to one another until they had finished their trek back to the van, loaded their bags in the back, sat in the front seat, and closed the doors. The first sound was a unified sigh of relief.

"Okay," Rio finally said, still showing signs of exasperation. "Now what?"

"Back to CYOI to collect ourselves?" Luke asked, unsure what Rio's response would be.

"Perfect," Rio agreed, just happy to have a plan.

Luke started the engine, relieved that he and Rio were on the same page. He felt the need to get back to home base. CYOI felt safe because it was familiar and he knew Isaac would be their biggest ally if they found themselves in a position where they needed one.

Feeling like they could finally talk freely, the conversation on the way back to the ministry was full of what ifs. None of them came as a surprise to Luke. He had discussed most of them with Isaac and Jacoba when agreeing to help Rio keep her anonymity as long as possible.

What ifs almost always come from a place of fear and worry.

This was no exception. Rio was worried about people finding out about her abilities. She feared what that would mean for the remainder of her life. She also wondered if it was wrong for them to run. She heard someone yell the name of that goddess they had learned about and worried that God would have wanted them to stay and face the crowd so that they could correct the misunderstanding and let them know that this was not an action taken by some false god.

Luke was worried, too. He joined in the what ifs at first. But, by the time they arrived at CYOI, He had started to calm things down by reassuring Rio that God would continue to take care of them. He had proven Himself in the woods with the rain and there was no reason to doubt Him now. The reminder helped Rio a lot. The entire life of faith was new to her but, she was beginning to get it.

They stopped to pick up another round of Luke's favorite spicy beef and took it back to CYOI where they unloaded all their gear and discussed the next steps while they ate in the cafeteria. They decided to keep the camping equipment out and available but not to take it with them the following day. They would drive to the last place they hadn't been where they knew Sota had visited, the Kunōzan Tōshō-gū Shrine on the Suruga Bay in Shizuoka. Luke was guessing it was a solid three-hour drive in each direction. Still, they decided that after their visit, regardless of the outcome, they would plan on returning to CYOI so Luke could get a good night of rest and Rio would have access to running water in one form or another.

After dinner, Luke and Rio said goodnight at the door to the girls' dormitory. There was no awkwardness this time. Neither of them were anticipating a kiss. However, each of them still wanted one.

Instead, Rio gave one last wave as Luke entered the boys' dorm and turned around to face the payphone. She had decided a couple of hours earlier, while riding in the van, that this would be the night she would finally call her mother and give her progress report number two. Although, the way Rio was feeling, it would be more of a "lack of progress" report.

On top of feeling like she hadn't accomplished what she set out to do, Rio had to have a tough conversation with her mom about her family history and hadn't decided whether to include the fact that she had developed the ability to control water. This could be a pretty long conversation. She sat in front of the phone for several minutes, just staring at the keypad. Finally, without any decisions made, she took a deep breath, exhaled, pulled out her calling card and reached for the receiver.

CHAPTER FORTY-FOUR
The Last Shrine

The phone call went better than Rio had anticipated. Of course, Toki was excited to hear from her daughter. But, she was also very interested to learn about the journey so far. And, to Rio's surprise, her mother thought that she had made a tremendous amount of progress. Rio decided to leave out all the parts of the water-related miracles she had been involved in. She knew that conversation was coming. She just wasn't quite ready yet.

But, even without those details, Toki was amazed by the adventures that Rio had already had. She was blown away by Rio's time in Shingu. She cried when she learned her father was dead. Sorrow and regret would overwhelm her in the days to come. But, for now, it was suppressed by a watershed moment for her tear ducts as she learned that Rio had been given the opportunity to finally meet, sit, and talk with her grandmother.

Decades of pent-up emotion spilled out. What had previously caused her fear and anxiety began to transform into thanksgiving and gladness. Toki couldn't help but wonder if she too would have the chance to see her mother again.

It further stunned Toki to learn that Rio had met Yoshito. But, the thing that blew her mind more than anything else was when she learned that Sota had been so upset by her departure that he had disappeared on a soul-searching mission to become a better man and had possibly been bouncing around from shrine to temple to monastery and who knew where else ever since. That news rendered Toki very nearly speechless.

The one thing Rio expected about the call that turned out to be accurate was the fact that it was a long one. When Rio realized that more than an hour had passed, she promised to call again soon and to stay safe but told her mom she had to hang up or her calling card would run out. She couldn't help but cry, as she took her long shower, thinking about what her mom must have been going through emotionally almost four thousand miles away. And, she was sure that more pain was coming. But, she hoped that this trip would also bring a great amount of healing.

Rio tried to distract herself by testing her abilities in the shower. She raised the pooling water on the shower floor, like she had done from the bridge at the Kifune Shrine, and created two small fists that she caused to punch each other and shatter in the air. The distraction worked for a moment but her mind soon started racing again.

After the shower, Rio laid prostrate on her bed and read another large part of the Bible. She was surprised when she recognized the first eight verses of the third chapter of Ecclesiastes from a song called "Turn! Turn! Turn!" by The Byrds. She also found herself reading the few chapters of the book of Daniel that she had come across and the book of Jonah like thrilling novels. But, the verses that stuck out most to her, encouraged her, and felt personally applicable that night were from another Psalm. They comprised the first four verses of Psalm 46 and read:

> "God is our refuge and strength,
>   an ever-present help in trouble.
> Therefore we will not fear, though the
>   earth give way
>   and the mountains fall into the
>   heart of the sea,
> though its waters roar and foam
>   and the mountains quake with their
>   surging.
> There is a river whose streams make
>   glad the city of God,
>   the holy place where the Most High
>   dwells."

After an uneventful but rewarding swim in the morning hours that followed, Rio joined Luke for the three-and-a-half-hour drive to the Kunōzan Tōshō-gū Shrine in Shizuoka. The drive was made a little longer than originally estimated by a stop for gas and breakfast. Rio asked Luke if he would mind her passing the time by reading the Bible instead of listening to music. He told her it was fine if she was willing to read aloud. Luke enjoyed hearing Rio read the Word of God so much that he was almost disappointed when they arrived at their destination on the steep peak of Mount Kunō above Suruga Bay.

But, the most disappointing thing about that day was the fact that their last lead turned out to be another dead end. While they talked to two different men who both remembered Sota, neither of them had any idea where he might have gone when he left Shizuoka. He was described as a quiet man but, not because of any vow and, that's where the new information ended.

By the time they had exhausted all possibilities at the Kunōzan Tōshō-gū Shrine, Luke and Rio were quiet, too. They were in a beautiful place and had been dealing with wonderful people. But, the amazing momentum that started in Shingu, where answers seemed to be handed out in abundance, continued in Kyoto and then slowed down at the Buddhist monastery on Mount Kurama, had now come to a screeching halt.

Standing at the top of the longest, most twisted staircase they had been to yet, overlooking the gorgeous bay, Rio finally said the only thing she could think of to say.

"Maybe it's time for me to accept the possibility that God didn't bring me to Japan to find Sota."

Luke was silent and neither of them looked at the other.

"I'm disappointed," Rio admitted as she continued, still pondering the contradictory feelings of desire to accomplish the goal that brought her to Japan but not wanting to let go of the things that had her wanting to stay there. "I'm discouraged. I haven't found what I'd hoped for. But, what I have found is better. So, I can count this trip as a victory no matter what happens or doesn't happen next. That has to be enough."

Luke knew that she meant what she said but he could also tell that she was trying to convince herself that things would be okay. He appreciated it and knew this was a step in the right direction when it came to learning to trust God with the path for her life. He put an arm around Rio and pulled her in to his side. She placed her head on his chest and they both smiled peacefully even though Rio still felt a bit on edge. However, her anxiety was only present because Rio was completely unaware of the fact that, not only was Sota very much alive but, they would learn of his exact whereabouts the very next day.

CHAPTER FORTY-FIVE
Sanctuary

The long car ride back to CYOI allowed Rio time to do some more reading aloud. That day, Luke heard a lot of Rio's voice and by the time they pulled into the parking lot, Rio had completed her reading of the Old Testament. Her favorite book was Esther. Rio imagined Esther to be a precocious and charming young girl and there was something about the story of a beautiful and intelligent Jewish teenager becoming queen of Persia, who conquered Babylon while the Jews were in captivity there, and saving her people that Rio found absolutely thrilling. She felt a connection to Esther that was somehow deeper than the other people she had read about that day. Perhaps it was the fact that the young girl was in a position that she hadn't sought out. A position that was unique to only her. And, she used that position to do something great. It inspired Rio and she hoped to do something great with the position she found herself in, too.

The main thing that Rio took away from the story, however, was not unlike what she took away from a lot of the stories she had read in the Bible. God is sovereign and loving in all circumstances. That was a point that was being driven home repeatedly as she read the scriptures. It was a good thing, too. This point was something that Rio would need to remember during the events that were coming her way. Discouragement, after all, had already set in. And, things would soon get even more devastating.

But, before they did, she would enjoy a nice dinner with Luke. They stopped at the same place that they had picked up the spicy beef the night before. But, this time, Rio insisted on getting chicken while Luke stuck with his old favorite. She teased him about being a creature of habit and told him that she couldn't do the same dinner two nights in a row. Luke, however, hit her with the timeworn expression 'if it ain't broke, don't fix it.' Rio laughed and found the logic hard to argue with, especially since she realized that it also applied to her own desire to drink nothing but water.

The mood stayed relatively upbeat but, Luke could tell that Rio was simply powering through because she thought that was what she was supposed to do. He understood, too. He felt a little discouraged by the three dead ends in a row and knew that it had to be a hundred times worse for Rio. Not only was finding Sota

Tanaka her entire reason for coming to Japan but, she also didn't have the experience walking in faith that Luke did. Not that, that experience made it easy but, it certainly helped.

They discussed the uncertainty of what to do next in the search for her father but were unable to come up with a satisfactory plan. So, they finally said goodnight and, for the first time, went their separate ways without a game plan for the following day. While Luke said a particularly long prayer about all of it before closing his eyes, he went to sleep feeling certain that God would guide them but without a clue as to where they were headed.

Rio went through her usual CYOI bedtime routine of showering and then reading the Bible on top of her bed. Having finished the Old Testament that day, she read the four gospels over the course of the night. By the time the wise men were offering gifts to the newborn King of Kings, her eyes were already welling up with tears. When Jesus said that He was the way, the truth, and the life, the tears began to fall. As Jesus' disciple, Judas, betrayed him with a kiss for thirty pieces of silver and it led to his tortuous crucifixion on a cross, the tears became an uncontrollable sob. But, then the tears became joyous when women bearing myrrh found the tomb empty. And, by the time Jesus ascended into heaven, Rio was on her knees thanking God for his mercy and grace and telling Him that she knew He had a plan for her and that she trusted Him with her life.

Almost immediately, Rio felt overcome with anxiousness. She couldn't shake the feeling that something was wrong. It surprised her because, if anything, she would have expected to have been overcome with joy at this moment. But, joy was not what she felt brewing inside of her. This was more of an uneasiness. Rio felt restless and concerned but didn't know what was causing it or why it was happening to her. She went for a swim to calm down but, it didn't work.

What is going on? Rio wondered.

Swimming had always calmed her down. It had been a constant source of peace her entire life. But, it was clear that wasn't going to cut it this time. So, she got ready for the day and found herself knocking on Luke's door just before 5:30am. Luke answered, still looking half asleep.

"Rio. Everything okay?"

"No," Rio answered abruptly.

"What's wrong?"

"I don't know."

"What do you mean?"

"I mean, something's wrong but I don't know what it is."

"Am I dreaming?" Luke asked. "Because, this makes no sense."

"You're definitely not dreaming."

"Then, tell me what happened. Just start at the beginning."

"I prayed," Rio answered but then found herself unsure of how to continue.

"That's a good thing. Right?"

"Of course."

"What did you pray about?"

"I told God I trusted Him and I wanted Him to take control of my life."

"You mean, like the sinner's prayer?"

"The what?"

"It sounds like you accepted Jesus."

"I did. I do."

"Well," Luke started, still feeling confused, "that's great. Right? I don't understand what the problem is."

"The problem is, we have to go."

"Go where?"

"I don't know."

"Go . . . Why?"

"I don't know. Something's wrong."

"I heard you say that but, what's wrong?"

"I don't know."

"Do you feel like we're in a comedy routine right now? This sort of feels like a 'Who's on first' type of vicious cycle kind of thing. Just tell me what you think is wrong."

"I can't explain it but, it's dangerous for us to be here right now. We have to leave CYOI and we can't come back right away."

CHAPTER FORTY-SIX
Goodbye, CYOI

That morning, Luke got ready faster than he ever had before in his life. They were in the van, with their bags, the camping gear and food supplies loaded in the back, and cranking the engine, with no idea where they were headed, before 6:00am. Departing the parking lot, Luke continued with the line of questioning he had started while they were packing up.

"So, you're sure no one here is in danger."

"No," Rio countered. "I'm not really sure about anything. But, I feel like you and I are in danger if we stay. It feels like it has specifically to do with us. Or, at least me. But, I think everyone else is okay. I don't know. I can't explain it. It's a weird feeling. I just knew we needed to leave. That's all."

"It seems like I should be warning Isaac."

"About what?"

"I don't know . . . Great, now you've got me saying it."

"I really don't believe he's in any danger."

"I still think I'll call him in a few hours when I know he'll be in his office."

"Go for it."

"At least check on him to make sure he's okay."

"Sure."

"Now what?"

"Do you really want me to say it again?" Rio asked with a curl of her lip.

"Right. You don't know. How about breakfast? Or, at least a cup of tea."

"Sounds good. But, let's get down the road a bit first."

"Fair enough."

Luke didn't have a specific place in mind and he knew Rio was right in not wanting to stop too soon. They should get a good distance away from CYOI in case her feeling about it being dangerous for her to be there proved to be correct. He still didn't understand how that could be the case but, he had also learned that his understanding wasn't necessarily required. She could still be right. And, without specific knowledge of what the danger was and when it would arrive, the old adage Rio had thrown out about him carrying around tents for two days that they never used, "better safe than sorry," seemed more appropriate than ever and was now ringing in his brain.

So, he started off driving east but soon decided to head south. About an hour down the road, he found himself just inside the Osaka Prefecture in an area called Takatsuki. Luke pulled the van up to a tea house across the street from a train station.

"How does that look?" he asked Rio.

"Works for me," she said as she opened her door.

They climbed out of the van and went inside. It was a quaint little café with flowery wallpaper and lots of dark wood – including the floors. Some of the tables had tablecloths but, not all of them, and none of them matched. The chairs were mostly the same but some of the cushions were red and some were white. Some of the chairs didn't have cushions at all. Had they been focused on it, Rio and Luke may have considered the possibility that this establishment and the one in which they had the infamous tea of tendaiuyaku could have shared the same decorator.

The truth is, at that moment, Luke and Rio couldn't have cared less. They were just happy to be there. Once they had agreed to find a bite to eat and some tea, the ride that brought them to the tea house had been a quiet one. Rio was reflective and did a little reading of the New Testament, beyond the gospels, to learn about the Holy Spirit coming at Pentecost, the severe persecution of the early Christian church, and Saul's miraculous conversion in which his name was changed to Paul.

When she read that section, Rio couldn't help but think about her mother transforming her life and changing her name from Mei to Toki. She particularly enjoyed the book of James and Paul's letter to the Galatians. The Bible seemed to be landing heavier with Rio this morning, as if it had previously been educational and informative but, starting last night, the effect had changed and the words were now being imprinted on her heart.

Meanwhile, Luke was just plain tired. He had mostly driven in silence and let Rio read to herself. An hour was about all he could handle without fear of his eyes closing. So, being anywhere without a steering wheel in his hands was good as far as he was concerned. Seated inside of the tea house, the influx of caffeine from the green tea began to get Luke's brain working and he finally re-launched the conversation just before the food arrived.

"I'm excited," Luke said out of nowhere.

"You don't seem excited," Rio shot back with a grin on her face.

"I'm exhausted so, it's not showing yet. But, I am. Your prayer last night is a big deal. It changes everything."

"I know it does."

They were interrupted by a warm and friendly man who delivered their grilled shishamo (a small saltwater fish,) steamed rice, miso soup, and small portions of tsukemono (pickled vegetables) and natto (fermented soy beans.) Luke started on the miso soup as soon as the man was gone. But, that didn't stop him from asking a question that sent the conversation in a totally new direction.

"Any thoughts on where to go next?"

"A few," Rio considered out loud as she nibbled on the natto. I was thinking, on our way here, that the last place we know of Sota spending some time was at the Kunōzan Tōshō-gū Shrine."

"Right," Luke agreed but with a tone in his voice that signaled he was waiting for more information.

"Maybe he left Kurama, went to the Kunōzan Tōshō-gū Shrine in Shizuoka, and then kept heading north."

"Got it," Luke said as he sucked down another mouthful of miso soup.

"I know that doesn't narrow it down very much but, at least it's a little bit of direction."

"True," Luke agreed but got hung up on the direction itself. "So, you're saying that when I took us an hour south this morning, we were clearly on the exact same page."

"No," Rio said with a chuckle, "I'm glad you brought us back to Osaka. I think we should finally do what you've been wanting to do since you learned about the woman who prophesied to my mom about me."

"You mean, we're going to the bench?" Luke asked with an

enthusiasm that hadn't been seen yet that morning.

"I think it's time," Rio admitted.

"That's awesome. That's the right call. I don't know what it is about that bench but, I swear it's the right thing to do. Answers are coming . . . "

"I hope you're right."

"Oh, I'm right. I'm definitely right about this. And, it's probably only thirty or forty minutes away. This is awesome."

Luke and Rio finished their breakfast, got back in the van, and headed deeper into Osaka where they would finally get some of the answers that they had been seeking.

CHAPTER FORTY-SEVEN
The Bench & The Rumor Mill

The ride in the van after breakfast was much livelier. Both Luke and Rio were excited to find out what was waiting for them at the bench where Mei, long before she changed her name to Toki and escaped to Hilo, had met the mysterious elderly woman who prophesied that she would give birth to Rio and that Rio would be a gift, not just to her but, to everyone. Luke drove the van, on Route 43 which paralleled the Hanshin Namba Railway Line, across the Yodo River. He got off at Dempo Station and continued south until he reached Kōshin-dō Temple. He decided that, although they weren't sure of the exact distance to the bench from there, that it was likely the best place in the area to park for free.

So, they walked along the Yodo River for what turned out to be a little over two miles. Along the way, they realized that they probably could have found a closer place to park. They passed a shipyard, an elementary school, two parks, countless shipping containers, a grocery store and a café before arriving at the Osaka North Port Marina which, as it turned out, had a free parking lot of its own. They quickly found out that it was also known as the Hokko Yacht Harbor as they stared at all the beautiful boats. Most were docked but there were several coming and going as well.

The setting was tranquil. They stood and just looked around in silence for a couple of minutes. But, then Rio noticed a nearby bench. Her gaze fixated on it and the smile on her face grew.

"There it is," Rio said without moving.

Luke spun his head around to see what Rio was looking at. He glanced at Rio, then the bench, then back at Rio.

"How do you know?"

"That's it," she said calmly. "It's exactly how Momma described it."

Rio finally took a step forward. Then another. She approached it slowly, almost reverently. Luke watched as she stood next to it, then turned to look at the view of the Yodo River.

"This is where it all started," Rio said as she turned back to look at Luke and he finally walked forward to join her.

"Maybe you should sit down," he said as he stepped up to the back of the bench.

"Yeah," Rio agreed before taking a seat in the exact spot where her mother had been sitting when the elderly woman had approached her twenty-five years earlier. She felt a peace wash over her like she was exactly where she was supposed to be at that moment.

The two of them were silent and still as the minutes passed. The sun warmed their skin and the view was magnificent. Finally, Rio broke the silence.

"Are you going to sit with me?"

"Maybe in a few minutes," Luke answered. "I think I'm going to head back toward the café and the grocery store. See if I can't find a pay phone and check in on Isaac."

"Okay."

With that, Luke did exactly as he said. And, just as he suspected, there was a pay phone outside of the grocery store. He picked up the receiver, put the money in, and dialed. Luke was relieved when Isaac picked up on the other end.

"Isaac," Luke started right in, "as strange as it may sound, it's good to hear your voice."

"Not strange at all," Isaac joked. "I get that all the time. I've been told I should have gone into radio. Of course, that may have been more of a commentary on my looks than anything else, but hey . . . "

Luke laughed before trying to explain himself.

"Well, what I really meant was that, we got out of there in a hurry this morning because Rio had a feeling that she was suddenly in some kind of danger. So, I'm relieved that she was either wrong or, at the very least, she was right that it was a danger that doesn't impact anyone else at CYOI. At least not yet."

"Huh," Isaac responded somewhat conspicuously. "She may have been on to something."

"What do you mean?"

"I mean, I was greeted at the door this morning by two NPA agents."

"National Police? What did they want?"

"First of all," Isaac started, "they weren't your typical, local police officers. These were information gatherers at the national level."

"And, what kind of information were they gathering, Isaac?"

"They were asking about Rio. They just don't know who it is they're asking about, specifically. Believe me, they had more questions than answers. But, that doesn't mean there isn't cause for concern."

"What, exactly, sparked their curiosity?"

"They said they were investigating an incident that happened up at the Kifune Shrine a couple of days ago. You know anything about that?"

"I do. But, how did they track that back to Rio?"

"They didn't. Not precisely anyway. They said that they were told a young woman saved a boy's life by controlling the water in a small river. People called it a miracle. Then someone told them they had heard about another miracle where a fisherman's life was saved on Ise Bay several days earlier. I assume that fisherman is the camper's father who called me the day before Rio saved Zee."

"Fair assumption."

"Anyway, apparently, most of the people at the Kifune Shrine were trying to credit a goddess named Tamayori-hime but, the person who knew about Ise Bay was a friend of the fisherman who was saved. They said he was a Christian who said that the young woman who saved him was with a young man who works here at CYOI. The other witnesses at the Kifune Shrine confirmed the young woman was with a young man there, too. So, they came asking questions."

"What did you tell them?"

"As little as possible without lying."

"To protect Rio?"

"Of course. But, also to protect the ministry."

"What do you mean?" Luke asked, concerned.

"We both know the Japanese government has never really wanted us here. They see Christianity as a potential disruption to the way of life in Japan. I don't know how they could use this against us, exactly, but I know they would if they could. I just don't want to give them an excuse to force us into closing our doors."

"Got it. So, what exactly did you tell them?"

"The first thing I did was I tried to convince them that it sounded like little more than the rumor mill cranking out stories. They didn't seem to buy into that theory though. Too many eye-witnesses."

"What do they know?"

"Enough to move forward. Thankfully, they still don't know her name but they do know a young woman has been staying here. Obviously, they can't be sure she's the one they're looking for but, they'll keep digging unless they somehow decide she's not. They also know that you have been helping the young woman search for her long-lost father. They don't know his name either. But, if they start asking questions at some of the places you've been, someone will remember who you two were looking for. So, it won't be long and they'll have that. You might want to either stop looking or make sure you find him before they do. Otherwise, they'll be waiting for you when you get there. And, if they are, they may just kick us out of their country and take Rio."

"I'd never see her again."

"It's a possibility."

"I can't let that happen."

"I'll be praying for you two."

"Thanks, Isaac."

"I told Rio her secret was safe with me and I meant it. But, I think that secret is about to get out anyway."

"I'm afraid you're right."

"Good thing you two got out of here when you did. Probably bought yourself a little more time. The two of you need to decide whether it's worth the risk to try and find her father first but, either way, I think you need to put her on a plane as soon as you can. Her best protection is to go home."

"Definitely," Luke reluctantly agreed. "Thanks, again."

"You bet."

"I'll be in touch soon."

"Be safe."

"We'll do our best. Bye."

"Bye."

Luke hung up the phone and walked back toward the bench, sadness overwhelming him, as he thought about how to convince Rio they needed to get her to the airport right away. But, when the bench came into view, he saw the same elderly woman from Ise Bay approaching Rio.

CHAPTER FORTY-EIGHT
Disclosure

"How's Isaac?" Rio asked when she heard footsteps behind her. She expected to hear Luke's voice in response but, was surprised to hear the voice of a woman instead.

"Isaac is, and will be fine, dear."

Rio spun around to see the elderly woman, whom she immediately recognized from the airport in Hilo, step around the opposite side of the bench and calmly take a seat next to her.

"You . . ." was all Rio could get out at first. Her mind was racing so fast that her mouth was frozen. But, after a few seconds, she was finally able to blurt out some more words.

"You were at the airport in Hilo. And, Luke said he saw you that day on Ise Bay."

"True," the woman said.

Rio was surprised that the woman spoke in perfect English because her mom had said she had spoken to her in Japanese.

But, Rio would eventually surmise, all that was happening was clearly by way of divine purpose and nothing, as had already been proven, is impossible for God.

"I was at the ministry's pool," the woman continued, "the okonomiyaki restaurant and the Kifune Shrine, too. Truth is, I have always been there. I just haven't always let you see me. Lovely. The water is just lovely, isn't it?"

"It is," Rio agreed as she looked away from the woman and took in the beautiful Yodo River view once more. Only seconds later, she returned her gaze to the woman beside her.

"You sat here with my mother twenty-five years ago, didn't you?"

"I did," the woman said in a calm voice. "She was so nervous. Far more than you are."

"What did you two talk about?" Rio asked in a fishing expedition.

"You know what we talked about," the woman said plainly. "She already told you. We talked about you, Rio. We talked about the fact that you are a gift. A gift to her, of course. To your whole family. A gift to Luke, too. Isn't love wonderful? Human love is one of the most magnificent things God ever designed. Don't you agree?"

Rio smiled.

"Of course you do," the woman continued. "How could you

not? But, you being a gift goes well beyond just a handful of people. You, sweet girl, are a gift to everyone. A gift to the whole world. What an honor you have been given . . . "

"I agree. It is an honor. But, how am I a gift?"

"Listen."

Rio looked around and tried to hear any noises that the woman could be referring to but didn't notice anything that she thought was related to her inquiry.

"To what?" she finally asked, hoping that the woman would choose to answer this second question.

"Listen to that still, small voice. Listen and you'll know the answer."

Rio closed her eyes and began to silently pray that God would open her ears and let her hear so that she could know what His purpose was for her and how that purpose made her a gift to the whole world. She heard nothing audible but, as if the answer had been in her heart all along and her heart was suddenly free to inform her mind, her purpose abruptly became clear.

Rio opened her eyes and looked at the woman as she spoke, "I'm supposed to show the world that miracles still happen."

"Indeed," the woman replied.

"Why me?"

"Why not you, dear?"

"How do I do it? When? Where? Or, have I already?"

"Think of what you've done so far as the rehearsals before the big show. You'll know the when and the where of that big show at the right time but the how should be obvious by now. What's happening to you is a gift. And, by way of being the vessel of that gift, you, Rio, are yourself a gift. Therefore, when it is time to be a gift, you should use the gift you've been given to do it."

"That's awfully close to a riddle," Rio chuckled. "But, I think I get it. I guess, for now, I stick with the goal that brought me here. The rest will just fall into place, huh?"

"Sounds like wisdom to me."

"I sure wish you could just tell me where Sota is," Rio said, flippantly. "That would make things a lot easier."

"I certainly can tell you where Sota is," the woman said, never veering from her calm and peaceful demeanor.

"What?" Rio exclaimed as she looked at the woman with great anticipation. "You can? Seriously? Why didn't we have this conversation sooner?"

"It wasn't time until just now."

"Well, if it's time now, then by all means, start spilling!"

"You'll find Sota Tanaka in the same place he's been for almost two years now. The Jorakuzan Mantokuji Temple in Tateyama. It's three hundred and sixty-five miles away. But, if you hurry, you'll be speaking to your father before nightfall."

"Are you kidding me?"

"Not at all, sweet one. Go get Luke, who's been watching us this whole time, and find Sota. God has great plans for all three of you. As for me, I'll be right here enjoying this lovely water. Of course, I'll also be where you are. You'll see me again. Run along now and enjoy your time with that precious young man."

"Thank you," Rio told the woman as she got to her feet.

"That's what I'm here for. That's what I've always been here for."

Rio and the elderly woman shared a knowing smile. Then, Rio turned and started sprinting toward Luke whose eyes grew wider as Rio got closer.

She practically tackled him with her enormous bear hug as she yelled, "I know where Sota is!"

"You do?" Luke gasped as the wind was practically knocked out of him and he immediately knew that there would now be no convincing Rio to go to the airport and fly home. "That was her, wasn't it?"

"Yeah," Rio said as she spun around to look at the elderly woman and realized that she had vanished into thin air. "It was."

"I knew it. But, I didn't want to interrupt. Now, tell me everything."

"Fine. On the way to the car though. We have like a seven-hour drive ahead of us."

"Where're we going, Tokyo?"

"A place called Tateyama."

"I don't know where that is. Good thing we have a map."

"I'm told it's three hundred and sixty-five miles."

"Wow. You two had a really specific conversation."

"Not all of it."

"Well, at least you know where Sota is. Isaac's fine, by the way but we still need to talk about something."

"I know."

"You do?"

"She told me Isaac was fine, too."

"Oh. Did she tell you the National Police were at CYOI this morning?"

"Nope. That's new. Guess we do have some catching up to do."

"Guess so. And only seven hours to do it in."

"Seven hours. Then I finally meet my father."

CHAPTER FORTY-NINE
Revelation

Sota woke up feeling fine that morning but, shortly after breakfast, he had developed a stomach ache. As the nausea gradually worsened, his body heated up and he began to perspire. Finally, he decided that he needed to lie down. As he crawled back into bed, he wondered if he had eaten something bad or contracted a horrible virus. He would soon learn that neither was causing the symptoms of his suffering. The illness had an entirely unforeseeable purpose.

The fever was rapidly growing worse. His sheets were soaked in sweat, he suddenly felt completely fatigued, and he found himself wishing he had brought a bowl to bed with him in case he vomited. Considering an attempt to crawl to the bathroom, despite his absolute exhaustion, Sota tried to open his eyes. But, instead of light creeping through the openings of his eyelids, everything went black as he fell into a deep sleep.

"Sota Tanaka," he heard a gentle voice whisper as he slowly regained consciousness while his body remained motionless. He suddenly realized he no longer felt ill and quickly decided that he must be having a dream. A split second later, he remembered that he had never been conscious of dreaming while in the middle of a dream before.

What is happening to me? he wondered.

"Sota Tanaka," the voice came again.

Who's here? he continued to wonder. *Who's inside of my head?*

"Sota Tanaka," Sota heard the voice say one more time.

Finally, Sota could open his eyes and total darkness was banished by a brilliant light.

"Yes?" Sota answered, in his native tongue, as if he wasn't sure he wanted to admit who he was.

A thirty-three-year-old Jewish man stepped out of the light and leaned over him.

"Who are you?" Sota asked hesitantly as he slowly felt his ability to move returning. He decided that this was, in fact, a dream. Or, at least, he was in a dream-like state.

"I am the Nazarene called Yeshua," the man answered in perfect Japanese.

His voice was still gentle but it was no longer a whisper. It was deeper now and Sota felt the power of His name penetrate his chest.

"I am the root and the descendant of David," Yeshua continued, the paradoxically tender and authoritative words now shaking Sota to the core of his being, "the bright morning star. I am the way, the truth and the life. I am the Alpha and the Omega, the first and the last, the beginning and the end, who is, and who was, and who is to come, the Almighty."

As Yeshua reached his right hand forward, inviting Sota to stand with him, Sota shrunk back in shame. He curled up in a ball and closed his eyes tightly, turning his head away from Yeshua, and trying to hide.

"You know who I am," Sota said, suddenly feeling naked and exposed. "You know what I've done. I can feel it. How can you offer me your hand?"

"I love you, Sota Tanaka."

Sota heard the words and began to weep uncontrollably.

"I died. But, now and forever, I live. I have done this so that you too can live, and live life abundantly."

Sota finally turned and opened his eyes to look at Yeshua's face. His smile was the most genuine and adoring smile Sota had ever seen.

"Why would you do this for me?" Sota begged, knowing he had done nothing to make himself worthy of such a sacrifice.

"Because you couldn't do it for yourself," Yeshua said with a hint of sadness. "You have tried harder than most. But, I have already succeeded where you could not. I am here to offer you the peace you have been seeking all these many years."

"How?" Sota asked with the urgency of a poisoned man begging for the elixir that would save his life. "I'm not worthy of your presence. You know the things I have done. Clearly, I am a man tortured by a heart of darkness."

"And I am the light of the world," Yeshua responded with a calm authority Sota had never seen or heard before. "The peace I offer you comes only from my Father and no one comes to the Father except through me."

"What do I have to do?" Sota asked, still pleading for his life.

"Do you believe me?"

"Yes," Sota nearly shouted. "You are the truth. I feel it bursting out from within you. I feel it piercing my heart. For the first time in my life, I truly believe. There is nothing I believe more than you. What you have, what you offer, I have searched everywhere to find. But, I have failed. Until now. You are my Lord, my God."

"Then follow me."

Tears still streaming down his face, Sota reached out and took the hand Yeshua was offering.

"Your sins are forgiven," Yeshua told Sota as he stood up and pulled him to his feet.

Suddenly, Sota was back in his room and standing up, out of

bed, feeling healthier than he ever had in his life. He spun around looking for Yeshua but, instead, he found an unfamiliar elderly woman sitting in his chair in the opposite corner of the room.

"I've already met my Lord," he told the woman. "Who could you possibly be?"

"Our Lord's humble messenger," the woman stated, matter-of-factly.

"What does my Lord wish for me to do?"

"Pack your things. There is no reason for you to be here any longer. Tell whoever you need to that you're leaving and you won't be back. When you have done all this and you finally reach the parking lot, it will be time to meet your daughter."

"My daughter?" Sota was mystified. He didn't have a daughter. Not that he knew of anyway.

"Mei was pregnant when she left, Sota. She left out of anger, yes, but she also left out of fear for the safety of your daughter."

"I never knew."

"Of course you didn't. How could you? But, now you do. You will meet her, and the man she loves, very shortly. And, she will need your help."

"I'll do anything."

"I know. You've paid a heavy price for your sins, Sota. But, the price your Lord paid was even heavier. Your heart is clean now. You can be the father your Lord always intended you to be.

Move quickly. Rio is on her way."

CHAPTER FIFTY
Renewal

Luke's mom had always gotten a kick out of telling people, particularly Luke's potential girlfriends, that Luke had gone through a very short phase, at the age of fifteen, where he was a real pain in the neck. But, when he got his driver's license and they helped him get his first car, he went right back to being his old sweet, easy-going self again. She said it was clear, to her, that he had just reached an age where he needed his independence. And, he had earned it by being a good kid, for at least fourteen years, who his parents felt could be trusted to make good choices.

Short of a couple of fender-benders, he never proved them wrong. Luke had always enjoyed driving. When he was a kid, his dad let him sit in his lap and steer as they drove through their neighborhood. Occasionally, once his feet could reach the pedals, Luke's dad would even take him to empty parking lots and let him drive around and practice parking the car. So, by the time he was old enough to get a learner's permit, Luke was ready to get out on the road. Maybe that's where some of the pent-up frustration in his fifteenth year had been coming from. Regardless, driving was a happy place for Luke.

Good thing, too. He'd done a lot of driving since Rio arrived in Japan. He liked long drives and especially enjoyed having Rio along with him. But, the trip from Osaka to Tateyama had worn Luke down. Two gas and bathroom breaks were not enough to keep Luke's eyes open forever. And, as much as he enjoyed both the Bible and the sound of Rio's sweet voice, Luke kindly hid how glad he was when she finally finished reading the New Testament.

The truth is, Rio was glad, too. Not for the same reason, of course, but she was glad. In fact, she brimmed with enthusiasm. Rio had read the entire Bible, as predicted, in less than a week. Early that same morning, she had invited Jesus into her life. On top of that, she was with Luke and they were on their way to finally meet Sota Tanaka. Quietly, she decided that this would likely go down as the greatest day of her life.

However, that's when Luke decided it was time he informed Rio about what he and Isaac had discussed regarding the National Police. He told her it was a very real possibility that, if they captured her, they could take her away never to be seen again whether it was to protect the people from what they didn't understand or to use her for her gift. Rio insisted that God was going to protect both her and CYOI and that she didn't want to talk about her departure again until after they had found Sota. She was determined that nothing would ruin this day.

So, Luke announced that he needed to put on some upbeat music and roll the windows down. He put in the CD that he had taken out of the player the day he first met Rio, *Jesus Freak* by dc Talk. And, as the song "So Help Me God" started to play, Rio understood why he thought this would help keep him awake. She liked the music a lot. It was a cool blend of rock and hip-hop. The lyrics were great, too. She bobbed her head to the beat and listened as she looked out her open window at the beautiful water.

They were crossing Tokyo Bay on the bridge-tunnel combination known as the Trans-Tokyo Bay Highway and the view was utterly gorgeous. By the time the song "In The Light" had finished and "What Have We Become" started to play, they were in the small coastal town of Tateyama, which fills the southern tip of Chiba's Boso Peninsula.

They had to pause everything for a moment and soak in the breathtaking view of Mount Fuji. It was approximately a seventy mile straight shot across the Tateyama and Sagami bays and neither Luke nor Rio had ever seen anything like it. Japan's tallest peak looked truly magnificent from their vantage point and it wasn't until Luke heard a horn honking from behind them that he started driving again.

As they pulled into the parking lot at Jorakuzan Mantokuji Temple, Luke and Rio shared a smile.

"Are you ready?" Luke asked Rio.

"Yep," she responded enthusiastically. "A little nervous, of course. Butterflies are going crazy. But, I'm excited. Ready for anything."

"Good. You've earned this. You deserve it. So, let's go do it."

The shared smile grew even wider and they both opened their doors to climb out of the van. As the doors shut, Rio stopped and took a couple of deep breaths. She closed her eyes and began to pray. *Lord, you knew I'd be standing here before I was even born. Please go before me and prepare Sota's heart to greet me with kindness. And, thank you for providing me with Luke. I don't know where I'd be right now if you hadn't sent him into my life. He will always be a reminder to me that you were taking care of me before I even knew you. Thank you for that. Thank you for loving me before I even believed you were real. I'm a bit anxious right now but, I trust you. I have no reason not to. So, I know I'll be okay no matter what happens next. Thanks for that, too.*

Rio opened her eyes with a widening smile and immediately saw Luke waiting for her at the back of the van.

"Now I'm really ready," she told him.

As they started walking toward the temple, Rio spotted a man carrying a duffle bag in the distance. He was coming toward them and was too far away for most people to see but, Rio was not most people. Her vision zoomed in on his face. He was, of course, older than the most recent picture she had seen but, there was no doubt, it was Sota.

"That's him," she said to Luke.

"Seriously? Already?"

"Yep."

Luke and Rio picked up their pace.

So did Sota.

Everyone walking briskly toward one another, they soon stopped just a few feet apart. Luke looked on, wide-eyed. Rio's smile hadn't faded and Sota's matched his daughter's. He was the first to speak and only chose one word but, it shocked both the others.

"Rio."

CHAPTER FIFTY-ONE
Sota Tanaka

Sota could hardly believe the tremendous blessing that was being bestowed upon on him just hours after his encounter with Yeshua, the holy God who had forgiven his sins after more than two decades of self-imposed penance. When he woke up that morning, he had no idea that he had a daughter and there he was, at this moment, in her loving embrace.

After proper introductions were made between the three of them, Luke and Rio stood in the parking lot and listened to Sota explain the story of his salvation. The whole conversation was in Japanese but Luke and Rio hung on every word.

Their discussion went on for nearly an hour before Luke finally butted in and suggested that they pile into the van and go find a place to eat dinner. Everyone agreed but then Sota went right back to it. He was so excited that he couldn't stop talking. Rio chimed in occasionally, to ask questions but, otherwise, Sota sounded like a man set free from a two-decade vow of silence. The explanation flashed back and forth between what he had experienced that morning and everything he had been through since the day his father had told him he would be marrying Mei Awkagawa. His story continued over dinner at a nearby ramen restaurant that Luke chose without consensus because he couldn't get a word in. The story was filled with laughter and tears, guilt and anger, heartache and joy, repentance and redemption.

About half way through dinner, Rio got an approving nod from Luke and then offered to give the Bible she had just finished reading to Sota when they got back to the van. Sota's eyes lit up as Rio explained some of the things she had recently learned about the amazing Messiah he had just had the honor of meeting. Shortly thereafter, Sota turned the table and asked Rio countless questions about her. He wanted to know everything and Rio held almost nothing back. Even Luke learned some things he didn't know before.

One thing none of them could possibly know, which would have likely dampened the festive mood, was that while they were eating, two National Police agents were at the Jorakuzan Mantokuji Temple asking questions about Sota. It was the same two that had visited Isaac earlier that morning. Both were men. Agent Fukuda was average height and slender but out of shape, even for the age of fifty-eight, while Agent Watanabe was shorter, rounder but surprisingly agile and energetic, even for thirty-two years old.

About an hour after they left CYOI, they received word that a police officer out of the Kyotofu Chukyo Police Station had obtained the name of the man the young woman in question was searching for: Sota Tanaka. With that new piece of information, the NPA agents could access a database most people, even in Japanese law enforcement circles, didn't know existed and track Sota Tanaka down at the Jorakuzan Mantokuji Temple. They discovered upon their arrival that Sota had decided to leave less than two hours before they got there and that he mentioned having just learned that he had a daughter.

The agents searched Sota's room and, at first, they didn't find anything because Sota had cleared his stuff out. But, as they were walking out of the room, one of the agents decided to drop to his knees and peek under the bed. There, amongst stacks of books and documents pertaining to the Shinto and Buddhist religions, was an old, framed wedding photo of Sota and Mei. Sota had hauled that picture around for more than two decades as a reminder of what he had destroyed. But, the moment he was set free from his pain and guilt, Sota had forgotten all about it. And now, after confirming it with others at the temple, the agents had a photo of one of the people they were looking for.

It wasn't until dinner was over and she felt she could find a private spot to give Sota a demonstration that Rio decided to tell him the one thing that she had kept mum about at dinner: her new ability to control water. They went to the van to show the Bible to Sota. He had learned English when he was younger because his father had mandated it for business purposes. However, he knew reading the Bible in English would be difficult because he hadn't practiced his English proficiency in over twenty years. Despite his rusty language skills, however, he was still excited and wanted to start reading immediately. But, Rio suggested they leave the van there for a little while and take a walk. Luke and Sota agreed but, Sota decided to bring the Bible with him just in case he got a chance to peruse it a little.

She found their private spot by suggesting they go down to the beach at Heisaura Bay. They walked up the beach for about a half of a mile until she felt that it was safe. The cover of night was helpful, too, even though the night sky was clear and the moonlight shining off the ocean created a beautiful gleam that illuminated the area far more than normal. Had Luke and Rio been alone, it would have been the perfect place for their first kiss. However, Rio's mind was on other things.

At first, Sota looked at Rio in disbelief as she explained the story of how she had discovered that she had this ability and how much it had evolved since that first morning. But, when Rio reached her hand out and a wave was paused mid-crash, Sota's brow furrowed and his eyes darted back and forth between the water and his daughter.

"How are you doing that?" he asked her.

"I'm not exactly sure," Rio admitted before dropping her hand and allowing the wave to finish crashing. She proceeded to tell Sota everything about the prophecy, including the fact that Rio was confident that it had been delivered by the same woman he had met in his room. The same woman who had told her where to find him that day.

Suddenly, this fantastic tale made everything about his marriage to Mei, the fact that she couldn't get pregnant, and her disappearance, make sense. He found himself thanking God for the revelation of truth at the same time Rio was thanking God that finding Sota had turned out to be such a joyous experience.

It was about then that Agents Fukuda and Watanabe were showing the wedding photo around town and asking everyone they could find if they had seen the man, who would be about twenty years older, that evening. After showing it to nearly one hundred people and getting nowhere, they finally got a positive response from a young couple coming out of the same ramen restaurant that Sota had dined in with Luke and Rio earlier. The man told the agents that Sota was with a younger couple and that they were leaving the restaurant while he and his girlfriend were arriving. The man glanced up and noticed the van in the parking lot, pointed and told the agents that he noticed they were getting something out of the van when he and his girlfriend entered the restaurant. Then, finally, he told the agents exactly what they wanted to hear:

"Van's still here. They couldn't have gone far."

CHAPTER FIFTY-TWO
Washed By The Water

Luke, Rio and Sota stood on the beach and talked, for over an hour, about the amazing journeys that had led them to the time and place that they found themselves in at that moment. Sota also mentioned that the elderly woman had told him they would need his help. They surmised that it might have something to do with the fact that the National Police Agency was now trying to locate Rio. All three of them feared what they might do to her or how they might try and use her if they managed to bring her in.

Rio wanted to ignore the horrific possibilities being discussed but, as the conversation continued, she couldn't help but picture herself imprisoned in a deep, dark hole somewhere. She knew that she meant no one any harm but, she had seen too many movies like "E.T.: The Extraterrestrial," "Powder," and "Escape to Witch Mountain" to believe that people wouldn't do horrible things to her just because they didn't understand her abilities or where they came from. They all agreed that her capture would most likely include, at the very least, indefinite imprisonment. Or, it could even result in government experimentation or an attempt to use her for nefarious purposes. The latter two seemed less likely but, not totally out of the realm of possibility. Regardless, she knew that, like Sota and Luke, her first choice was to not find herself in the hands of the National Police. Now, she had to trust God to protect her and try to accept the fact that, whatever His plan was, it was the right one.

Luke and Sota both argued that it was time to get Rio back on a plane and headed home before the NPA discovered her identity and made travel impossible for her. However, while Rio agreed that it made logical sense to escape while she could, she knew in her heart that God's purpose for her was in Japan and she was determined to stay and see it through.

It was clear to all three of them that divine providence was at work and none of them wanted to step in front of that. This conversation led Sota, once again, to begin asking questions about what Rio had learned in her readings of the Bible. He was obviously anxious to read it himself but, in the meantime, wanted to soak up as much as he could by any means available. Rio's grasp on the scriptures after only one reading was remarkable but, naturally, Luke had to fill in a few holes and explain some things.

One of the things that Rio mentioned having noticed was that in the book of Acts, a lot of new followers in Christ were baptized the same way that John the Baptist had baptized Jesus Himself. Luke explained that the act of baptism is a way for us to identify ourselves with the death and resurrection of Jesus Christ by being immersed into the water and then raised back out of it, symbolizing the dying of our old self and then being raised in a new life with Christ. He told them that it is an act of commitment a lot like a wedding, a signal of the covenant relationship we are entering into with Jesus Christ, and a commissioning to go forward as the light of Jesus in this dark world.

"I am ready," Sota said as if an invitation had just been extended. "My commitment to Yeshua is firm. We must not wait. The time for this baptism is now."

Luke looked at Rio, thinking she would share in his surprise. Instead, she was nodding in agreement with Sota.

"Absolutely," she said. "Luke, can you baptize us?"

"Yeah . . . " Luke said, realizing that he was the only one who seemed at all taken aback. "Sure. I mean, typically, there are more witnesses. It's kind of a public statement of faith. But, under the circumstances, I think we can . . . Now, as in right now, huh? Well . . . Yeah. Okay, let's just go ahead and kick our shoes off and wade out into the water."

Less than three minutes later, their feet were stepping into the sixty-five-degree water. The higher up the body the water got, the colder it felt. They eventually walked out far enough that the water was reaching Rio's waistline but their enthusiasm kept them warm. The moonlight was bright enough that they could see each other's faces and they were all wearing big smiles.

"I know I've already heard your confessions of faith," Luke started, "but, just to be clear, have you each accepted Jesus as your savior and come to believe that he died for your sins?"

"Yes," Rio and Sota answered, almost in unison.

"Then it is an honor and a privilege to baptize you in the name of the Father, the Son, and the Holy Spirit."

Luke lifted Sota's left hand up to his nose so he could hold it closed, then put an arm behind his back and laid him backwards into the water, dunking him under, and then pulled him back up. He then repeated the same process with Rio.

"You have both been raised to walk in a new life," Luke told them as they all exchanged hugs and shared in the excitement of the moment. "Now, let's get out of the water and I'll pray as we start to dry off."

The three of them walked back to the shoreline, talking and laughing joyously. Luke put an arm around each of them and prayed. He confessed that there is nothing like the contagious zeal of new followers of Jesus and thanked God for the inspirational obedience in taking the faith-step of baptism in the walk with Him for both Sota and Rio. He asked God to continue leading, guiding and directing them as He had clearly already been doing. He also asked God to use their lives for His purpose and glory.

As he ended the prayer, Luke remembered what Rio had done the day he learned about her abilities and asked, "Hey, can't you dry us off like you did after saving Daichi?"

"Oh," Rio said as she realized he was right, "I can."

Rio waved her hands in front of them and the water collected in a sphere, levitating three and a half feet in the air between the three of them. Sota's eyes grew wide as he realized he was completely dry, including his clothes, and he was staring at a levitating ball of water that his daughter had complete control of. Then, suddenly, Rio waved a hand and the ball of water zoomed into the ocean and disappeared.

The trio walked back toward the parking lot to get the van, talking about how amazing everything was that was happening around Rio and what a privilege it was to be a part of it. They also decided they would have to find a campground or something to spend the night in and then figure out where they would go from there. Unfortunately, they were not yet aware of the fact that they would never get that far because Agents Fukuda and Watanabe were staking the van out at that very moment.

CHAPTER FIFTY-THREE
Tokkō

Following a socialist-anarchist plot to assassinate Japanese Emperor Meiji in 1910, The Home Ministry of the Empire of Japan established the Tokubetsu Kōtō Keisatsu (Special Higher Police.) This branch of law enforcement, often called Tokkō or "peace police," was specifically established to investigate and control political groups and ideologies deemed to be a threat to public order. Tokkō acted as a civilian counterpart to the military's Kempeitai and Tokkeitai, combining both criminal investigation and counter-espionage functions in a similar fashion to that of the Federal Bureau of Investigation in the United States of America. However, in less charitable circles, it has often been compared to Nazi Germany's Gestapo secret police and called by the unflattering term "Thought Police."

The decade that followed the establishment of the Tokkō

saw historical events such as the Russian Revolution, the Samil Uprising in Korea as well as major unrest in Japan due to the Rice Riots of 1918 and an increase in strikes due to the labor movement. So, under the administration of Hara Takashi and subsequent prime ministers, the Tokkō expanded significantly. Charged with suppressing "dangerous thoughts" that could threaten the state, the Tokkō was primarily concerned with socialism, communism and anarchism. But, the scope of its attention gradually increased to include all religious groups and anyone of extreme thought on either the left or the right.

By 1936, the Tokkō had arrested 59,013 people. But, in October of 1945, the Allied Occupation authorities eliminated the police force. Or, at least, that's what the public was told. The truth is, they were never fully disbanded. The branch did shrink considerably, however, and they went underground so that they could operate far more covertly, effectively becoming a concealed, formidable shadow of law enforcement. When they were in public, as agents Fukuda and Watanabe were on this occasion, they simply identified themselves as being from the National Police Agency. This, of course, was technically accurate. They just didn't make it known that they were from a clandestine branch that everyone, except for a select few at the very top of the NPA, thought had been abolished more than fifty years earlier.

In Japan, it was rare that police cars were not readily identifiable by their paint and lights and all officers wore uniforms. However, agents Fukuda and Watanabe were wearing business suits and sitting in a black, unmarked, four-door 1996 Toyota Corolla. Parked across the street and waiting for the trio to return to the old church van, they were discussing what they knew about the case so far.

They knew that there was a young woman in search of her long-lost father, Sota Tanaka, who had turned out to be a deeply religious man of both the Buddhist and Shinto faiths. They also knew that she was connected to at least two major events that were unexplainable by the laws of nature and that she was being escorted around Japan by a Christian missionary. They did not know who she was, where she had come from or, whether there was any truth to the claims of miraculous events that seemed to follow her around. They suspected she was somehow committing fraudulent behavior in either an attempt to gain some sort of religious following or, perhaps because she had "daddy" issues and was trying to gain the attention of one Sota Tanaka. Either way, with all the different religions involved, the acts performed publicly, and the rumors that were already spreading in the public conversation, she was considered a threat to the state and needed to be brought in for questioning before things got out of hand.

Between their access to an exclusive database of public

location, behavior and ideology back at headquarters and the upcoming opportunity to interrogate all three of the people of interest that they were currently waiting for, agents Fukuda and Watanabe were confident they would be able to get to the bottom of things in the next twenty-four hours or so. But, first, they had to apprehend those persons of interest.

So, for now, they had to exercise some patience which had never been a strong suit for either of them, particularly Agent Fukuda. He was the kind of guy who got fidgety when the coffeemaker was taking too long to brew. Waiting for these people to return to their van was enough to drive him crazy. He had already chewed all his fingernails, cracked the bones in his fingers and neck until nothing would pop any longer, and chewed a pen cap until he had rendered it unrecognizable. Agent Watanabe, on the other hand, had adjusted his seat several times and, having worked through dinner, was starting to wonder if it was too soon to bring up the possibility of leaving his partner there to continue surveilling while he went in search of something to eat.

"Here we go," Agent Fukuda said as he watched a man who looked like he could be around the age of fifty enter the parking lot with another man and a woman, each of whom were about half the age of the first man.

Agent Watanabe glanced over to see what his partner was

referring to. He was skeptical because Fukuda had already gotten prematurely excited several times that night. But, as Watanabe looked closer, the older man appeared to be a possible match for Sota Tanaka. He had filled out some since the wedding photo they were viewing by flashlight. He wasn't fat, just thicker. But, that's what age does to a lot of men. The younger two fit the descriptions as well. At night and from that distance, they just couldn't be sure until they saw if the group approached the van.

"Come on," Agent Fukuda spoke again, as if he could somehow coerce them into proving they were who he hoped they were, even though they couldn't hear his voice.

Finally, as the group talked and laughed, they meandered their way to the van and stopped.

Agents Fukuda and Watanabe both leaned forward and grabbed their respective door handles without looking away.

Luke stuck his key in the door lock and the agents instantly opened their doors to approach their persons of interest.

CHAPTER FIFTY-FOUR
Fugitives

Sota was the first to spot the agents as they advanced but he didn't immediately recognize them as being law enforcement.

"Excuse me," Agent Fukuda said in Japanese as he flipped open his badge, gaining the attention of Luke and Rio. "National Police. We'd like to ask you a few questions."

Suddenly, the gate valve on a fire hydrant, less than twenty feet away, burst open. The cap shot into a car door and water went everywhere. The noise was as loud as the firing of a gun and caused the agents to spin around as they tried to figure out what it was and where it came from.

"Run," Rio said with determination in her voice.

Luke and Sota looked to see Rio drop her arm from having caused the fire hydrant incident. She turned to run and they quickly followed her lead as she hurried toward the restaurant where they had eaten dinner hours earlier.

The agents spun back around and saw the trio fleeing. Immediately, they sprinted after them.

"Find a back exit," Rio said as she held the front door to the restaurant open so Luke and Sota could hustle inside. If she had the time, she would have noticed how surprisingly calm she felt considering the circumstances. There was a confidence inside of her that was new and stronger than anything she had ever felt before. It was a sense of peace in a situation that would cause most people severe anxiety. Somehow, she knew that everything was going to work out fine. God had a purpose for her in that place and at that time. And, because that purpose was God's, and not some whimsical desire she was trying to fulfill for herself, nothing could stop it. But, she also felt confident that her purpose didn't include sitting in a police interrogation room. In fact, that could possibly keep her from it.

Following Sota and Luke toward the kitchen, Rio looked back at the entrance just in time to see the agents surge through the doorway. She spun around and made a motion with her arms that looked like a conductor leading a symphony into the crescendo of a beautiful song. But, instead of hearing music, the audience got to witness every ounce of liquid in the dining area leap out of various containers and form a large sphere in the middle of the room. The ball of liquid then hurled toward the agents and erupted all over them. The force was so strong it knocked them back through the door and sent them floundering to the ground. Rio hurried into the kitchen to catch up with Luke and her father.

"Where's the exit?" she heard Sota yell in Japanese.

She saw a cook pointing and they all dashed for the door at the very back of the room. Sota and Luke piled out first and Rio saw the agents entering the kitchen just before she was going to exit.

Rio stepped outside, then stopped and turned around again. She pointed her left hand toward a faucet and rapidly wiggled her fingers, building the pressure inside the pipes. Next, she raised her right arm and made a sweeping "S" motion before making a similar move with both arms to the one she had just made in the dining room. Every faucet, hose, bottle, can, jar, pitcher, pot and pan in the room sprayed liquid in all its forms. Even ice and steam were blowing through the air. The room looked like a bomb was exploding. Everything was, once again, feeding into a sphere that hovered in the middle of the kitchen. No matter what stage it was in at first, it was all liquid by the time it reached the ball. Realizing that she could change gasses and solids to liquid gave Rio a new idea.

The agents stopped running and waited to see what the sphere was going to do. Everyone else in the room cleared out, running to the dining room.

Finally, the agents started to inch their way toward Rio as the size of the water ball continued to grow, quickly filling the room. Their eyes were darting back and forth between Rio and the ball trying to determine if they could gain any control over either.

Standing just outside of the doorway, Rio suddenly brought her hands in front of her face and then threw them out toward the walls. The water ball immediately spread in four directions, soaked the agents on the way through them, and splattered all four walls. By the time the water hit the walls, it began to freeze. Within seconds, the walls were frozen solid, trapping the agents in a room sealed by ice that was more than a foot thick.

Rio looked at the ice, with a little bit of wonderment. She had just discovered she could do something she was unaware of less than a minute earlier. Realizing she didn't have time to be impressed, she let the door close, ran down the steps, and joined Sota and Luke in the back alley.

The trio continued running, out of the alley and onto a street. Rio turned around and looked for the third time since they exited the restaurant. No sign of the agents.

The ice must be holding them for now, she thought to herself before speaking out loud as they continued to jog. "We need to find a place to hide."

When they were a couple of miles from the restaurant, Rio took the trio down a street that led toward the beach. "Let's try and find something down here," she said to Luke and Sota who were starting to slow down and fall behind.

She had looked over her shoulders a couple of dozen times and never saw any sign of the agents so, she was confident the pursuit had ended. Or, at least, the ice prison in the kitchen had forced the agents to hit the pause button. This would allow the trio enough time to find a proper spot to hunker down and catch their collective breath.

Sota had fallen the furthest behind. Finally, he stopped, while the other two continued jogging. He was heaving deeply as he put his hands on his knees and closed his eyes, facing the pavement.

"I," Sota tried to speak. "I just . . . need . . . a minute." He finally got his sentence out and then promptly threw up.

Rio turned back and rushed to his side. "Are you okay?" she asked.

"Better now," he answered while unsuccessfully attempting to force a smile. "I just need to stop running."

"I know," Rio admitted. "I think it's safe for the moment. Let's walk until we find something. Can you do that?"

Sota nodded affirmatively and they began to search for a place where they could lay low until they were able to figure out the next step. Unfortunately, the next step wouldn't be entirely up to them.

CHAPTER FIFTY-FIVE
Healing

The search for a place to hide from the authorities continued and, ultimately, Rio was the one who spotted what looked like a vacant vacation rental cabin about a block from the beach.

"How about there?" she asked out loud, somewhat rhetorically.

"That house?" Luke asked, surprised.

"Yeah," Rio acknowledged. "Why?"

"That's breaking and entering," he stated emphatically.

"No one's there," she argued.

"Still breaking and entering."

"It's a vacation rental."

"That we didn't rent."

"No one will even know we were there."

"We'll know."

"Yeshua will know," Sota added.

Rio nodded her head in agreement before a mental lightbulb went off and she asked, "What if we leave a rental fee on the counter with a thank you note? We just need a place to lay low for a while and none of us owns any property around here, am I right? Or, does someone have something they should have shared with the group an awful lot sooner?"

There was a pause as Luke and Sota realized she was right. Going inside of any building would, technically, be breaking and entering. At least this way they had the opportunity to do it in a way that they could honestly justify.

"I can get behind that plan," Luke finally agreed.

"Me too," Sota added.

"Good," Rio sighed in relief. "Now that the hard part is over, how do we break in?"

After a shared chuckle at Rio's humorous attempt to ease the tension, the trio walked around the property and couldn't find any doors or windows that were unlocked. But, standing at the top of a staircase on a second story deck in the backyard, Rio remembered what she had just learned about her abilities before fleeing the restaurant and an idea came to mind. She walked back over to the window that they had tried to nudge just moments earlier and stared at the kitchen sink just below it on the inside.

"I think I've got this," Rio said as she put her right hand up in front of the glass.

The Gift of Rio

Luke and Sota looked on as water began to pour out of the faucet and, just like it had at the drinking fountain in Hilo, bent mid-stream and inched toward the window. But, instead of heading for Rio's mouth, the water worked its way toward the lock and began to solidify, creating a long and thin arm made of ice.

"That's new," Luke said as his eyes widened.

"Yeah," Rio admitted, "I learned this when I was locking the agents into the restaurant kitchen. This just involves a little more precision than that did."

The ice-arm forced the lock open and Rio slid the window open with her left hand. She then pulsed her right hand like she was gently tossing something and the ice turned back to water as the stream splashed down into the sink. Immediately, the water stopped pouring out of the faucet. Rio took the screen out of the window, climbed up and through it, stepped down onto the counter, and hopped off onto the kitchen floor.

"I'll let you in through the sliding glass door," she told the men before closing the window and locking it.

Luke put the screen back into the window sill as Rio unlocked and opened the sliding glass door in the dining area next to the kitchen as she added, "Come on in. Make yourselves comfortable but try to touch as little as possible with your fingers. Don't turn on any lights and stay away from windows. I need to call my mom."

"Guess we know who's in charge," Luke told Sota.

"Sounds like she knows what she's doing," Sota agreed with a shrug. "Maybe there's more for me to learn about my daughter."

"I think she's just smart," Luke said with a smile before pointing at the heavens. "And, maybe receiving a little guidance."

"Even more reason to follow her lead," Sota said as he patted Luke on the arm.

Rio found a phone in the master bedroom at the back of the house, picked it up using a wash cloth that she had carried in from the kitchen, set her calling card down in front of it, and used the bottom of her shirt to form a pseudo-glove for dialing, as she called her mom. She knew this was going to be her most difficult call yet. Of course, part of that was because she had finally found Sota. But, on top of that, she knew that it was time to tell her mom about her abilities. And, the thing that made it the hardest was the fact that, deep inside, she knew that this was the last call she would be making before "the big show," as the elderly woman had called it.

She was right, too. It was a tough conversation. Her mom expressed some skepticism when she first heard about Rio's abilities. But, as Rio continued to explain all that she had experienced, Toki began to accept it as truth. And, relief set in that she finally had answers after twenty-five years of waiting and wondering. The kicker, for her, was hearing that Rio had met the same elderly woman while sitting on the same bench. That's when the tears began to flow.

A similar reaction occurred as Rio talked about accepting Jesus into her heart. Toki, at first, was skeptical. But, she knew her daughter and, she could hear in Rio's voice that the experience she had been through was an authentic one. By the time that part of the conversation was over, Toki had promised Rio she would get her hands on a Bible and read it.

Probably the most surreal moment of the conversation, for Rio, wasn't really conversation at all. It was the moment that she put her calling card away and handed the wash cloth-wrapped phone off to her biological father so that he could speak to her mother. It was such a small action and something she assumed that most kids would consider common. But, she had never done it before and the significance of it was not lost on her. She was simultaneously nervous, happy, and sad.

Rio left the room so her parents could talk in private. She heard Sota's sobbing almost immediately after she closed the door and she went to sit with Luke. Rio snuggled in close and put her head onto Luke's chest. He liked the fact that she had grown so comfortable with him and he felt an emotional tingle as a wave of romantic feelings rose inside of him. Clearly, Rio was emotional. Understandably so. But, Luke could tell there was more to her actions and he wondered if that should make him anxious. Little did Luke know, he was right to wonder because the Holy Spirit within Rio had already begun to prepare her for the event that was coming soon.

Sota and Toki, although he couldn't stop calling her Mei, talked for over thirty minutes. There were a lot of tears on both ends of the line but, as forgiveness began to take root, so did freedom. Toki was amazed as Sota told her about his encounter with Yeshua and she suddenly began to look forward to keeping the promise she had made to her daughter earlier in the conversation. As Rio's calling card began to run out, Sota gave Toki the phone number that he found printed on the phone. She called right back and they continued their conversation like two old friends. Toki noticed that it was the friendliest that they had ever been.

When Sota and Toki had finished their conversation, Rio got back on the phone to say goodbye to her mom. She fought back tears so she didn't have to explain her sadness because she knew that her mom wouldn't understand. After asking her mom to give her love to Anthony and Hani, Rio finally hung up the phone and turned around to open the door. As she did, she saw the elderly woman standing in the corner. They shared a knowing smile and the woman promptly vanished. Unshaken, Rio opened the door, walked out of the room and re-approached her father and Luke.

"It's almost time," she told them.

"For what?" Luke asked with more than a hint of trepidation.

"My time is almost here. But, before it arrives, I need to give you some guidelines for the days that lie ahead."

CHAPTER FIFTY-SIX
Opening

By the time Rio had finished explaining what she needed Luke and Sota to do over the days to come, it felt like something had bumped the house. It was just noticeable enough to give everyone a small pause. But, then the house started to roll and shake. It began weak and slow, but escalated and grew stronger quite quickly.

"What is this?!" Luke exclaimed.

"Don't you recognize an earthquake, California boy?" Rio shot back at him as she braced herself between walls in the hallway. "When it's over, I have to get to the beach."

"For what?" Luke asked, not really wanting to know the answer. He got into a doorway on the other side of the living room and braced himself just like Rio was doing.

Sota did the same in the entryway to the kitchen.

"Just trust me," Rio said as she looked at Luke. "This

earthquake is just the catalyst. The beach is where I'm supposed to be for the miracle that I was created to perform."

After staring into Luke's somber eyes for a moment, she looked at her father. Thankfulness for the time she had been granted was coupled with a deep sadness that everything was about to change.

Luckily, Sota broke the mood because his nerves caused him to start giggling uncontrollably and it was contagious. It seemed like an inappropriate time to be laughing but, like little kids in a church service, once they got going they couldn't stop and the three of them laughed their way through the rest of the seven-minute earthquake, even as various items fell off shelves and out of cupboards and came crashing to the floor. What could have been a scary moment turned out to be one that would be remembered fondly in the future.

Still, or perhaps even more so because of that moment, Rio wasn't ready to say goodbye to the two men she had quickly grown to love. The same was true when she had said goodbye to her mother, and to the rest of the family back in Hilo, on the phone a little more than ten minutes earlier. But, when the massive earthquake finally settled, she knew it was time to do exactly that.

The trio put some money on the counter and wrote an anonymous thank you note for the owners as they had promised each other they would do. They quickly wiped down everything they could remember touching before they went outside to survey the damage left behind by the earthquake.

Luke and Sota followed Rio out of the house. Sota locked the door and closed it behind them. They were certain there was extensive structural damage, and some they could see, but they were surprised it wasn't worse. They wouldn't know any details right away and they could only hope no one had been severely hurt or even killed. Everything was dark. The power was out and a dust cloud was already blocking a lot of the light from the night sky. Rio continued to lead the men down the street, out onto the beach and up to the shoreline. She stopped and looked at the beautiful ocean in front of her. Emotion overcame her and she closed her eyes.

Before Rio turned around to open her eyes and face her father, the tears were already falling. She hugged Sota tightly and told him how glad she was that she had finally met him and spent time with him. It was the first instance in her life where she got to tell her biological father that she loved him. And, she also told him that she looked forward to seeing him again one day.

Sota thanked Rio for finding him as the tears began to fall from his eyes as well. He gave her a warm hug and kissed her cheek before telling her that he loved her, too. He said that, in fact, he only wished he had known she and Yeshua sooner so that he could have felt the love he had in his heart for a longer period of time but that he was grateful to know that it was a love that would never fade.

When Sota and Rio finally let go of one another, she turned her attention to Luke. Her tears were uncontrollable and his were starting to stream down his cheeks as well.

"I . . . " Rio started before Luke interrupted her.

"I love you," Luke blurted out. "Not just as my sister in faith. Not just as friends. I have absolutely, without any doubt, fallen completely head over heels in love with you, Rio."

Luke reached out and gripped Rio by the arms, slowly pulling her toward him. He moved his left hand up and placed it on her right cheek, wiping tears away with his thumb. He then leaned in, closed his eyes and kissed her more deeply and passionately then either of them had ever kissed anyone before. Rio knew instantly that if she could choose a single moment in which to spend eternity, that this was, hands down, the one that she would have picked. Unfortunately, it couldn't last forever.

"I couldn't let you go without telling you," he said as he slowly pulled away.

"I'm glad," she said before opening her eyes. "I love you too, Luke. Like I never imagined possible. This isn't a forever goodbye though. I will see you again."

"I know," Luke replied as both welled up with tears again.

"It still hurts."

Rio nodded in agreement as tears continued to fall. She clinched her jaw, unable to speak, in a losing battle against the tears. Rio closed her eyes tightly and then opened them again, releasing a new stream of waterworks. Adding insult to injury, the release of so many tears cleared her vision and she suddenly spotted Agents Fukuda and Watanabe in the distance.

Rio slowly started backing up. Her feet were in the water and she hadn't even bothered to remove her shoes.

"Where are you going?" Luke asked and then spun around to see what she was suddenly focused on. He spotted the agents, too. He could barely make them out in the cloudy darkness but he immediately knew who they were.

"Is that the NPA?" Luke asked as he turned back to Rio, who was nodding affirmatively.

All he could do was close his eyes and let the tears fall. He knew that he had to accept God's plan but that didn't make it easy. The phrase from the book of James, chapter one, verse 6, "he who doubts is like a wave of the sea, blown and tossed by the wind," came immediately to his mind and quickly pierced his heart. This was the most difficult moment of his life so far and the anticipation of the moments that were going to immediately follow made the whole thing nearly unbearable. He didn't know the details of what was about to happen but, he knew that his time with Rio had finally run out. Had he not known that God is sovereign and had he not appreciated the gift that his precious interlude with Rio had been to him, he may not have been able to handle either that moment or what he suspected might be coming next.

CHAPTER FIFTY-SEVEN
Closing

Luke stood, motionless, facing Rio, as the agents approached from behind him. Rio had stepped far enough backward that the water was up to her shoulders. Sota was standing off to the side with his eyes darting fearfully back and forth between the agents and his daughter.

"You need to come with us," Agent Fukuda spoke in Japanese and with authority as he and Agent Watanabe stopped just short of the waterline.

"I can't do that," Rio said calmly, continuing the conversation in Japanese. "I won't."

"It's not up to you," Agent Watanabe chimed in.

"It's not up to you either," Rio informed the agents.

"Excuse me?" Agent Fukuda asked, incorrectly taking Rio's statement as an act of defiance.

"I'm staying right here," Rio insisted. "This is bigger than any of us. There is a massive tsunami coming and God Himself has tasked me with stopping it."

"What tsunami?" Agent Watanabe asked. "We had a very large earthquake. And, yes, a tsunami could possibly be created as a result. That's why most people are already headed for higher ground. But, you couldn't possibly know what will happen. And, how would you be able to stop it if you did, anyway? This god of yours can't do it but you can? Come on. Let's go."

The water began to quickly recede from the shoreline.

"This tsunami," Rio calmly said as everyone looked at the water.

The disappearance of the water swiftly exposed Rio's body and the ocean floor became visible. She felt her body sink lower as the sand withdrew from beneath her shoes and was carried away.

"God is going to stop it. He's just going to do it through me. Since you don't believe me and you can now see that a tsunami is in fact coming, it would be logical for you to go now."

The agents began backing away as the amount of exposed ocean floor rapidly increased, meter by meter, behind Rio.

"Actually," Rio said as she looked at her father and Luke, "you should all go."

Sota stepped forward and put an arm around Luke as the agents turned and started to run away from the coastline.

"I'll see you again," Rio assured them before turning around to face the task ahead.

As Rio started walking toward the receding water, Sota and Luke slowly backed away but they couldn't bring themselves to take their eyes off Rio. She continued her march into certain danger until she could see the wave in front of her begin to develop and come roaring back toward her.

There was no panic. No hesitation. The wave was massive but Rio's resolve was strong. She didn't have time to focus on it but she quickly estimated that it was two hundred feet high. Still undaunted, she quickly lifted her arms and stretched them out in the shape of a "V" as she began to tenaciously concentrate on the water in front of her. The force behind the wave was incredible, and the strength required from Rio was immense. But, her connection to the water was profound and she immediately felt in her soul that what she had to resist and take control of extended way beyond just what she could see in front of her.

The tsunami waves being generated by the gigantic earthquake extended all along the eastern coastline of Japan. They reached further South than Rio's newly encountered family members in Shingu and considerably further North than she had been, even as far as Kinkasan Island. But, the worst damage would have been near where she was standing at that moment as the waves would have ravaged the land beyond Sagami Bay and absolutely decimated the surrounding areas of Chiba and Tokyo after the water funneled in through Tokyo Bay. With a population of more than 12.6 million people, the death toll in Tokyo would likely have climbed to well over 100,000.

Behind her, Sota and Luke looked on. They were equally amazed, proud and already grieving what they could tell was likely about to happen. Behind them, many people who knew it was already too late to get to higher ground had begun to watch the terrifying wave rushing through the darkness. With the lights out and all of the dust in the air, the wave may have gone unnoticed if it had been smaller. But, it was so massive in size that it was too obvious to miss.

People were on rooftops with binoculars. Others were inside with telescopes. Most were just watching with their own eyes. None who could see her, understood why this young woman was facing the ferocious seas. The few who tried to guess assumed suicide but they couldn't have been more wrong.

Rio stood in the path of certain destruction as long as she was able to stay on her feet. Every ounce of energy she had was being used to fight the power of the monstrosity before her that, without her interference, would devastate around seven hundred miles of coastline as well as the buildings and people that inhabited it. The water rose above Rio and stopped, making her look like she was standing in front of a twenty-story building made of water.

The darkness kept people from being able to see the living creatures swimming in the giant mass of sea. From the shoreline, it looked like the water froze. But, it was still moving, still fighting to move beyond where Rio had drawn the proverbial line in the literal sand.

Finally, it brought Rio to her knees as she gave it everything she had inside of her.

People all along the eastern coastline of Japan, awakened late at night by the shaking of the earth beneath them, witnessed the amazing site of water that seemed to be frozen in time. But, only a select group beneath Mount Daisen, at the southeastern tip of Tateyama Bay, were given the chance to watch the young woman who was causing a tsunami to stand still.

Those watching Rio, including her father and the man who had, minutes earlier, confessed his love for her, also had the unfortunate chore of watching the water come crashing down on top of her and take her lifeless body out to sea as the ocean suddenly became eerily calm and Japan was left at peace.

CHAPTER FIFTY-EIGHT
After The Show

Both Sota and Luke continued to be filled with pride and grief over the days that followed Rio's passing. The grief was expected but the pride came from observing the outpouring of gratitude from the citizens of Japan. Flowers were laid up and down the coast in honor of the young woman who had quickly become a global, albeit anonymous, hero by giving her life to miraculously save countless others.

Of course, Luke and Sota had to go through the Tokkō's interrogation process with agents Fukuda and Watanabe but, per Rio's instructions, they gave them very little additional information. Besides, it was clear that Rio was gone and any "damage" she was going to cause had already been done. The rumor mill was cranking and Rio was already becoming legendary. Even the Tokkō could not argue that Rio had saved tens of thousands of lives, if not hundreds of thousands and, ultimately, they had no choice but to let Luke and Sota go.

Also per Rio's instructions, Sota set out to reunite with his family and, once that had been accomplished, intended to return to the many shrines and temples where he had lived over the previous two decades to tell their occupants about his encounter with Yeshua and the fact that his daughter was the young woman God had sent to save the people of Japan. His life had changed forever and he was bursting with enthusiasm to give others the same opportunity that he had been given.

Rio had instructed Luke to gather her things and return them to her family. But, she insisted, he should go and see his own family first. This was both because they had been expecting him before Rio changed his plans, and because she assumed the NPA would be watching and she didn't want him leading them to her family. So, she insisted that he wait until he was in California to purchase his plane ticket to Hilo.

So, three days later, Luke found himself on his way to the airport in Osaka where he had first met the woman he had loved and then lost. He took out the third CD she had brought with her and put it into the player in the old church van. It was a homemade mix CD full of songs like "Near You Always" by Jewel, "Hold My Hand" by Hootie and the Blowfish, "Head Over Feet" by Alanis Morrisette, and "Everybody Hurts" by R.E.M. Luke chuckled to himself as he decided that, while she hadn't even met him yet when she made the mix, Rio must have designed the CD specifically to make him cry.

Meanwhile, Daichi was back in his favorite fishing spot on Ise Bay when he saw something beneath the surface out of the corner of his eye. He looked over the side of the boat as the large creature breached the surface and grabbed on to the side of his boat.

"Arigatō Rio," Daichi said with complete joy on his face as he reached for her hand and pulled her into his boat.

Rio climbed in, dried herself off the same way she had after she rescued Daichi and after she and Sota had been baptized by Luke. She then explained that it was critical that he keep this encounter to himself and that she needed him to get her to the airport in Osaka as fast as he could. Daichi kept his word on both counts.

Two hours later, Rio approached the table at Kona Kafe where Luke was, once again, eating Pipikaula.

"I'm going to need you to remain calm," she said quietly.

Luke slowly looked up and tears formed in his eyes. His hands started to shake and he set his fork down. Luke's mouth began to quiver and a tear rolled down his cheek. He swallowed hard, which included a partially chewed bite of his lunch, as he tried to muster the ability to speak without sobbing.

"What?" was all he could get out and, even that caused his

voice to crack.

"Can I join you?"

Luke used his napkin to wipe his eyes and tried to keep from drawing attention.

"Please."

"Thank you," Rio said with a warm smile.

"Where . . ."

"Where have I been?" Rio finished Luke's sentence because he clearly couldn't finish it himself. In fact, all he could do in response was to nod affirmatively.

"I think you, of all people, know the answer to that. Still, it's difficult to describe."

"Try," Luke said through happy tears.

"The ocean, quite literally, swallowed me up. I'm sure you saw that."

"I did," Luke confirmed.

"I'm sorry."

"You're here now."

"I am. The water crushed me instantly and my body was dead until just a couple of hours ago but my soul was alive the entire time. My soul . . . My soul has never been more alive. When I died, it felt like I was immediately snatched out of the ocean and taken someplace else."

Luke's smile continued to grow but his tears didn't slow

down.

"There's so much to tell you. And, now we'll have the time to do it."

Luke nodded appreciatively. He had thought his time with Rio was brief but, it had only been the beginning. *Thank you,* he silently prayed before speaking out loud.

"Let's get started."

"Like my father," Rio said as tears of joy formed in her eyes, "I got to meet Yeshua face-to-face. If only I could put it into words. It's nearly unfathomable. He's regal, and yet, he's relatable. He's adamant, and yet, loving and kind. He's just . . . There is no one else like Him."

"I'm going to have a million questions about that," Luke said with wide eyes.

"Oh, there's so much to tell you. I learned so much while I was gone. Where I was, there is no time. At least, not in the sense of being restricted by it. Life here has such a limited view. We're like people who live in valleys. We can't see any valley but our own. But, there, you live on a mountain and see all the valleys. That's the perspective of time there. You can see it all at once. It's amazing."

Luke gave Rio a knowing smile. He had imagined what heaven would be like and he looked forward to experiencing it for himself one day. How remarkable that Rio had been there and returned. The elderly woman had been right in calling her a gift but, it was also true that, she had been blessed with many gifts herself and that was one of them.

"I met three others like me. The same way I control water, Matias controls fire, Amanda controls the winds, and Tyler controls the earth. The world will see their miracles in the days ahead. In fact . . ."

"Let me guess, the fire, I think you said his name was . . . Matias . . ."

"Right."

"His miracle is second."

"It is. How did you . . ."

Luke pointed at the TV on the wall behind Rio. She turned around and saw that it was showing a breaking news story about a massive fire that had started in the Central Chilean Andes Mountain Range and should have consumed the capital city of Santiago but the fire seemed to abruptly go out. She turned back around in her chair and calmly faced Luke again.

"I got to meet them. It felt good, to know that it wasn't just me."

"I'll bet it did," Luke agreed. "I want to hear everything."

"You will," Rio said with a huge smile as she reached across the table and took his hand.

Luke squeezed her hand and silently thanked God a second

time for returning her to him. He felt more grateful than he had since the day he first came to know the Lord.

"What comes next?" he finally asked.

"For now, we wait. We let the next miracles take place."

"Do you get to live a normal life now?"

"Define normal," Rio said with a chuckle. "Nothing will ever be normal again but, yes. For now. Not forever though. A war is coming. It's a spiritual war that was declared over the very first humans millennia ago. It's a war for the souls of people everywhere and throughout all of time. Humans were not able to see it before but, that's all going to change. The final battle will be fought, very soon, right here, across the globe, and no one will be able to escape it."

"And I'll have a million questions about that too," Luke admitted as he tried not to feel too overwhelmed by what she was telling him.

"So, you can still do all of those things?" he asked.

"You mean, with water?"

"Yeah."

"Absolutely. The stuff I did before? Honestly? That was really just the beginning."

THE GIFT OF RIO

THE GIFT OF THE ELEMENTS SERIES
BY C.S. ELSTON

Rio's Chronological Reading of the Bible

Night One

Genesis 1:1-5:32; 1 Chronicles 1:1-4; Genesis 6:1-10:5;
1 Chronicles 1:5-7; Genesis 10:6-20; 1 Chronicles 1:8-16;
Genesis 10:21-11:26; 1 Chronicles 1:17-27; Job 1:1-42:17;
Genesis 11:27-21:34, 25:12-18; 1 Chronicles 1:28-31;
Genesis 22:1-24:67, 25:1-4; 1 Chronicles 1:32-34;
Genesis 25:5-6, 25:19-26, 25:7-11, 25:27-28:9, 36:1-43;
1 Chronicles 1:35-54; Genesis 28:10-35:29; 1 Chronicles 2:1-2;
Genesis 37:1-46:9; 1 Chronicles 5:1-6; Genesis 46:10-12;
1 Chronicles 2:18-55, 4:1-23; Genesis 46:13; 1 Chronicles 7:1-5;
Genesis 46:14-18; 1 Chronicles 7:30-40; Genesis 46:19-25;
1 Chronicles 7:6-12; Genesis 46:26-50:26; Exodus 1:1-6:27;
1 Chronicles 6:1-4a; Exodus 6:28-40:38

Night Two

Leviticus 1:1-27:34; Numbers 1:1-26:34; 1 Chronicles 7:14-19;
Numbers 26:35-37; 1 Chronicles 7:20-29; Numbers 26:38-36:13;
Deuteronomy 1:1-31:29; Psalm 90:1-17; Deuteronomy 31:30-34:12;
Joshua 1:1-19:9; 1 Chronicles 4:24-33; Joshua 19:10-21:45;
1 Chronicles 6:54-81; Joshua 22:1-24:33;
Judges 1:1-3:6, 17:1-18:31, 3:7-13:25, 19:1-21:25;
1 Chronicles 6:4b-15; Ruth 1:1-4:22; 1 Chronicles 2:3-16;
1 Samuel 1:1-2:10; Psalm 113:1-9; 1 Samuel 2:11-21;
Judges 14:1-16:31; 1 Samuel 2:22-14:52;
1 Chronicles 8:1-9:1a, 9:35-44, 5:7-10,5:18-22; 1 Samuel 15:1-17:58;
Psalm 144:1-15; 1 Samuel 18:1-20:42

Rio's Chronological Reading of the Bible

Night Three

Psalm 5:1-12, 59:1-17, 133:1-3; 1 Samuel 21:1-15; Psalm 34:1-22;
1 Samuel 22:1-5; 1 Chronicles 12:8-18; 1 Samuel 22:6-23;
Psalm 52:1-9, 109:1-31; 1 Samuel 23:1-29;
Psalm 13:1-6, 17:1-15, 22:1-31, 54:1-7; 1 Samuel 24:1-22;
Psalm 7:1-17, 35:1-28, 57:1-11, 142:1-7; 1 Samuel 25:1-44;
Psalm 18:1-50; 2 Samuel 22:1-51; Psalm 14:1-7, 53:1-6;
1 Samuel 26:1-25; Psalm 31:1-24; 1 Samuel 27:1-12;
1 Chronicles 12:1-7; Psalm 56:1-13; 1 Samuel 28:1-2, 29:1-11;
1 Chronicles 12:19-22; Psalm 40:1-17, 69:1-36, 86:1-17, 131:1-3;
1 Samuel 28:3-25, 30:1-31:13; 1 Chronicles 10:1-14;
2 Samuel 4:4, 1:1-3:5; 1 Chronicles 3:1-4a;
2 Samuel 3:6-4:3, 4:5-5:5; 1 Chronicles 11:1-3, 12:23-40;
Psalm 2:1-12, 78:1-72, 16:1-11; 2 Samuel 5:6-10;
1 Chronicles 11:4-9; 2 Samuel 5:17-21; 1 Chronicles 14:8-12;
2 Samuel 23:13-17; 1 Chronicles 11:15-19; 2 Samuel 5:22-25;
1 Chronicles 14:13-17; 2 Samuel 5:11-12;
1 Chronicles 14:1-2, 13:1-14; 2 Samuel 6:1-11; Psalm 101:1-8;
2 Samuel 6:12-23; 1 Chronicles 15:1-16:43;
Psalm 15:1-5, 24:1-10, 65:1-13, 68:1-35, 110:1-7, 19:1-14;
2 Samuel 8:1; 1 Chronicles 18:1; 2 Samuel 21:15-18;
1 Chronicles 20:4; 2 Samuel 23:8-12; 1 Chronicles 11:10-14;
2 Samuel 21:19-22; 1 Chronicles 20:5-8; 2 Samuel 10:1-19;
1 Chronicles 19:1-19; Psalm 33:1-22; 2 Samuel 11:1;
1 Chronicles 20:1a; 2 Samuel 11:2-12:24a;
Psalm 6:1-10, 32:1-11, 38:1-22, 51:1-19, 103:1-22;
2 Samuel 12:26-31; 1 Chronicles 20:1b-3; Psalm 21:1-13;
2 Samuel 12:24b-25, 8:2; 1 Chronicles 18:2; 2 Samuel 23:20a;
1 Chronicles 11:22a; 2 Samuel 8:3-4; 1 Chronicles 18:3-4;
2 Samuel 8:7-8; 1 Chronicles 18:7-8; 2 Samuel 8:5-6;
1 Chronicles 18:5-6; Psalm 124:1-8, 108:1-13, 60:1-12;
2 Samuel 8:9-14; 1 Chronicles 18:9-13; Psalm 44:1-26, 20:1-9;
2 Samuel 23:18-19; 1 Chronicles 11:20-21; 2 Samuel 23:20b-39;
1 Chronicles 11:22b-47; 2 Samuel 8:15-18; 1 Chronicles 18:14-17;
2 Samuel 7:1-29; 1 Chronicles 17:1-27;
Psalm 138:1-139:24, 145:1-21; 2 Samuel 21:1-14, 9:1-13;

Rio's Chronological Reading of the Bible

Night Three (continued)

Psalm 8:1-9; 2 Samuel 5:13-16; 1 Chronicles 14:3-7, 3:4b-9;
2 Samuel 13:1-15:6, 24:1-25; 1 Chronicles 21:1-30;
2 Samuel 15:7-36; Psalm 3:1-4:8, 11:1-7, 23:1-6, 26:1-12;
2 Samuel 16:1-14; Psalm 12:1-8, 36:1-37:40, 9:1-10:18;
2 Samuel 15:37, 16:15; Psalm 27:1-28:9, 39:1-13, 41:1-43:5;
2 Samuel 16:16-17:23; Psalm 55:1-23, 58:1-11, 61:1-63:11;
2 Samuel 17:24-26; 1 Chronicles 2:17; 2 Samuel 17:27-18:33;
Psalm 64:1-10, 70:1-5, 84:1-12, 141:1-10, 143:1-12;
2 Samuel 19:1-20:26; Psalm 140:1-13; 1 Chronicles 22:1-19;
Psalm 29:1-30:12;
1 Chronicles 23:1-23, 6:16-30, 23:24-25:31, 6:31-53, 26:1-29:22;
1 Kings 1:1-40; Psalm 25:1-22; 1 Kings 1:41-2:9; 2 Samuel 23:1-7;
1 Kings 2:10-11; 1 Chronicles 29:26-30; 1 Kings 2:12;
1 Chronicles 29:23-25; 1 Kings 2:13-3:15; 2 Chronicles 1:1-13;
1 Kings 3:16-28; Psalm 72:1-20, 50:1-23; Song of Songs 1:1-8:14;
Psalm 45:1-17; 1 Kings 5:1-12; 2 Chronicles 2:1, 2:3-16;
1 Kings 5:13-18; 2 Chronicles 2:2, 2:17-18; 1 Kings 9:15-16, 9:20-23;
2 Chronicles 8:7-10; 1 Kings 6:1-38; 2 Chronicles 3:1-17;
Psalm 127:1-5; 1 Kings 7:1-51; 2 Chronicles 4:1-5:1; 1 Kings 8:1-21;
2 Chronicles 5:2-6:11; 1 Kings 8:22-61; 2 Chronicles 6:12-7:3;
1 Kings 8:62-66; 2 Chronicles 7:4-10; Psalm 132:1-18; 1 Kings 9:1-9;
2 Chronicles 7:11-22; 1 Kings 9:10-14; 2 Chronicles 8:1-3;
1 Kings 9:24; 2 Chronicles 8:11; 1 Kings 9:25; 2 Chronicles 8:12-16;
1 Kings 9:17-19; 2 Chronicles 8:4-6; 1 Kings 9:26-28;
2 Chronicles 8:17-18; 1 Kings 10:22; 2 Chronicles 9:21;
1 Kings 10:1-13; 2 Chronicles 9:1-12; 1 Kings 4:1-19, 4:29-34;
Proverbs 1:1-31:31; 1 Kings 4:20-28, 10:14-21; 2 Chronicles 9:13-20;
1 Kings 10:23-25; 2 Chronicles 9:22-24; 1 Kings 10:26-29;
2 Chronicles 1:14-17; 2 Chronicles 9:25-28; 1 Kings 11:1-40

Rio's Chronological Reading of the Bible

Night Four

Ecclesiastes 1:1-12:14; Psalm 73:1-28, 88:1-18; 1 Kings 11:41-43;
2 Chronicles 9:29-31; 1 Kings 14:21; 2 Chronicles 12:13-14;
1 Kings 12:1-19; 2 Chronicles 10:1-19; 1 Kings 12:20-24;
2 Chronicles 11:1-4; 1 Kings 12:25-31; 2 Chronicles 11:13-17;
1 Kings 12:32-14:18; 2 Chronicles 11:5-12, 11:18-23;
1 Kings 14:22-28; 2 Chronicles 12:1-12; Psalm 89:1-52;
1 Kings 14:29-31; 2 Chronicles 12:15-16; 1 Kings 15:1-8;
2 Chronicles 13:1-20a; 2 Chronicles 13:21-14:1a; 1 Kings 15:9-11;
2 Chronicles 14:1b-7; 1 Kings 14:19-20; 2 Chronicles 13:20b;
1 Kings 15:25-31; 2 Chronicles 14:8-15:7; 1 Kings 15:12-15;
2 Chronicles 15:8-19; 1 Kings 15:33-34, 15:16, 15:32, 15:17-22;
2 Chronicles 16:1-10; 1 Kings 16:1-33, 15:23-24;
2 Chronicles 16:11-14; 1 Kings 22:41-46;
2 Chronicles 20:31-34, 17:1-18:1; 1 Kings 16:34, 17:1-19:21;
Psalm 104:1-35, 114:1-115:18;
1 Kings 20:1-21:29, 22:51-53, 22:1-35; 2 Chronicles 18:2-34;
1 Kings 22:36-40; 2 Chronicles 19:1-4a; 2 Kings 1:1;
2 Chronicles 19:11-20:30; Psalm 46:1-49:20, 83:1-18, 91:1-16;
1 Kings 22:47-49; 2 Chronicles 20:35-37;
2 Kings 1:2-18, 3:1-3, 2:1-25, 3:4-27; 1 Kings 22:50;
2 Chronicles 21:1-3; 2 Kings 8:16-25; 2 Chronicles 21:4-20, 22:1-6;
2 Kings 8:26-9:37; 2 Chronicles 22:7-9; 2 Kings 10:1-27, 11:1-3;
2 Chronicles 22:10-12; 2 Kings 11:4-21; 2 Chronicles 23:1-21;
2 Kings 12:1-16; 2 Chronicles 24:1-16;
2 Kings 10:28-36, 13:1-3, 13:22-23; 2 Chronicles 24:17-25a;
2 Kings 12:17-18, 4:1-44, 13:4-8, 8:1-6, 13:9-11,12:19-21;
2 Chronicles 24:25b-27; 2 Kings 14:1-6; 2 Chronicles 25:1-10;
2 Kings 14:7-14; 2 Chronicles 25:11-24; 2 Kings 5:1-7:20, 8:7-15;
2 Kings 13:14-21, 13:24-25, 13:12-13, 14:15-16, 14:23, 14:17-20;
2 Chronicles 25:25-28; 2 Kings 14:21-22, 15:1-5;
2 Chronicles 26:1-21; Amos 1:1-9:15; Hosea 1:1-5:7;
2 Kings 14:24-28; Jonah 1:1-4:11; 2 Kings 14:29, 15:8-12, 15:13-20;
1 Chronicles 5:23-26; 2 Kings 15:6-7; 2 Chronicles 26:22-23;
2 Kings 15:21-29; Isaiah 6:1-13; 2 Kings 15:32-38;
2 Chronicles 27:1-9; 1 Chronicles 5:11-17; 2 Kings 16:1-9;

Rio's Chronological Reading of the Bible

Night Four (continued)

2 Chronicles 28:1-21; Isaiah 7:1-10:4, 17:1-14; Hosea 5:8-7:16;
2 Kings 16:10-18; 2 Chronicles 28:22-25; 2 Kings 15:30-31, 17:1-2;
Hosea 8:1-14:9; Micah 1:1-7; 2 Kings 17:3-23, 18:9-12, 17:24-41;
Isaiah 5:1-30; 2 Kings 16:19-20; 2 Chronicles 28:26-27;
2 Kings 18:1-2; 2 Chronicles 29:1; 1 Chronicles 4:34-43;
Isaiah 13:1-16:14; 2 Chronicles 29:3-31:1; Psalm 66:1-67:7;
2 Chronicles 31:2-21; Isaiah 18:1-23:18; 2 Kings 18:7b-8;
Micah 1:8-7:20; 2 Kings 18:13-19:37; 2 Chronicles 32:1-23;
Psalm 75:1-77:20, 80:1-19, 87:1-7, 125:1-5;
Isaiah 1:1-4:6, 10:5-12:6, 28:1-38:22; 2 Kings 20:1-11;
2 Chronicles 32:24-26; 2 Kings 20:12-19; 2 Chronicles 32:27-31;
Isaiah 39:1-8; 2 Kings 18:3-7a;2 Chronicles 29:2; 2 Kings 20:20-21;
2 Chronicles 32:32-33; Isaiah 24:1-66:24; 2 Kings 21:1-17;
2 Chronicles 33:1-9; Psalm 82:1-8; 2 Chronicles 33:10-19;
2 Kings 21:18-26; 2 Chronicles 33:20-25; 2 Kings 22:1-2;
2 Chronicles 34:1-3; Zephaniah 1:1-3:20; 2 Chronicles 34:4-7;
Jeremiah1:1-6:30, 13:1-27, 16:1-17:27; 2 Kings 22:3-20;
2 Chronicles 34:8-33; Nahum 1:1-3:19; 2 Kings 23:1-28;
2 Chronicles 35:1-19; Psalm 81:1-16; Jeremiah 47:1-48:47;
2 Kings 23:29-30; 2 Chronicles 35:20-36:1; Jeremiah 22:1-17;
2 Kings 23:31-37; 2 Chronicles 36:2-5; Habakkuk 1:1-3:19;
Jeremiah 8:4-9:15, 9:22-10:16, 26:1-24, 7:1-8:3, 11:1-17, 15:10-21;
Jeremiah 22:18-23, 35:1-19; 2 Kings 24:1-4; 2 Chronicles 36:6-7;
Jeremiah 36:1-32, 25:1-38, 45:1-5, 46:1-28; Daniel 1:3-21;
2 Kings 24:7; Daniel 2:1-49; 2 Kings 24:5-6; 2 Chronicles 36:8;
2 Kings 24:8-9; 2 Chronicles 36:9; 1 Chronicles 3:10-16;
Daniel 3:1-30; Jeremiah 9:16-21, 10:17-25, 12:7-17, 19:14-20:18,
22:24-23:8; 2 Kings 24:10-17; 2 Chronicles 36:10; Jeremiah 49:1-33

Rio's Chronological Reading
of the Bible

Day Five

Obadiah: 1:1-21; Jeremiah 14:1-15:9, 18:1-19:13, 24:1-10, 29:1-32;
2 Kings 24:18-20; 2 Chronicles 36:11-14;
Jeremiah 49:34-39, 50:1-46, 51:1-64, 11:18-12:6, 23:9-40;
Jeremiah 27:1-28:17; Ezekiel 1:1-23:49; Jeremiah 21:1-14;
Ezekiel 24:1-25:17; Jeremiah 37:1-38:28;
Ezekiel 29:1-16, 30:20-31:18; Jeremiah 32:1-34:22; 2 Kings 25:1-21;
2 Chronicles 36:15-21; Jeremiah 39:1-18, 52:1-30;
Psalm 74:1-23, 79:1-13, 85:1-13, 102:1-28, 120:1-7, 137:1-9;
Lamentations 1:1-5:22; 2 Kings 25:22-26; Jeremiah 40:1-44:30;
Psalm 71:1-24, 116:1-19; Jeremiah 30:1-31:40; Ezekiel 26:1-28:26;
Ezekiel 33:21-39:29, 32:1-33:20, 40:1-48:35, 29:17-30:19;
Daniel 4:1-37; 2 Kings 25:27-30; Jeremiah 52:1-34;
Daniel 7:1-8:27, 5:1-31; 2 Chronicles 36:22-23; Daniel 9:1-27;
Ezra 1:1-4; Daniel 6:1-28; Ezra 1:5-2:20; Nehemiah 7:4-25;
Ezra 2:21-70; Nehemiah 7:26-73a; Ezra 3:1-13;
Psalm 92:1-15, 126:1-6; Daniel 10:1-12:13; Psalm 93:1-100:5;
Ezra 4:1-5, 4:24; Haggai 1:1-2:23; Zechariah 1:1-8:23; Ezra 5:1-6:18;
Psalm 118:1-29, 129:1-8, 148:1-150:6; Ezra 6:19-22;
Zechariah 9:1-14:21; Esther 1:1-10:3; Ezra 4:6-23;
Psalm 105:1-106:48; Ezra 7:1-10:44; 1 Chronicles 3:17-24;
Nehemiah 1:1-7:3; Psalm 1:1-6, 107:1-43, 111:1-112:10, 117:1-2;
Psalm 119:1-176, 121:1-123:4, 128:1-6, 130:1-8, 134:1-136:26;
Psalm 146:1-147:20; Nehemiah 7:73b-11:36; 1 Chronicles 9:1b-34;
Nehemiah 12:1-13:31; Joel 1:1-3:21; Malachi 1:1-4:6

Rio's Chronological Reading of the Bible

Night Five

Luke 1:1-80; Matthew 1:18-25; Luke 2:1-20; Matthew 1:1-17;
Luke 3:23-38, 2:21-40; Matthew 2:1-23; Luke 2:41-52; Mark 1:1-8;
Matthew 3:1-12; Luke 3:1-20; John 1:1-28; Mark 1:9-11;
Matthew 3:13-17; Luke 3:21-22; John 1:29-34; Mark 1:12-13;
Matthew 4:1-11; Luke 4:1-13; John 1:35-51; Mark 1:16-20;
Matthew 4:18-22; Luke 5:1-11; John 2:1-4:42; Mark 1:14-15;
Matthew 4:12-17; Luke 4:14-15; John 4:43-46a; Luke 4:16-30;
Mark 1:21-28; Luke 4:31-37; Mark 1:29-39; Matthew 8:14-17;
Luke 4:38-44; Mark 1:40-45; Matthew 8:1-4; Luke 5:12-16;
Mark 2:1-12; Matthew 9:1-8; Luke 5:17-26; Mark 2:13-17;
Matthew 9:9-13; Luke 5:27-32; Mark 2:18-22; Matthew 9:14-17;
Luke 5:33-39; Mark 2:23-28; Matthew 12:1-8; Luke 6:1-5; Mark 3:1-6;
Matthew 12:9-14; Luke 6:6-11; Mark 3:7-12; Matthew 12:15-21;
Mark 3:13-19; Luke 6:12-16; Matthew 4:23-7:29; Luke 6:17-7:10;
Matthew 8:5-13; John 4:46b-54; Luke 7:11-35; Matthew 11:1-19;
Luke 7:36-8:3; Mark 3:20-30; Matthew 12:22-45; Luke 11:14-26;
Mark 3:31-35; Matthew 12:46-50; Luke 8:19-21; Mark 4:1-20;
Matthew 13:1-23; Luke 8:4-18; Mark 4:21-34; Matthew 13:31-35;
Luke 13:18-21; Matthew 13:24-30, 13:36-52; Mark 4:35-41;
Matthew 8:23-27; Luke 8:22-25; Mark 5:1-20; Matthew 8:28-34;
Luke 8:26-39; Mark 5:21-43; Matthew 9:18-26; Luke 8:40-56;
Matthew 9:27-34; Mark 6:1-6a; Matthew 13:53-58; John 5:1-47;
Mark 6:6b-11; Matthew 9:35-10:42; Luke 9:1-5; Mark 6:14-29;
Matthew 14:1-12; Luke 9:7-9; Mark 6:12-13; Luke 9:6; Mark 6:30-44;
Matthew 14:13-21; Luke 9:10-17; John 6:1-15; Mark 6:45-56;
Matthew 14:22-36; John 6:16-59; Mark 7:1-23; Matthew 15:1-20;
Mark 7:24-30; Matthew 15:21-28; Mark 7:31-37, Matthew 15:29-31;
Mark 8:1-10; Matthew 15:32-39; Mark 8:11-13; Matthew 16:1-4;
Mark 8:14-21; Matthew 16:5-12; Mark 8:22-30; Matthew 16:13-20;
Luke 9:18-21; John 6:60-71; Mark 8:31-9:1; Matthew 16:21-28;
Luke 9:22-27; Mark 9:2-13; Matthew 17:1-13; Luke 9:28-36;
Mark 9:14-32; Matthew 17:14-23; Luke 9:37-45; Mark 9:33-37;
Matthew 18:1-5; Luke 9:46-48; Matthew 17:24-27; Mark 9:38-41;
Luke 9:49-50; Mark 9:42-50; Matthew 18:6-9, 18:10-35; Mark 10:1;
Matthew 19:1-2; Luke 9:51-62; Matthew 8:18-22; Luke 10:1-20;

Rio's Chronological Reading of the Bible

Night Five (continued)

Matthew 11:20-24; Luke 10:21-24; Matthew 11:25-30;
Luke 10:38-11:13, 11:27-13:17, 13:22-16:17, 16:19-18:14;
John 7:1-10:21; Mark 10:2-12; Matthew 19:3-12; Luke 16:18;
Mark 10:13-16; Matthew 19:13-15; Luke 18:15-17; Mark 10:17-22;
Matthew 19:16-22; Luke 18:18-23; Mark 10:23-31; Matthew 19:23-30;
Luke 18:24-30; Matthew 20:1-16; John 10:22-11:57; Mark 10:32-45;
Matthew 20:17-28; Luke 18:31-34; Mark 10:46-52; Matthew 20:29-34;
Luke 18:35-19:10; Mark 11:1-11; Matthew 21:1-11; Luke 19:28-44;
John 12:12-19; Mark 11:12-26; Matthew 21:12-22; Luke 19:45-48;
Mark 11:27-33; Matthew 21:23-27; Luke 20:1-8; Matthew 21:28-32;
Mark 12:1-12; Matthew 21:33-46; Luke 20:9-19; Matthew 22:1-14;
Mark 12:13-17; Matthew 22:15-22; Luke 20:20-26; Mark 12:18-27;
Matthew 22:23-33; Luke 20:27-40; Mark 12:28-34; Matthew 22:34-40;
Luke 10:25-37; Mark 12:35-37a; Matthew 22:41-46; Luke 20:41-44;
Matthew 23:1-36; Mark 12:37b-40; Luke 20:45-47; Matthew 23:37-39;
Mark 12:41-44; Luke 21:1-4; Mark 13:1-23; Matthew 24:1-28;
Luke 21:5-24; Mark 13:24-31; Matthew 24:29-35; Luke 21:25-38;
Mark 13:32-37; Matthew 24:36-25:30; Luke 19:11-27;
Matthew 25:31-46; John 12:20-50; Mark 14:1-11; Matthew 26:1-16;
Luke 22:1-6; John 12:1-11; Mark 14:12-17; Matthew 26:17-20;
Luke 22:7-14; John 13:1-20; Mark 14:18-21; Matthew 26:21-25;
Luke 22:21-23; John 13:21-30; Luke 22:24-30; Mark 14:22-26;
Matthew 26:26-29; Luke 22:15-20; John 13:31-35; Mark 14:27-31;
Matthew 26:30-35; Luke 22:31-38; John 13:36-17:26; Mark 14:32-42;
Matthew 26:36-46; Luke 22:39-46; Mark 14:43-52; Matthew 26:47-56;
Luke 22:47-53; John 18:1-11; Mark 14:53-72; Matthew 26:57-75;
Luke 22:54-71; John 18:12-27; Matthew 27:1-10; Luke 23:1-12;
Mark 15:1-5; Matthew 27:11-14; John 18:28-38; Mark 15:6-15;
Matthew 27:15-26; Luke 23:13-25; John 18:39-19:16;
Mark 15:16-20a; Matthew 27:27-31; Luke 23:26-32; Mark 15:20b-21;
Matthew 27:32; John 19:17a; Mark 15:22-41; Matthew 27:33-56;
Luke 23:33-49; John 19:17b-37; Mark 15:42-47; Matthew 27:57-61;
Luke 23:50-56; John 19:38-42; Matthew 27:62-66; Mark 16:1-8;
Matthew 28:1-8; Luke 24:1-12; John 20:1-13; Matthew 28:9-10;
John 20:14-18; Matthew 28:11-15; Luke 24:13-43; John 20:19-31;

Rio's Chronological Reading
of the Bible

Night Five (continued)

Matthew 28:16-20; John 21:1-25; Luke 24:44-53; Mark 16:9-20

Day Six

Acts 1:1-11:18; James 1:1-5:20; Acts 11:19-14:28;
Galatians 1:1-6:18; Acts 15:1-18:17; 1 Thessalonians 1:1-5:28;
2 Thessalonians 1:1-3:18; Acts 18:18-19:41;
1 Corinthians 1:1-16:24; Acts 20:1-6; 2 Corinthians 1:1-13:14;
Romans 1:1-16:27; Acts 20:7-28:31; Ephesians 1:1-6:24;
Colossians 1:1-4:18; Philemon 1:1-25; Philippians 1:1-4:23;
1 Timothy 1:1-6:21; Titus 1:1-3:15; 1 Peter 1:1-5:14; Jude 1:1-25;
2 Peter 1:1-3:18; 2 Timothy 1:1-4:22; Hebrews 1:1-13:25;
1 John 1:1-5:21; 2 John 1:1-13; 3 John 1:1-14;
Revelation 1:1-22:21

Also by C.S. Elston

Now Available:

    "The Gift of Tyler"

    "The Four Corners"

    "The Four Corners of Darkness"

Coming Soon:

    "The Four Corners of Winter"

    "The Gift of Matias"

    "The Gift of Amanda"

After award-winning stage work in the nineties, Chris Elston moved to Los Angeles where he wrote more than two dozen feature film and television screenplays. He has been invited to participate in screenwriting events for Cinema Seattle and Angel Citi Film Festival. In 2013, Chris left Los Angeles for the suburbs of his hometown, Seattle, Washington, to get married and start a new chapter in his own story. Five and a half years later, the journey of the chapter that followed landed he and his wife in Prescott, Arizona where they now reside.

You can learn more at:
cselston.com
twitter.com/cselston
facebook.com/cselston

www.ingramcontent.com/pod-product-compliance
Lightning Source LLC
Chambersburg PA
CBHW071148020726
47502CB00002B/321